BEL MOONEY

Intimate Letters

WARNER BOOKS

A *Warner* Book

First published in Great Britain in 1997
by Little, Brown and Company

This edition published by Warner Books in 1998

'The *Darling* Letters' is taken from *The Other Country* by
Carol Ann Duffy, published by Anvil Press Poetry in 1990.
Reproduced by permission.
Extract from *The End of the Affair* by Graham Greene,
published by Heinemann, is reproduced by permission.

The moral right of the author has been asserted.

*All characters in this publication are fictitious
and any resemblance to real persons, living or dead,
is purely coincidental.*

A CIP catalogue record for this book
is available from the British Library.

ISBN 0 7515 2261 9

Typeset by M Rules in Janson Text
Printed and bound in Great Britain
by Clays Ltd, St Ives plc

Warner Books
A Division of
Little, Brown and Company (UK)
Brettenham House
Lancaster Place
London WC2E 7EN

This is Bel Mooney's fifth novel. She is also the author of many best-selling books for children, and is well known for her searching interviews on Radio 4 and television, as well as for a successful career as a journalist. She is married to Jonathan Dimbleby and together they develop projects for their independent production company Dimbleby Partners. They live with their family on a farm outside Bath where Bel Mooney is currently working on a new novel and an animated film.

Also by Bel Mooney

Fiction
The Windsurf Boy
The Anderson Question
The Fourth of July
Lost Footsteps

Non-fiction
The Year of the Child
Differences of Opinion
(with Gerald Scarfe) Father Kissmas and Mother Claws
Bel Mooney's Somerset
From This Day Forward/The Penguin Book of Marriage
Perspectives For Living

Children's Books
Liza's Yellow Boat
The Stove Haunting
A Flower of Jet
The Voices of Silence
The Mouse With Many Rooms
Joining the Rainbow
The Green Man

Kitty Books
I Don't Want To!
I Can't Find It!
It's Not Fair!
But You Promised!
Why Not?
I Know!
I'm Scared!
I Wish!
Why Me?
I'm Bored

for Bernard Levin

              . . . Nobody burns them,
the *Darling* letters, stiff in their cardboard coffins.

Babykins . . . We all had strange names
which make us blush, as though we'd murdered
someone under an alias, long ago. *I'll die
without you. Die.* Once in a while, alone,
we take them out to read again, the heart thudding
like a spade on buried bones.

                        Carol Ann Duffy

When I am dead and gone, stay clear of my grave,
Keep off the grass,
Lest I should burst into flames as before,
And scorch you as you pass.

                        Cretan mandinade

Prologue

When Rosa McKee's husband forgot their twenty-second wedding anniversary, she locked herself in the bedroom and put on her recording of *Carmina Burana*. Later, when he knocked softly on the door she turned the volume up. Giving up at last, he went outside to wander in the garden, regretting the inevitable desolation that resulted from her wish to leave things wild. A formal garden will keep its structure, even in winter, he thought.

Exactly two days and three hours later, he was dead. Simon McKee was climbing down from the new van, seed catalogue in hand, favourite old trowel in his jacket pocket, when his heart decided it had had enough. He had already apologised, of course, and given her the *amalanchia*, but she had not yet enjoyed the full luxury of forgiveness. In the days that followed – which folded in on themselves, night into day, a continuum of disbelief, rather than grief – Rosa sobbed continually that it was all her fault.

'Mum, Mum, don't punish yourself. How can it be your fault?' cried Kathy, who had driven overnight from Edinburgh. 'It just . . . happened, that's all. Oh, poor Dad . . .' They clung to each other.

'We quarrelled. Or at least . . . I quarrelled with him. He forgot our anniversary. I was hurt . . .'

'He never forgot things. He was so . . . sorted,' sobbed Kathy.

'That's the point. There must have been something wrong; he must have been ill already and I made it worse. I was so stupid. What does it matter – an anniversary? No more now . . .' Rosa's voice choked away and her body shook as she ground her nails into the palms of both hands.

Kathy McKee cradled her mother, crying for her father, but also (in the most secret, shameful corner of her mind) wishing for deliverance. The university bars, the tutorial groups, the parties started to recede. Terrified of imprisonment, guilty at that terror, and feeling all the time the inconsolable loss of the child, she whispered, 'I won't go back, Mum, I'll stay with you.'

She thought of the father – the quiet, faultless confidant who had held her hand, who had first planted seeds with her, who used to make her patterns for colouring with a spirograph, who smelt of skin and soil, who was always just *there* – and was rocked by panic. Her father was shrunken to an old blue sweater, draped on the back of a study chair. It could not be true.

'Of course you'll go back,' said Rose. 'I'll be fine. It'll just take time.'

'Do you . . . ? I mean . . . will we . . . ? *Does it go away?*' wailed her daughter, so that suddenly their positions were reversed, and Rosa was glad to be the parent again, administering comfort.

'I suspect it never goes away,' she said, so softly that her daughter did not hear.

Later, when Kathy had gone to sleep, Rosa stood looking

down over the city. Simon had chosen their home, in one of the less famous crescents, for its view: at night a regular pattern of light and dark. Rosa had yearned for a country house, a small rectory maybe, which she said would make sense for the business. No, he argued, there was no need for a vast garden in order to design such things for other people. No time. Better to survey perfection from above each day, drawing inspiration from the idea of order which flourished in the bright daylight of Georgian England.

Behind their house was a garden, not too large, which Rosa claimed as her own. Simon would have built a parterre, surrounded by low box hedges, and separated from the house by stone flags on which would be placed low wooden containers for shaped bay. But Rosa cultivated wildness. In vain did Simon protest it did not suit the house or surroundings, and beg for espaliered peaches along the stone walls. She allowed the corners to remain unstrimmed, the shrubs to loll across each other, and thyme to sprout with dandelions and valerian between the stones of a winding path which led nowhere. Her husband sighed and dismissed her garden as a jungle. Rosa smiled serenely and said there was nothing wrong with jungles.

'It's the only thing we quarrel about,' she once said to her closest friend Kit – whose idea of gardening was a window box. 'But I told him he could exercise his will with other people's gardens – build his formal walks and all those things he loves so much – but give me ours.'

'If that's all you quarrel about, you're lucky,' laughed Kit.

Simon McKee had set up SIROSA Garden Design not long after Kathy was born, twenty years ago, when they had been married just a year. Rosa was unsure about the union of names in the title, suspecting vulgarity, but people seemed to respond to the Mediterranean softness, and business went well. Simon had always loved plants; in his solitary childhood, he said, they had been his company. If he regretted abandoning his dreams of sculpture he did not show it, not even to his wife. He had a child, he shrugged, and must needs earn a living. 'Michaelangelo believed the marble not yet carved held the form of the sculpture,' he told Rosa, 'and it isn't so different to imagine the untamed or neglected land holding the finished garden – waiting to be coaxed out.'

'He always *accepts* things,' Rosa told Kit, with a mixture of pride and exasperation, 'when other people moan and rebel.'

'It's impossible to imagine Simon rebelling against anything,' laughed Kit, 'but compared to Paul he's positively racy!'

Gradually Simon built a reputation, and after a couple of articles in gardening magazines the commissions came quickly. From time to time, Rosa helped him on site, once Kathy was at school, and she realised she had no desire at all to start work as an art teacher, as she had intended. Good at plants, she gave him her advice, and they disagreed on most things except roses. SIROSA Garden Design was the two of them now. But only in name. In the last few years Simon had begun to spend more and more time at his computer, summoning the ghostly images of gardens in spring, summer, autumn and winter, so that he would always be able to predict so much as the fall of a leaf on to a path, knowing how that would alter the whole.

Rosa disliked the neat little plans he printed out. 'It's like cheating, almost,' Rosa complained, 'and there's no surprise left. No romance.'

She hated the computer. He laughed at what he called her 'technofear'. Kathy went away to study law, taking her own computer with her, and for a while Rosa would find herself drifting out to the autumnal garden, that first term, and wondering where her daughter's childhood had gone, and what was she to do with her days? At forty-four she felt old. Friends had always said Kathy was lucky to have such a young mother, and how admirable that Rosa ignored career to concentrate on the girl, and what a close couple the McKees were . . . And so on.

Once her daughter had gone away for her first term, Rosa was left gazing into the impenetrable thickets at the edges of her garden. She did not know what to do.

She looked up at the office window on the first floor, saw her husband in profile, working at his computer, and yearned to be the other side of his screen, looking out at him, begging to be redesigned, so that her paths would lead somewhere, in a new direction. Or, in any direction. The only way seemed backwards, and Rosa was prone to sentiment. So she would take out the albums, and smile at her mini-skirted wedding photographs, then at the sudden pictures of her baby, her toddler, her child, her teenager, her daughter. The growing, the unprunable change upwards and outwards, the cutting off. Putting the albums back in the sideboard cupboard, she chose to cry.

Simon became exasperated. 'You have to learn to let go,' he said.

'Why?' asked Rosa, setting her face against him.

'Because that's how it is,' he said gently.

Rosa tried to paint again on the kitchen table, washing areas of colour on to handmade paper, and letting it bleed, like clouds. One painting she called 'Edge', imagining the sea: a bulbous mass of washed-out ultramarine beneath a front of grey-blue sky, the sea edge the paper, left white, as if the light dazzled. She showed it to Simon, who praised her work, rather because it showed her determination to do something once more, than for its own sake. Remembering her drawings of flowers, each stamen delineated with surgical skill, Simon looked at this wishy-washy confusion of blues and greys, and sighed. She asked why.

'I wish you'd kept it up,' he said.

'I had to do colouring in with Kathy,' she smiled. 'All those lines! Why is it that we made children so afraid of going over the edge? And those dreadful paint-by-numbers sets people used to buy . . .'

'They were reassuring,' he said.

'Kathy was like you,' said Rosa, not listening. 'She liked parameters.'

'Or perimeters?' he said.

'Borders, boundaries, banks,' she laughed, looked at her picture with absent-minded pleasure.

Simon walked upstairs to his office, and studied the screen. She had given him the answer to the problem that had been bothering him all morning.

So Kathy's first year came and went, and Rosa adjusted, and SIROSA Garden Design made money, despite the recession, and Rosa was even asked for help – more and more in fact, as the commissions came in and Simon required her colour sense. She liked it. They were a proper partnership now, she said.

Then, in the February of Kathy's second year, he forgot the anniversary, and died. Again and again Rosa would summon up the images as if upon a screen: his face as he realised he had forgotten, and the sight of the door-handle turning in vain, and the way she had snapped up the volume on the portable music machine (as he called it) that had been her Christmas present.

O Fortuna! . . . they sang.

She had heard his footsteps retreating, then peered from behind the curtain, down to where he wandered in her garden, pausing from time to time to examine or adjust. Occasionally he shook his head slightly, as if in despair at the lack of control in his wife, or in that wild garden. Rosa hated him then, for hurting her, for not understanding her needs, for withholding the small amount of attention that would sustain her for a year. Surely it should be easy? She vowed not to forgive him too quickly, or else how would he learn? If you don't guard the little things within a marriage, how to protect the important ones? She counselled herself toughly, and had not fully relented when the policeman was at the door.

On the day of Simon's funeral Rosa refused to wear black. Kathy's choice of sober jacket and skirt was an implicit criticism of her mother's green and purple. 'I want to wear the colours he liked, the colours I wore when we met,' cried Rosa, folding her arms about herself as if in protection against her daughter's conservatism.

'Dad liked you in black,' whispered Kathy.

She knew even more. He had told her once that though her mother had chosen to go on wearing the mirrored Indian waistcoats and trailing skirts she had indeed worn twenty years ago, he had a secret admiration for what he called tailoring. He had called it 'grown-up', and had complimented Kathy on the neat straight skirt and classic argyle sweater she happened to be wearing at the time. Kathy had agreed that the trouble with her mother was that she locked herself into a shapeless hippie style. They had smiled together, father and daughter in collusion, patronising the woman they both loved with their criticism of her taste. That Christmas, Simon had bought Rosa a simple, structured jacket in the darkest of blues, with mandarin collar and buttons of dull silver. It cost more than the rest of her wardrobe in total, but she rarely wore it.

'It's not *me*,' she had confessed to Kathy, 'but don't tell him.'

'If you never wear it, he'll know!' Kathy had remonstrated.

'I'm not really a classical person,' Rosa had said.

Now, on the day of the funeral, Kathy took the jacket from the wardrobe and held it out towards her mother. 'Why not wear this?' she said.

Tears sprang in Rosa's eyes, and she shook her head vehemently. 'He'll know,' she said. 'He'll know I'm just doing it to please him, and that'd be false, Kathy. Don't you see that? Dad doesn't want me to change, not now. He wants me to wear my usual things. He liked that. He did! He does now!'

The rising note in her mother's voice, and her use of the present tense, pierced Kathy, allowing resentment to trickle through again. Thinking about her role – *the daughter* – on that terrible day, she thought for a second, How can she do this to me? She should be comforting me; he was my father, he's left me alone . .

Unable to play the child, as she wished, she laid the despised jacket down on the bed, and took her mother firmly by the shoulders.

'Mum,' she said quietly, 'Dad's dead. He's dead. *You* can wear what you like – but don't think it's got anything to do with *him*! I can't bear it when you talk about him as if he can see, as if he cares what you're going to wear! Dad's dead, Mum.'

'How do you know?' said Rosa, lifting her chin.

Kathy whispered, 'Oh God, Mother – why are you doing this to us?'

In the church, Rosa bowed her head. She closed her eyes, but still saw the simple coffin, on which she had laid a simple spray of white freesia. She refused to let it reproach her, even though she knew she had not obeyed his wishes. Simon had always asserted his atheism, putting (as he said) all his faith in human reason. But Rosa clung to a wistful semi-belief – never going to church to worship, but haunting holy buildings, as if somewhere in piscina or screen or vaulted porch the answers might be found. But to what? When he asked her, she would smile vaguely, and ask how he could *know* anything.

'I know I want to be burnt with a minimum of ceremony, and my ashes scattered somewhere in a garden,' he had said cheerfully.

'Whose garden?' she had asked.

He had looked away for a second. Then shrugged.

'One of mine. They're all mine,' he had said. 'But don't let's lose sleep over it. I don't intend to hang up my trowel for a good few years!'

Rosa remembered that. It was as if her life with Simon ran continually before her eyes, like a speeded-up video, almost comical sometimes in its movement towards death. Head down, hearing his words, his favourite sayings, his jokes like distant bursts of gunfire in the wasteland of her memory, she heard nothing of the short address. She was aware of Kathy clutching her arm, and of the vibrations in her own chest as she suppressed sobs. The vicar was gazing at her with intolerable compassion; she felt exposed and battered by its indiscriminate kindness.

There was a stillness in the small nave, beyond silence. Each person's mind returned again and again to the contemplation of sudden death, and quailed at the horror. There to mourn their relative, friend or associate, they grieved for themselves, and felt humble in the face of eternity – or, at least, fate. There were many faces neither Rosa nor Kathy recognised – people for whom, as the vicar said, 'Simon McKee created beauty as rich as any hung in an art gallery – a living, changing beauty of flower and leaf, of shrubbery and path.'

There were nods. Then, in the silence before the last hymn, Rosa heard a sudden intake of breath choking to a jagged sob. It came from far behind her. She attempted a slight turn to see who made the noise. The angle was wrong; she was too late. As the quick footsteps echoed, Rosa was aware of a flurry of black, like the blur at the corner of a photograph when someone has moved, or a faking of ectoplasm. Then the old door clunked shut.

Kit was in Rosa's eyeline. She inclined her head gracefully for a moment, in sympathy. Rosa noticed that she was gripping Paul's arm with both hands, as if afraid he too might slip away. She felt surprised; it was not her friend's style to cling. Then she turned back and fixed her gaze on the coffin that held her own husband. That was surprising too. Nothing fitted; nothing made sense. The order of acanthus on the stone pulpit, like the liturgy itself, was called into question by the chaos of the coffin. So sudden.

And *who* was it who had gone?

Someone had rushed to him, in that car park. There were no trees or flowers near him then. His last words were to a passer-by who, in her own distress, had barely heard. He was dead when they reached hospital, so that was it: the last message in the car park to a frightened stranger. The woman said she thought he had whispered, 'I love you.'

The vicar led the way to St Mary's churchyard, down the lane. Just outside the city, five minutes' drive from their house, this place gave an illusion of absolute rurality, and Rosa loved it. Once every couple of months she came here on a Sunday morning – despite Simon's incredulity – which is why the vicar had, with some reluctance, given in to her request for a 'proper' funeral. She lied to him. She told him it was what her husband wanted, even though he was not a worshipper – and said the same to Kathy, who was in no mood to argue, despite her doubts. 'Daddy mentioned to me that he liked the idea of being laid to rest in a garden,' Rosa fibbed – then cried. And so it happened, beneath scrawny yews, under a sky of slate.

When at last the mourners had all walked away, relieved the thing was done, Rosa pulled away from Kathy's arm, and retraced her steps.

Already earth was rattling down on her husband's coffin. She watched herself watching; she heard herself say, 'Goodbye, my darling'; she witnessed her own stumbling steps away from the void, a tiny figure in emerald and purple, against a grey background, colours bleeding into the wet. There was no form. She knew that she was right to have embraced randomness, because all Simon's borders, his plans, had crumbled into the vast mudslide of the universe.

From her abstract height, dizzy with the impossible, absolute whiteness of light, Rosa McKee pitied that small, inappropriately bright person walking from the grave, catching up with other black figures, and not noticing another dark creature, bent with grief, resting in the shadow of a tree. A white face looked up for a moment, then buried itself once more. Nothing was said. Nothing was known.

Except that the small, human Rosa's grief would last forever, throbbing beneath the surface of her skin. Knowing that, the inhuman, invisible Rosa could not help rejoicing that it was she, not Simon, who remained alive.

Chapter One

It was one way of beginning, one step away. But it is impossible. I am here, and can no longer hide. I should begin: *my name is Rosa McKee and I killed my husband.*

It is one truth. Who is to say it is not the truth? Wives do kill – with subtlety over the years, gently mortifying the flesh with small strokes of love, until at last the strain of survival is too great. Or by clinging on, with hooks of affection and need so tiny that death is imperceptible, by a thousand pricks. Or by squatting softly on his crown, adding to the daily burden, until at last the beloved head bows lower, and lower, until the stem snaps . . .

I put to death my husband Simon by all these methods, but the *coup de grâce* was my rage at his absent-mindedness. He forgot our anniversary, making me feel like a thing of no account, and for that I punished him. I closed my ears to his apologies. With the ferocity of my gaze, I wilted the small tree he finally offered, and yet all the time I thought myself the victim, not him. I chose to listen obsessively to the wild, profane songs:

> I bemoan the wounds of Fortune
> with weeping eyes,

> for the gifts she made me
> she perversely takes away . . .

because the energy of Orff's music always spoke to me of the untamed world and, besides, Simon detested it.

But I did not mean to kill him; it was not my intention. I did not put the trowel in his pocket that would become his route to the earth. I did not select the tweed that would become his shroud. Nevertheless, in the days and weeks that followed Simon's funeral I accepted my responsibility. My intention (because I have finally learnt how to use this machine) was to pretend that this is a novel, not the truth. I wanted to create myself anew: the poor creature in purple, the victim – seen from afar with pity. Yet it will not do. I can no longer distance myself from my rage – or my responsibility. Because now, so long after these events, living with him each day, I confront my faults as well as his. You can even get to like them in the end. It is like picking a scab.

Do you know about grief? I had never thought about it. When my parents died, I was sad, of course, but they were old, and we had never been close. I cried because I knew I had to step forward and take their places in the line, like a volunteer at the last stand before a massacre. Or a martyr. Still, I had Simon to protect me. I could hide behind him, and hope that death would not spot me. Which is exactly how it happened. The gunfire got him first, and – yes – even in the cemetery, the perfect grieving wife, I could smell the wet earth and be glad it was him, not me.

You see? Whichever way I turn, it lurks there, blaming me.

After they had all gone I was relieved. Kit and Kathy cleared the glasses, and crusts of sandwiches, and I fell into a slightly drunken sleep in which I heard him calling to me. It was

Kathy, shaking me to see if I wanted tea. I sent her away. I wanted to wrap myself in misery, to be alone in the house with him. I pulled photographs from my drawer, and wallowed in them – wandering back slowly through the stages of our life together, not now lingering sentimentally over our daughter, but focusing on the man who held her up in his arms, smiling in full colour at the camera I held with occasional shake, as if in premonition.

It's strange how you forget what someone looks like, when you live with them every day. Asked to describe my husband, I would have shrugged and demurred, then would have said that he was about five ten, slimly built, with tanned skin, sandy-brown curly hair, hazel eyes – nothing to distinguish him, no scars, no facial tics. Yet he had an evenness of features that was pleasing – the kind of man women liked, but who aroused in them no frenzy of curiosity or desire. Ordinary, I would have said.

Then, in death, he became a mystery to me. Our family snapshots (bundled in drawers recently because I could not be bothered to keep up the ritual of sticking them in albums) held the key. Simon was dead; these were the only remaining signs of him, and must be studied like the entrails, to indicate what had been, and what would be.

That is a stupid way of putting it.

I mean: I needed to *see* the man I had been married to for twenty-two years, needed to remember precisely what he was like, in order to understand myself. I could not separate us in my mind; therefore how could I stand alone? I felt that by looking back, thinking about him, dwelling at length on the qualities that set him apart from other men, I could create for him a monument within my memory that would, in the end, serve to set me free. I would become his priestess. I would have a role.

Apart from studying the photographs, I also tried to draw his portrait, from memory at first and then from the snapshots. I took my pencil around the planes of his jaw and cheeks; I shaded the hollows beneath his eyes, wondering why I had not noticed them before, and whether they were the intimation of death. I marvelled at the shape of his ears – so neat! But his eyes and mouth eluded me. Again and again, I screwed up my face, and burst into tears of fury, throwing my pencil on the table. I was unworthy, you see. I could not capture the exquisite kindness that marked him out, nor the slight lifting of the corners of his mouth that betrayed some deep, hidden amusement he could share with no one. What was it? What amused him? I could not remember.

It's hard to remember those days. I made Kit return to London, and then, after two weeks, forced Kathy back to Edinburgh, insisting I would be fine alone. I said her father would have wanted her to get on with her studies; he wanted nothing more than for her to become a lawyer; if she worked hard she would be doing it for him. She was so like him, my Kathy. She understood the call of duty and obeyed.

Each morning I woke around five, and lay waiting for birdsong, and experiencing all over again, each twenty-four hours, the pulling in my chest and stomach, as if a rope were being tightened around the neck of a sack, the oppression dragging me down and down, which I thought I must carry forever. Most days I cried. Sometimes, though, I just lay unable to move, unable to feel my skin, pinch though I might, aware only of that dead weight and my own voice repeating his name aloud.

'Simon. Simon. Simon. Oh, Simon. Simon. I love you, my dearest Simon.'

On and on, like that, until it seemed to me that I inhabited a world devoid of all sensation apart from the numbness of mind and flesh, and in which the only sound was the litany of my pain. That is grief: a tedium merciful in its anaesthesia, alternating with the most acute, white hot agony. No one can expect it. No one can know what it is like until it is there.

I decided to make a project out of his grave. It would be so different from the vulgar graves all around, with their head-stones of shiny granite and rigid plantings of nasturtiums and anemones. Why did people always choose screaming reds and yellows? Did they think they would cheer the dead? No – Simon's grave would be a wild flower garden, with no headstone. He deserved fritillaries and cowslips. His plot would be full of poetry. Meanwhile I went each week and placed fresh flowers in the coffee jars I embedded at the head and foot, sadly enjoying the ritual which brought me close to him. We would be alone there, with just the birds in the shivering branches above, and the sound of distant traffic, and my own voice whispering his name again and again. Sometimes I would sit back on my heels, in a daze, until the agony in my limbs brought me back to life. I would wonder where he had *gone*. It was impossible that he was under the earth.

Then, one morning, two months after the funeral, I heard the birds more loudly than ever. I looked out of the window at the burgeoning in the garden, and felt an unexpected tremor; a sharp pain, like the stirring of roots. This was different to grief. I felt it in my head, not my abdomen.

I ran downstairs, unlocked the back door, and looked. It was palpable, this shifting and heaving of the earth, the spikiness of green lances, the slash of yellow daffodils, the star-points of white jagged against dark bark, the whole garden sharp – as if to touch any part would hurt, and flesh would part and bleed. I walked outside, shivering with excitement. I saw the colours and shapes, and heard the wild chorus in the branches, and thought of what I might do. My garden was beautiful. Simon was wrong; he had not given me my due. The doleful untidiness of winter was over; my creation sprang to life, and I knew I wanted to make more like it. I too could create gardens. They would be a memorial to Simon, even though perhaps he would not approve the new direction SIROSA Garden Design would take. This I would do – for him. For you, my love, my Simon.

Back inside, I found the right band on the CD and followed the translation of the Latin. It was so right! My delight was immeasurable. I felt a part of that medieval awakening, after the long dark winter.

> The sun warms everything,
> pure and gentle,
> once again it reveals to the world
> April's face,
> the soul of man
> is urged towards love
> and joys are governed
> by the boy-god.
> All this rebirth
> in spring's festivity
> and spring's power
> bids us to rejoice;
> it shows us paths we know well,
> and in your springtime
> it is true and right
> to keep what is yours.
> Love me faithfully!
> See how I am faithful
> with all my heart
> and with all my soul.
> I am with you

even when I am far away.
Whoever loves this much
turns on the wheel.

I knew I would never stop loving Simon, but that I had to create a new life, to please him. I was bound to the wheel, and yet it would still turn. It's impossible to communicate the utter simplicity, yet enormity of that thought. It is the moment when the widow realises that she can walk without the frame, weak though her limbs might be.

Still, I was afraid, and needed help. There was one person, only one, I could tolerate seeing and she was always the first I turned to. I went into the kitchen and picked up the phone.

Kit Jordan and I had known each other for years, and, although many months might pass between our meetings, we lazed into conversation like someone slipping on an old coat. We had met in the first term of art college. She was my opposite, my alter ego, and my love for her (I thought later) was almost a form of narcissism; I adored what I wanted to be.

I used to joke that I had become a provincial lady, and dressed accordingly – whereas there was no skirt too short, or tights too shiny, or jacket too cropped for Kit to buy, and wear with confidence. When I reached forty I had my hair cut to a bob, because I thought it time. Kit was derisive; she indulged in a wild perm and a red rinse, and looked like a Mucha model. She lived in Islington, worked as a freelance photographer of some reputation, and lectured me from time to time about not being a proper partner in SIROSA Garden Designs, about what she called 'letting go'.

As I tapped her number, I looked out of the window at Simon's van, with the logo in green on its side, and knew she would approve and help. Of course, she came down the next day.

'I knew you'd get there!' she said, lolling on my sofa. 'I was waiting for you to want to begin.'

'Begin what?' I asked, knowing perfectly well what she meant.

'The rest of your life, of course. You can't hide away forever, love.'

'It used to make me angry,' I said, 'the way people imply you've got to pull yourself together. I didn't want to! As if it could be so easy anyway. As if you could just shrug somebody off, after twenty-three years.'

'OK – granted – but better than shrugging *on* a shroud,' said Kit, briskly. Then she leant back and gave the old laugh, that caught in her throat like a growl, 'Mind you, if Paul was your husband, you'd think you were actually married to a shroud!'

'Oh, Kit, that's so mean,' I murmured, smiling all the same.

'You know I don't mean it.'

The trouble was, I didn't know that. Once, years ago when we were both drunk, I told her that in general the world considered Paul 'not up to her', and asked her how come she fetched up with a dependable solicitor whose hair greyed prematurely, and who took upon himself the domesticity which bored her.

'It just happened,' she replied in her deliberately brittle tone. 'You wake up one day and realise that this person loves you so much he's offering you your freedom, in fact. You realise it's cold and lonely out there, and that there's nothing so lonely as your own bed in the morning with some guy in it you only wanted to screw. You know how long Paul had been around! So I thought, why not? He's like an island, and I'm a bird. I settle for long periods then I fly off, but I always come back. You know how it is.'

I didn't know that either. My friend's life was a mystery . . .

but then, increasingly in the last few years, I'd come to think of all the lives of people I knew as mysterious. Only ours was clear to me – mine and Simon's, our marriage, our home. I knew that. Now, looking at Kit in her leather jeans and jungle-print shirt, I felt irritated. She married a man who loved her so much he even repressed his own desire for children, to please her. And he was alive.

'You know you're bloody lucky?' I said.

'I know,' she said quietly, hearing my tone.

I said, 'I think about Simon all the time – he's in this room, in these curtains, and in the cracks of the furniture. He'll never go away. And I don't want him to. I know you're thinking that it would have been easier if I had had my own career, like you. But the point is, I don't want it to be easier. I like him being here. I can talk to him.'

'Rosa—' she began.

I held up a hand, unusually shutting her up. 'Don't try to stop me! People always try to stop you talking about the person who's dead, but what you want is to talk about them all the time. You want to go through the detail. You want to fix it all permanently. You know, sometimes Simon seems more real now than he did when he was alive. Then he might be tucked away in his office for hours and hours, and ask not to be disturbed. Now I can disturb him whenever I like! I think of all the time we had together, and go back over all sorts of little things, and I sort of enjoy them more. I hear his voice . . . And it consoles me. Can you see that?'

'Dangerous,' said Kit.

'But why? If it can make me happy?' I asked, exasperated.

'We're going round in circles,' she said. 'When you rang me you were full of the fact that you want to try to carry on the business, for Simon's sake. You wanted me to give you advice. You said you were ready to move on. But all you're talking about is the past.'

For a moment I felt I'd made a mistake inviting her down. She could not possibly understand. When someone has died you need the past, you require it; you have to shore it up like concrete, so that it can take the combined weight of you and your memories. In addition to the burden of the dead.

'I'm talking about *now*,' I said.

'OK,' she said, in an uncharacteristically patient voice, as if she were talking to a sick person, 'feel what you want to feel, but take the next step. For Simon's sake. Pick up the business. You have to support yourself, Rosa! Find a qualified partner, if you think you need to, but with all your colour sense, and creativity, I think you can do it. You've still got all those young freelance gardeners to call on, haven't you? And the contractors – that "magic list", I think he called it?'

'Yes,' I said, reluctantly, 'I can pick it all up easily, the consultancy, the maintenance, the new designing . . . But do I want to? I thought I did . . .'

'Try, Rosa. Please try.'

I felt sullen. I had asked her down to tell me this, but now I didn't want to hear it. 'I said I would and so I will,' I muttered.

'You said on the phone that you'll need to find your way round his computer. That's my thing. So why don't we start with the office? Sort things there?'

'I hate machines,' I said, knowing my voice was childish.

'Jesus Christ, Rosa!'

That was better. I didn't like Kit when she was patient and understanding; it didn't suit her. She was in a hurry with her life; she had no time to be nursemaid. I needed the cold water of her impatience.

'Let's do it now,' I said, and got up, leading the way to the door.

Each day I stood at the door of Simon's office, willing myself to go in. I studied the small room carefully from the door; I knew the position of each book on his shelves: Gertrude Jekyll, Russell Page, Geoffrey Jellicoe, Charles Bridgeman, and the rest. Then the rows of plant books, and works by architects, and histories of garden design, and fat seed catalogues, and his sculpture library. His desk was as he had left it: tidy, with a tray each side piled with sketches and notes, and in between them the computer which Simon had predicted – accurately – would revolutionise his method. On the walls were the botanical prints he loved and one or two reproductions of engravings of famous gardens.

His favourite was Dyrham Park just north of the city, in Gloucestershire. In the seventeenth century William Blathwayt transformed it briefly into a formally ornate Dutch pleasure garden, before fashion dictated that it return to the wild. Simon used to joke that Dyrham represented the difference between us. From time to time we would walk in the deer park, and I would revel in the sweep of the land, while he liked to imagine beneath the soil the traces of parterre, cascade, formal pool and wall. I used to laugh at him, pointing to the corner in Kip's famous print, labelled 'Wilderness'.

'Some wilderness!' I'd crowed. 'Man-made, man-tamed and about as empty of soul as a cesspit.'

'Oh, there's beauty in cesspits,' he had grinned. 'I read a quote by Rilke; he said even in the worst aspects of humanity, there's a truth, a reality, that has to be embraced. I think that's true.'

'Tolerated, maybe, but not embraced,' I'd said.

He called me a romantic. He said that in the bright light of his eighteenth-century enlightenment all things had a place; and walls contained the worst excesses of human nature, without sweeping them away. I did not understand him.

He was so wise, so tolerant, so reasonable. I would lean in the doorway of my husband's study, surveying his things, concentrating on memory . . .

I turned. The sitting room was quiet. Kit was watching me.

'The last time I went to his office, he spoke to me,' I said.

'Oh, Rosa . . .'

'He did! You have to believe me. I was trying to remember his voice, and concentrated really hard, but then something strange happened. It wasn't that I heard him, because I expected to. It was just that . . . that he wasn't saying anything that made sense.'

'What did he say?' asked Kit, taking refuge in dryness.

'He said he was sorry.'

I'm sorry, Rosa, I'm sorry, my love.

This is absolutely true. You have to believe me. I told him it didn't matter about the stupid anniversary, that if I had only known he was going to die I wouldn't have been so selfishly obsessed with marking out each parcel of time as if it were a personal achievement. But somehow I sensed he wasn't apologising for that. I listened but he didn't speak again.

Kit was surveying me with her head on one side, and a slightly worried expression on her face. She got up. 'It sounds to me like we have to go to that room, and knock this thing on the head,' she said, 'like getting back on a horse when it's thrown you.'

'Oh, but I'm not *scared*,' I said.

We walked upstairs, and stood by Simon's desk. 'Gertrude Jekyll managed without a computer,' I said.

'I couldn't give a toss if she turned into Mrs Hyde at night and went howling round her garden – I'm telling you that I'm going to drag you kicking and screaming into the twentieth century, and into living for yourself!' Kit said firmly.

'I knew you'd be like this. That's why I asked you to come.'

'Wasn't she a funny old bat anyway?'

'Who?'

'That Jekyll woman.'

'Oh, Kit!'

'It's so good to see you laugh.'

I went to fetch another chair, and we sat down in front of the computer's blank face. Kit grinned. 'Same as mine,' she said. 'So I'll start by taking you through, with really easy language. Then we'll open up.'

After ten minutes I was caught between panic and petulance. My brain was like a glossy surface; her explanations slithered away. The concept of folders, files and documents immediately depressed me because of an order, a logic which Simon (and Kit, and Kathy) understood, even loved, but from which I was excluded. When Kit told me to visualise the screen as a desktop I glanced from its cold vacancy to the contents of Simon's table, and rejected the thought.

Kit squeezed my shoulders. 'You *will* learn, I promise you – even if I have to spend a week down here getting you over all the hurdles once. Then I'll write out the simplest of guides. You'll never get your head around the manual. Look, let's stop messing about – you can't stand the theory of it. We'll start by switching on and getting started, then I'll take you very slowly through all the functions. OK?'

I nodded gloomily.

Kit switched on, and the screen came to life. She started to explain, and I half listened, again and again, her hand guiding mine on the mouse – making me giggle like a child, enjoying my own ineptitude.

'I always thought of a menu as full of delicious choices,' I said.

'Once you get used to this one you'll love it,' said Kit firmly.

'But there's no oysters!' I said.

'Click on there – twice,' said Kit. 'Now, I'm terrified of losing some of Simon's key folders. I imagine he kept lists of clients and plants . . .'

'Drawings too – everything,' I said.

'So we'll have to open a folder that won't matter much, to take you through the functions. Then it won't matter if you lose anything. Let me see . . .' She was staring at the box of little folders on the screen desktop. I was avoiding looking, fascinated, despite myself, yet not wanting to admit it.

Then she said, 'Look – "Admin". That's got to be boring. We'll go for that.'

She told me to click twice, and we waited as the computer made its tiny, responsive whirr. Then I laughed. 'My God – a list of paint colours! That was when we were going to redo the whole house – about six years ago. That was when he first got this. Must have been keen!'

'OK, so it'll do just fine. We can use this to learn the basics of word-processing. I'll take you through, then let you play around and I'll make some simple notes for you. Then we'll have to hunt around for his design software instructions, cos I might find it beyond me. Now . . .'

Kit showed me how to type, insert words, and delete. I followed, unwilling at first to understand, then enthusiastic as the machine obeyed and I found it like a game.

'Yes, that's right – play!' Kit said, taking a piece of paper and writing the heading 'Foolproof Directions For Technophobes Like Rosa McKee' across the top. For a few moments the only sound was that of my fingers, clumsy and slow, on the keyboard.

'It's quite fun,' I said at last.

''Course it is! Are you OK?'

'Ye-es . . . but how do you move to another page?'

'It'll move itself, when you get to the bottom.'

'I just want to move on. I'm bored with this page.'

'OK, so you need to know how to scroll. Here's what to do.'

I watched as the paint page disappeared. The next one continued a list of possible house improvements, with likely costs. Somehow this tedious list made me sad. Was this how he spent his time? Did I make him do such mundane things? I said, 'Poor Simon, what on earth was he putting all this boring stuff on the machine for? We didn't do any of it – that's why the house is falling apart.'

'Scroll on,' said Kit.

I kept my finger down, and blinked, suddenly dizzy, as a page flashed before me too fast to register.

'Don't stare at it, and slow down!' said Kit.

I obeyed. The swift flow of words into oblivion slowed, until sentences could be read as they made their way up the screen. Then I saw it.

How can I tell this? Would it be better to step back, as though that third person might save me from the truth? (Humiliated forever, and hurt as I never thought I could be hurt . . .)

Try.

*

Both women leant forward at the same time to stare at the screen. 'What on earth is this?' Rosa asked, lifting her hand, like a teacher commanding silence from the class.

It was the stillness of absolute terror, they would both think later, although Kit could not grasp the significance of the moment, and Rosa McKee knew precisely, in the first second of revelation, that it meant the end of the life she had known.

'It's a *letter*,' Rosa whispered.

They both read what was on the screen before them, then Kit looked away, embarrassed. 'He was a romantic old thing then?' she said. 'Oh, sweetheart, don't read it. It'll only make you sad.'

'A love letter,' said Rosa slowly. Her face had become pale, as her eyes moved to and fro along the lines.

'*It's a love letter*,' Rosa repeated, with new intensity.

The words seemed to glitter before them both. '*My dearest, my darling*'.

'Rosa, don't read this,' Kit murmured, putting an arm around Rosa's shoulders – which began to tremble violently.

Rosa shook her off. She turned her whole body towards Kit for a moment, as if she might hit her, and cried. 'You don't understand!' Then she swivelled back to the screen, jabbed the correct key without hesitation, and scrolled to the next page. 'Look at it!' she whispered.

Then it was as if a spotlight switched on within Kit's mind, and she knew there was no power on earth that could change what she had unwittingly made happen.

Rosa leant forward, her shoulders hunched, her gaze fixed, like a gypsy looking into a crystal ball. There was a long silence, then she made a small sound like a sob, and swivelled abruptly towards her friend. Her face was set into a mask of pure pain, lines of tension etched deeply from nose to mouth, as if to relax would be to allow the contents of her brain to tumble out on to the table.

'You don't see – do you?' she said harshly. 'This is a love letter all right. But it's not to *me*, Kit. It's got nothing to do with *me*.'

Chapter Two

My dearest,
I have to steady myself. The unforeseen has
happened. In years to come I shall look back, like
someone staring at the sun, into the golden light of
our meeting. How can it happen? You go to see a
woman, you discuss terraces and hedges, you are as
professional as you have ever been, and yet the light is
blinding already – and you are lost. I am lost. You are
lost. Or rather we are both found at last. I want to run
around all the gardens in the world, my arms spread
wide, shouting my joy so that it echoes all around the
universe. I want to lie full length on a lawn, and weep.
I want to sing silly songs, and turn somersaults. Oh
my darling, how can I begin to express what you have
done for me? Are doing for me. Will do for me.

It seems absurd to be writing this on a wretched
machine – hardly the stuff of romance! Can you
imagine Keats sitting at an Apple, to write to Fanny!?!
Yet it pleases me in a strange way. I got the thing with
such trepidation; it took me ages to find my way
around it; now I can make it do things for me – and so

it is becoming like a friend, whose secrets only I hold
the key to. So I can confide in him (definitely a male,
this chap!) about you – my golden secret, my love, my
love.

Besides which (and I wouldn't be me if I did not
take refuge in the prosaic every now and then), the
truth is my writing is appalling – I'm ashamed of it,
especially when contrasted with your elegant
calligraphy. (What a joy it has been to tear open the
businesslike envelope – so tactfully done – and find
your beautiful words inside. *Thank you*.) So we will be
a trio, this machine and you and I.

Are you feeling the same as me? How long is it
now? I check the pages of my diary with disbelief and
see that it is only three weeks. How can it be that two
human beings can run hand in hand around the
world, and explore its strangest corners, all in the
space of three weeks? There must be a mistake.

What is happening to me? I can't bear not to see
you. I shall find a reason to come to you in the next
couple of days. Better still, YOU find a reason to
meet me in town on Wednesday. We'll have lunch,
and I shall gaze at your lovely face across the table,
wondering that you could have told me that you think
yourself 'ugly'. No – find a reason to walk past my
house tomorrow, so that I can just see you in the
street. Find a reason to come yesterday, last week, the
day I was born. Perhaps I have only just *been* born.
What *is* happening to me?

The silence in my study is so complete it's bursting
my eardrums. Yet somewhere in the house my
daughter is playing records, and I know that my wife
is making a clatter in the kitchen. But it all fades to

nothingness, and I am totally alone, thinking of you.
  With love, Simon

                              4th June 1988
  Darling,
It's difficult to decide whether our telephone calls are
joy or pain: joy for what they are, pain because they
remind me that we are apart. But I would hardly be
true to my principles if I let the pain outweigh the joy,
so I don't. And you are almost as marvellous with real
words on the phone as on paper.

  Monday was a day of dreams, its happiness still
with me – lighting the mundanities of everyday life
here. On my trip to Kent I thought of you
continuously, and wanted to come back straight to
you. But I couldn't; I had to come home – those are
the things we have to live with, my love. So I was
longing to see you, hear you laugh, kiss you, talk with
you, caress you and finally – no, not finally, for this is
an unending sequence – make love. You are magic and
I am enchanted.

  I lay awake for hours that night, revelling in you,
committing to memory every detail of the few hours
we were together. I shall go over them again and
again until we can be together again. 'We will carve
out precious chunks of time,' you wrote in your last
letter. 'There will never be enough, but . . .' You did
not finish the sentence, and you were right. We will

put a moratorium on time. We will live in the present. We will put a ban on Autumn and Winter, so that our flowers grow and blossom, and stay the same forever. You're my Paradise Garden.

I am armoured by my happiness, so much so that I know if I were never to see you again a great, irreducible chunk of joy would remain with me always. But I *shall* see you again – on Thursday when I have finished at the Wallstons' place. (Oh, that bloody pond! The other day I had a mad fantasy of throwing Mrs W in it, so that she would rise, spitting tadpoles, and no longer able to bleat of 'the spirit of nature' – as if I wanted to cut down a feeble little tree for the sake of killing it, rather than to open up a vista! But sorry, work talk is boring, although you are always so helpful. You would be such a business partner! In another life . . .)

Anyway, I should be able to be with you around four, in time for tea. Please be as understanding as you usually are, my darling, if I spill mine in my haste to cuddle you. Sadly R informs me she's got theatre tickets for that night, and so I can't stay long. That evening I shall be sitting smothered by red velvet, hearing actors and actresses speak someone else's lines, and I shall know the real meaning of the word 'playacting', since I shall be as artificial as they are – going through the motions when the real drama, the real passion, the real pain are in my 'life' with you.

My deepest love, Simon

Thursday – and for God's sake
I don't know the date!

O, you of little faith!
I know my moods are volatile, so that I can be
depressed and anxious and even despairing one
moment, and happy and calm and eager the next, but
neither affects the truth and depth of my feelings for
you, and the joy inseparably attached to those
feelings. Sometimes that joy is hidden behind a cloud,
and sometimes it fills the sky, but it can no more be
truly absent than the sun can.

I know I make demands on you that are unfair, and
I sometimes behave like a child when told that I
cannot after all go to the circus. But my longing for
the circus is not just greed; it is partly a recognition of
how few visits there will be time for, and how soon
the Big Top will be taken down and move on to the
next town.

But mainly, overwhelmingly, it is a measure of my
need for you to need me, and for us to be able to
share life and love – even if in fragments. That's why
I responded so badly when I suddenly found a little
parcel of time, but you had made other arrangements
and would not/could not shift them to suit my selfish
needs. You see, you say it is you who suffers most,
because you are there alone, whereas I have my
family, but you don't understand how afraid I am of
losing you. You'll say, 'Sorry, Simon, I'm not sitting
waiting around here for you to fit me in. Goodbye.'

The other day you told me you love me in tones
which suggested that the Third World War had
broken out and you had time to say only those words

before the big bang. Well, that is roughly what I feel
all the time, and it's no use telling me to be easy in
my mind and not fret and enjoy the hours we can
snatch, and not think about the future, because
although my head hears you my heart does not.
Every time I pass the circus, my heart trembles and I
clench my fists in case there is a notice up saying
LAST DAY. One day there will be – and I will know
at last that there is not the remotest possibility of the
tightrope walker, glittering in her finery, falling off
into my arms.

So I began by accusing you of having little faith,
and now I show how insecure I am myself. You said
to me, 'You will get bored of coming here, soon,
when the novelty has worn off', and I put my hand
gently across your mouth. Perhaps it's time we
reaffirmed what we said in the beginning: that we
will live in the present and not spoil it by worrying
away at what can't be.

I DECREE THAT THE FUTURE IS
ABOLISHED.

Love, love, love, love, love, love, love – and faith
too

S xxxxxxxxxxxxxxxxxxxxxxx

20th August 1988

My love,
Well, now you know why I use this! You've been
really honest – you loved my holiday letters but it

took you hours and hours to decipher single phrases. You imagined a demented french flea hopping all over the pages, probably drunk on Beaujolais, and producing the marks that landed on your doormat, under cover of a french stamp! I'm sorry. I did warn you! Anyway, now I'm back, and I shall see you at the end of this week, but in the mean time I have to write and tell you how happy I feel to be back within a few miles of you, so that if suddenly I could put on giant magic boots, I could step right into your garden.

I missed you so much. In the market at Bergerac I suddenly saw, through the crowd, a head like yours and I took a step towards her – but of course it wasn't you. I must have looked ill or something, because R asked me what was the matter. I said I felt hot. She insisted we went to sit in a café to have a citron pressé, which was sweet of her. But then Kathy started to moan and say she was bored (as always!) and we talked about where to go and what to do – and all I could think of was you.

Shall we do it one day? Shall I move heaven and earth to steal a few days with you? It would be like being given a present that could be opened and enjoyed forever. WE WILL DO IT. I owe it to you, because you're so patient and uncomplaining when I have to go to France to spend two long weeks with my family. I must have summoned up your face a hundred times a day, especially your expression when we said goodbye – which said, 'I will not complain because this man has another life.'

Am I right?

I think of you in your still, calm, beautiful sitting room, that day, bending your head over Yeats and reading me that marvellous poem – and I still feel a flicker of guilt because the power in me then was not aroused by the words, but by you. But I suppose Yeats would have approved. Living the feeling, not reading about it. Until Friday.

With all my love, Simon   xx – and the rest

4th September

My darling,

Those were magical hours, the more so for the fact that for once they were not brief ones to be snatched, but real ones to be savoured. They will keep me going. I shall write again tomorrow, I expect. And phone. In the mean time, I have amazing news which will transport you, as much as it has me. Kit has invited R and Kathy to stay, to go to some show or other, and I have made an excuse – which she understands!! So we will have a glorious weekend together. Black it out in red in your elegant little diary, decorate the red with silver stars – October 7th–9th!

In haste – S

20th September

Dearest heart,

It's all arranged and I am so excited I feel like a boy with a new train set. I've booked, and we can walk on the moor in the October sun (of course it will be sunny! How would it dare to be anything else!) and listen to water and eat delicious lunches, and return to make love as the afternoon dwindles into evening, and then drink some excellent champagne and dine and talk and talk and talk. Two nights and two days will be touched with magic, so that within those hours we encompass a whole history of loving. Time will be sent packing.

I've told the girls that I will be off out working all weekend, and if R tries to ring me late I will just say I left the answerphone on by mistake. We often do that anyway. I don't even think she will ring, as the time is so short. Oh, my love – should I feel guilty? We talked of this last time, even though I'd put a ban on such discussions. Sometimes I don't fully comprehend the complexity of my feelings. Oh God, this is no place to attempt analysis. All I know is that GUILT is a mean and unworthy thing, and I will not let my love be sullied.

I'll phone you tomorrow (when you'll have got this) between 5 and 6, and have a quick word, but we are going out for drinks (boring!) so I won't be able to talk long.

Love, as ever, Macky

12th October

Oh my darling,
I'm still reeling. Thank you, thank you for the most

wonderful time I have ever had. Never before in my
life have I known such intense happiness, except
maybe once when I was a child and my parents
bought me The Red Bicycle and it seemed to me that
a boy could not be prouder or happier than I.

Wasn't that the most perfect time? Do you
remember saying, as we looked across to the tor, that
you could happily die tomorrow, having known such
joy? I knew what you meant, and for a terrifying
moment I imagined dying with you. And then we
should be together for all time – or rather for no time,
for the time that is beyond time. But you see, that's
the trouble. NOT to be able to laugh like we did
when you got your feet wet in that stream, or gaze
over the gold and purple moorland as the sun was
slipping down, or wake curled round each other's
bodies like spoons, or . . . Well, you know all the
things I am thinking of, not least of which is reaching
a depth of intimacy with you, when I could explore all
the most secret parts of your body (and your soul)
without shame.

Imagine NOT being able to do those things! Even
if we never had such a chance again, we can live our
lives with the limitless possibility, can't we? And to
acknowledge that is to *accept* time, and life – for all the
shortfall in happiness we have to tolerate, because of
my situation. So we shall not slip into that easy way of
wishing for an end, even if the wish is only half
acknowledged. You and I, my love, we'll LIVE, if only
to be in love with each other. I look down at my hand,
see the veins blue-grey beneath the surface of the
skin, and reflect that I am forty now – FORTY, for
heaven's sake! You say I am being a child, and then

you embark on one of your own flights of insecurity. But I am so conscious of getting older (forty is crisis time) and it used to worry me. But now, when I look down at my veins and think of all the network of bones, and the blood beneath, and the essential strength of heart, kidneys, liver, I am awestruck because all that adds up to the whole creature who is Simon McKee, and who is there for YOU. I love my body and I will cling to my life – even if ten devils are trying to prise my fingertips off the cliff edge – for the sake of the time I can and will have with YOU. Thank you for coming to Devon. Thank you for loving me – for stirring the dull roots with Spring rain.

All my love forever, Your Macky

Chapter Three

I've been sitting wondering whether the words exist to convey how one human being feels about betrayal.

They write things like 'her face was set into a mask of pure pain', and it doesn't come close. 'Pure pain', as distinct from impure pain?

Would it be truer to stamp down a jumble of letters to symbolise the white noise inside my head? Would they spell the savage terror of the beast at bay? Or take us one step further away from meaning? The language does not exist to express the headlong tumble into the void.

Kit was sitting quite still, as if waiting. I could hear her breathing quite quickly, and sensed her face turned towards me. But I read on, scrolling very slowly.

'You've got to stop, Rosa!' said Kit. 'I'm turning this fucking thing off!'

She reached forward for the switch. I slammed my hand down on hers, hurting her. 'I've got to read it,' I said.

Kit jerked away. Then she got up quickly, sending her chair crashing back. In that second I thought that the noise must even waken Simon, setting all his nerves aflame once more.

'I can't bear it, Rosa. Please!' Kit said, jamming a cigarette between her lips with shaking fingers.

'*You* can't bear it?' I said. 'I'm really sorry, Kit. We come in here to give me a computer lesson, and we stumble across the bloody, stinking LIE my husband was living, for God knows how long . . . Oh, I'm really sorry it's upsetting you.'

'You don't know it didn't stop. It probably didn't last,' she mumbled.

At that I jabbed again and again, scrolling on and on, letter after letter, the year changing, the love sneaking onwards in those intimate letters between my husband and some woman, on and on . . .

I shouted out some noise, and crashed my right hand down on the whole keyboard, accidentally moving on the document to its last recorded entry – one month before he died.

'Look at that! So it was five years. Going on for six years. The bastard! He was unfaithful to me for FIVE BLOODY YEARS! Look at it, Kit! Don't bloody well turn away, it won't go away, it's been there all this time, locked in the machine, like a . . . like . . .'

I felt myself folding up, crumpling like someone shot in the street by a sniper. I was aware of Kit standing above me, her arms around me, cradling my head in her abdomen, as I shuddered there. For a while there were no words, except that once Kit said flatly, 'Oh, you fool, Simon. You fucking idiot!'

Then, from somewhere deep in my own gut (it seemed) I heard the creature sobbing. 'How . . . ? What did he . . . ? Oh, God, you bastard, you pig, you cruel vicious lying creep . . . All that *time*, you . . . Oh, Jesus Christ, oh Jesus, help me . . . help me!'

I heard her murmur, 'To write on the computer . . . The stupid, bloody *fool*.'

After a while I felt Kit disengage one of her arms, and

reach across to the computer, click once, then twice, then again (the procedures must be gone through, I had learnt that already) and at last switch off. Then she pulled me to my feet, very gently, helping me along like people do at a funeral after the outrage of sudden violent death.

'We're getting out of here,' she said.

We were at the door when I raised my head and pushed her away, so that she staggered slightly with the force of it. I ran at the computer; I screamed at it; I started to hit it with open palms.

'I hate you, I hate you, I hate you,' I yelled, as the monitor resounded hollowly to blows.

Kit pulled. 'Rosa, Rosa, come on! We'll go and talk this through. Come on . . . come with me now.'

She was crooning to me as if to a baby, leading me away downstairs.

I was cold. My teeth chattered, and I sat hunched in a chair, staring at my hands, which stung. Kit ran upstairs, brought down a duvet, and wrapped it around me. Then she went to the sideboard and poured a large brandy. I swirled it, trying not to retch.

It was Simon's drink, not mine. I imagined him settling himself back in his mistress's house, cradling a brandy balloon, hating his obligation to return here – to his home. *Macky* – of all the stupid names. I never had a nickname for him; he was always 'Simon', safe within his dignity, his whole presence, the selfhood that I knew, after twenty-two years . . .

'Drink it, Rosa – please!'

My hand was shaking so much Kit had to steady it with her own, guiding my head with her other hand – as she might a very old woman in hospital. The stuff burned my throat, but I got it down.

'How could he? How could he do that – to me?' I asked at last.

'Obviously he never imagined you'd find out,' said Kit, very quietly.

'Oh – so he could have gone on, for another six years, running us both? Lying to me every day, every hour? Wanting to be with *her* all the time he was . . .'

I remember rocking to and fro.

'Don't, Rosa, please don't. Look at me . . . go on! Look at me, Rosa.'

'What?'

'Rosa – we're going to face this together. We're going to talk about it, you and me, do you hear?'

I heard. I saw Kit's face as if from a distance, through mist. I nodded instinctively, polite as I was brought up, but there was no acquiescence in that movement. I knew nothing; my head was bursting with words and phrases – his words and phrases. His love for the mysterious Other – the woman I would never know.

I felt Kit untangle my fingers, and hold both my hands, very tenderly. Her hands were warm.

'You're like ice,' Kit said.

'Do you remember Roy?' I asked, staring straight ahead.

'Of course I do,' said Kit, sounding puzzled.

'He wanted to marry me,' I said.

'I know he did.'

Impossible to forget Roy Simpson. I went out with him in the first year, and most of the other girls were jealous. He was a third-year painting student, so quite a feather in my cap. And I adored him.

'I should have married him,' I said.

'You can't say that. You can never know what might have happened.'

'He was much better than Simon. He wouldn't have done this to me. I should have married him.'

Kit let out her breath impatiently. 'I'm not having this,' she said. 'We're into truth right now, so I'm going to knock this new lie on the head, in case you start to live with it. Are you ready? Roy slept around all the time you were going out with him. I went to bed with him once – yes, Rosa, I did, though I would never have told you! You weren't at the party; we both got pissed; I went back to his place, and we fucked each other's brains out, all night. The next day was fine; we liked each other before and we liked each other after, and he knew I wanted nothing to do with love – or even a relationship. But you did. You were the kind of woman men always thought of as A Relationship, whether they liked it or not. Roy was captured by you, he told me, like a fly in a sticky web. A clever little spider, he called you. He said all the others – yeah, me included! – were the kind of women he just slept with, but you were different. So of course he thought he might marry you. Then you met Simon McKee. You left Roy for Simon – and you made the right decision.'

I didn't want to hear any of this. I stared at her, and shook my head. 'Roy loved me. He wanted to marry me. He was *kind*,' I whispered.

'Simon was kind,' said Kit firmly.

Then all the hatred I felt for Simon transferred itself to her. 'How can you say that? How can you be on his side? Get out of here! Go on – get out! GET OUT!'

'I'm not going anywhere. I'm staying with you until we've talked this through, and I feel you can go on.'

'I want to die,' I whispered.

'Nonsense,' said Kit.

'Yes, I do!' I hissed. 'I want to die so that I can run after him forever. So I can find him wherever he is and hit him

and scream at him for what he's done. I want to hurt him –
forever – just like he's hurt me. Why should he be dead – and
safe? Why should he have left me here, to find all that . . . all
that . . . filthy, disgusting *stuff*, when he isn't here for me to
scream at?'

'Oh, Rosa – you always hated the computer . . . And how
could he have known he was going to die? We don't know.
None of us knows.'

'I hate him. I shall always hate him now. I'll tell Kathy so
she knows what kind of a man her father really was. She
idolises him, she thinks he was perfect. Perfect! A disgusting
liar! A cheat, an adulterer, a lying, snivelling bastard of a
cheat! He didn't give a bugger for us – for either of us!'

'Yes he did, Rosa.'

'How can you sit there and say that?' I shouted. 'Didn't
you read that stuff? Or were you being too polite to read
somebody else's love letters? Like watching through the bedroom window – and you wouldn't do that, would you, Kit?
You're much too well bred! Well, damn you for saying that
he cared for us. If you want to defend him – I told you – you
can get the hell out of here. I don't want you! You can go and
lie down on his grave and tell him what a brilliant person he
was. What a stunning specimen of humanity, to write to this
little tart he was in love with, and tell her that he hated being
with us. Go on, tell him!'

'Rosa – it's not my fault,' said Kit quietly.

'I'm sorry,' I said. 'It's just that . . . I don't know what to do.'

Across the chasm I watched my friend watching me, and
realised that there was no way she could reach me. I was
alone on my cliff, whipped by bitter winds. She wanted to
help me, that much was obvious. You do, don't you? Or perhaps that is another untruth; perhaps in reality we don't want
to help, but long to run from the alien, inconsolable pain. Yet

we do not, because of the deep knowledge that one day the men in black will be at our own door, and it will be terrible then to turn and find the room empty.

'Look, we'll talk it through,' Kit said, wondering where to begin.

'To think that it was all a lie, our marriage a lie, everything . . .' I said.

'But how do you know that?'

'You read those letters – there's more, there're hundreds of them, I bet. All hidden in that bloody thing. I'll read them all—'

'I'm going to go up there and delete the lot,' said Kit, half rising.

'Oh no,' I told her, 'you're not touching them, Kit. They're mine now. I inherited them, didn't I? Somewhere that woman's got her actual letters, tied up with pink ribbon no doubt, and she thinks they're all hers. Like she thought *he* was, probably – staying with me for the sake of duty, or God knows what. Why the hell didn't he leave once Kathy had gone away to university? He probably felt sorry for me. He probably talked about it with her – both of them feeling sorry for me.' I couldn't suppress a groan. 'But now I've got the letters too, and I'll read them all. I'll go on reading them forever, to try to find out.'

'What?' Kit asked.

'What he was like – to her. Did you read them? All that poetic stuff? All hearts and flowers and dearest darling shite! He wasn't LIKE that, Kit! He was never like that!'

Kit was looking thoughtful. 'Oh, I don't know . . . I remember how worked up he got about Moore and Hepworth. Actually, in those days I always thought of him as quite a romantic.'

God damn him forever, for a romantic, for a liar, for a

fool, I thought. I closed my eyes for a second, and imagined him staked out, arms and legs spread, and I was burning his naked flesh with a cigarette butt, while somewhere behind me a woman wept quietly. I could not turn to see her. I was too absorbed in inflicting pain where it was deserved. Oh, those medieval images of hell! I wanted dozens of black devils to spring up from the bowels of the earth and help me punish him, as was their duty: stuffing burning irons up his anus, cutting off his penis, impaling him. *Luxuria* – to be revenged fittingly. Sin, I thought; it was and is a terrible sin, yet nobody thinks so these days. Perhaps Her friends all knew. Perhaps our friends all knew, and yet nobody was shocked because adultery is what people do, and are forgiven. Why should they tell me? Nothing wrong with it!

Feeling sick, I swallowed air and opened my eyes. Kit was staring at me. 'Can you imagine what it's like?' I asked her. 'I feel as if I've just opened a door— No, it's like one of those screens they hang icons on, and there's the special, sacred door the priest comes through, and I feel as if I've gone through that door and found the devil sitting on the altar, in the holy place.'

'Oh, Rosa love – Simon wasn't a saint.'

'You don't say.'

'You know what I mean! He wouldn't ever have wanted to be thought of as a saint. He was just . . . human.'

'So – is it supposed to be human to lie to your wife for five years? And I'm supposed to excuse it? Say, "Poor you, Simon, you're dead now, so I forgive you everything"? Well, I can't say that, Kit. I'll never say it. Don't tell me he was human! Those letters read inhuman to me.'

'So you'll hate him forever now?' Kit's voice was tired, as if she had heard all this before, somewhere else, and knew less how to cope.

'YES! Of course I will! Anybody would!'

'What's the point?'

'Maybe it'll give me something to do. Maybe I'll spend my days working through those letters, then taking his study apart to find her letters to him – there must be some! Then I'll have her address, and I'll turn up on her doorstep, and ask her why she didn't keep her hands of my husband. She knew he was married; she should have sent him packing. Bitch! It wouldn't have happened if it hadn't been for her.'

'Oh, Rosa . . . it doesn't work like that,' said Kit quietly.

I ignored her, and went on. The only voice I wanted to hear was my own, because I knew I had the answer. 'I'm going to find out, you know. I'll take his room apart. Supposing she's somebody I know? Suppose she was at his funeral, watching me, thinking, "Ha, you stupid weeping cow, he was *mine*, he wasn't yours!" She must have been laughing at me all the time . . .'

'No,' Kit said.

'Of course she was!' I cried. '*Macky* – what a stupid name! He always hated nicknames – he said so, do you remember? So why'd he let her call him "Macky"? I don't understand. He must have gone mad.'

'People call each other silly names,' Kit said.

'*We* didn't call each other silly names,' I replied.

'Rosa, you have to think . . . I mean, maybe he loved you both in such different ways that he was torn in two. Maybe it did drive him mad, in a way.'

'But I'd have known! Surely I would have known? He was just the same as ever, he didn't change. I'd have noticed if he'd behaved differently, moped about, or something like that. No – he was like an actor. He just played his role, lying to me the whole time. I'll never, *ever* forgive him!'

'Some people lead two lives . . . because they don't

know what else to do. They're caught.'

'It's disgusting and dishonest. Why are you making excuses for him, Kit? I thought you were my friend.'

'Maybe I'm making excuses for myself.'

'What do you mean – for yourself?'

Kit shook her head. 'I don't know whether to tell you. I didn't ever want to tell you – because I didn't know how you'd respond.'

I felt something sharp twist in my side then, like an electric current. 'What are you saying? It wasn't . . . You're not saying . . . ? KIT! Was it *you* he wrote those letters to?'

'Don't be ridiculous, Rosa! Of course it wasn't.'

'How do I know? I don't know anything any more. Anything could be true. It's like I've gone into another country where everything is the opposite of what I thought. White is black. Good is most certainly bad.'

'Rosa – I give you my word of honour that I have never even contemplated having an affair with your husband. Look – that's what I was trying to start to tell you. The reason I'm not sitting here, as your friend, and pouring scorn and resentment on Simon, and calling him a liar and a cheat, is because I have no right to. You do – but I don't.'

'Yes, you do. You know he was a complete bastard, so why don't you say so – even to make me feel better,' I said.

'No – I'm not calling him names because *I'm the same as him*. That's what I want to tell you – I understand how you can live like he did. I've been there, Rosa. So maybe you can judge him – but I can't.'

I gazed at her. The look on Kit's face was out of character. The woman whose fine, bony features habitually settled into expressions of mocking merriment, or combative intelligence, was leaning forward now, her eyes pleading, stripped of all protection.

'I've been having an affair too, Rosa. It won't shock you, you know I'm not a plaster saint either. The odd one-night stand when I've been away, a guy in the office you might fancy for a couple of weeks . . . all that doesn't mean anything. But I fell in love, Rosa, and I'm still in love with him. It's a terminal doting passion – but I can't leave Paul. I can't. For nearly two years now I've been on the rack. Every moment I'm not with Mark is like torture. And I'm not with him an awful lot of the time.'

My first response was relief. In truth it was impossible to imagine Kit having an affair with Simon; he always used to joke that even as my friend she was just too much for him. Then I saw that she was looking for the comfort she should have been giving me. I said nothing.

'Rosa?' she prompted.

'Does Paul know?' I asked. My voice was cold. I couldn't help it.

Kit shook her head. 'He hasn't got a notion. You know what he's like. He goes to his office, and comes home, and starts to cook the meal he bought at lunchtime, and if I'm late he puts on a record and waits patiently, and— *Oh God, he's so bloody good!* He never asks where I've been or who with or anything. He loves me and he trusts me, and he doesn't know anything about me. I can't bear it!'

'Who is this man?'

'He's a feature writer. Young – he's twelve years younger than me – and so beautiful, Rosa! I can't take my eyes off him when we're together. He's funny and clever and sexy – and there's never been anything like it for me. Never. It's *the* great love.' She paused, shook her head sadly, and repeated, 'A very great love.'

'Like Simon's . . . for her,' I said.

'Yes! I mean – probably. What can I say? Simon deceived

you all that time, and I lie my head off to Paul, because . . . that's what you do, Rosa. You haven't got a choice. You get into this obsessive love, and you have to follow it to the darkest corners. A passion, like I said. Once, when we'd been together for about seven months, Mark tried to break it off. He went back to the girl he'd been with before, and she was fifteen years younger than me. Imagine how I felt! I felt old, and ugly, and rejected, and I wanted to die. But I couldn't tell anyone. Paul thought I was ill; I couldn't sleep, I used to wake up at four or five in the morning, and lie there staring into the darkness, aching for Mark. I tried to tell myself it was the best thing, because I could concentrate on my marriage again, and be fair to poor Paul. Then Mark rang, and I wanted to run down the road naked, screaming with joy. If he'd asked me to I would have crawled on my stomach from here to Scotland, eating dirt. It's terrifying. But you're *caught*, and once you realise it, it's too late.'

I shook my head. 'I'm sorry – I think all that stuff's just excuses. Saying we've got absolutely no control over anything. It's not good enough. Everybody would just do exactly what they wanted, all the time.'

'The point is – we don't do just what we want! What *I* want is to be with Mark, yet I stick with my bloody marriage! I was going to phone him later . . . I have to speak to him two or three times a day. And he writes me letters, Rosa! The most wonderful things, in this big curvy handwriting, and I read them again and again. I love them so much! And I want him more than I've ever wanted anything in my life. But I stay with Paul.' Kit paused, then added gently, almost persuasively, 'Simon stayed with you.'

'I wish he hadn't then!' I shouted. 'And you! You're staying with Paul because you feel sorry for him – or is it because you like the house? Don't you want to leave the luxury?'

'Oh for heaven's sake!' Kit shouted back.

We glared at each other; then at last she shook her head, rose quickly, and knelt at my side. 'I'm sorry for yelling,' she said softly, 'but we have to be able to talk. You have to let me reach you.'

I did not bend towards her. I held my head up stiffly, and when at last I glanced sideways, down at Kit's upturned face, I know my expression was set into coldness – and judgement. I would not give in. I would not forgive her either. I had to be on the side of her husband, because he and I were both victims.

'Do you think that's possible, Kit – really?' I asked. 'I don't think anybody'll reach me – ever. Not now. Maybe I should just go away somewhere and die.' Kit shook her head. 'And maybe the honest thing *would* be for you to leave Paul. I'm sorry, Kit, but it's all too easy for people like you and *him* – Simon. You want it all ways. And it's not fair. It's not bloody fair!'

She just looked at me. And as I stared back, I found myself studying the contours of her face, still beautiful although lines were beginning to show, and thinking that this was the face of someone who was somebody's 'very great love'. Was there just one such love for each of us?

I thought that must be true. In which case, Simon, no one else but Simon, was my own.

Chapter Four

Next morning I woke very early. For a second I wondered where I was, then remembered, and curled into a foetus. My mouth was coated, my breath sour. I knew if I were to rise the hangover would hit, so I half turned my face into the pillow and groaned aloud. After a short while, suddenly aware of saliva seeping about my face, I pulled myself up and reached for the clock. It was 4.30 am.

During the evening, Kit and I had got through three bottles of white wine, and played old records, and become (at one point) hysterical with laughter. What was it about? All I could remember was the desperation. We found it hard to meet each other's eyes, and were glad to retreat into reminiscence. The trouble was Simon was present in our shared past. At the end I'd collapsed in drunken tears over the last shot of whisky, wailing about Simon. Kit had – with some difficulty, given her own condition – put me to bed.

Outside a single bird trilled. The purity of the sound was unbearable; it pierced my brain. I wanted to call out to it, tell it to stop. I needed to hear the sound of my own voice in that room, in perfect silence, as though the slightest sound might muffle the words I wished to say. To him.

The light was chilly grey-blue, neutralising outlines, depriving the familiar of identity. I looked sideways, at the pillow I had not changed since he died. In the days after his death I'd clutched it, wept into it, smelt the most subtle scent of him, the essence. I had also picked it up and thrown it across the room, in rage and frustration at being left. When calmer, I'd cradled it in my lap and murmured, 'I love you, Simon, I love you. Can you hear me? I love you.' Now I reached out and laid my forefinger on the surface for a fraction of a second, before withdrawing it quickly, lest I become contaminated.

'How could you? How could you do it to me?' I said aloud.

So sorry Rosa my darling, I'm so sorry.

I listened. The bird poured its soul into the air, to be joined by another, then another. I hated them. How could I hear, with all that din? Sooner or later, though, I knew he would speak again, within my head, but this time I would not listen. This time I would pursue him, and tell him how much I hated him. I would disturb his grave. I would dig up what I had planted. I would kick and scatter the earth . . .

'NO!' I shouted aloud. 'Don't think I'll listen to your excuses, you bastard. You *bastard*, Simon – bastard, bastard, bastard, bastard, *bastard*.'

With each repetition I clutched at my knees through the duvet, and rocked in time. As a child I used to swear like that, like the rest of them, relishing the bad words: 'Damn, damn, double damn – two bloody hells and a bugger!' It was wicked, and satisfying, if meaningless. If they heard you at home, it set you apart and earned a rebuke; at school it was tame. They all said 'fuck' when I was not even sure what the word meant. Once, when I was ten, walking from primary school in a group, I had seen the word chalked on a wall.

'But what does it *mean*?' I had asked. One of the boys had smiled, half in derision, and knowingly raised two fingers.

'It means – that!' he'd said.

I had nodded, mystified, then attempted a wink, as if I understood.

Four letters on a wall, two fingers jerked upwards in the air . . . and then we had stripped privet twigs, to bend into loops for collecting spider webs. When I looked into the gauzy webs, layer upon layer, I saw my own reality, milky and distinct, but pure, far removed from that other confusing reality of word and sign. I had gone home and drawn pictures of fairies, and princesses in flounced gowns, and castles on tall hills, wreathed by cloud.

'That's lovely, my pet,' my mother had said, leaning over the table to look.

Encouraged, I'd created alternative worlds within the pages of Woolworth's sketch books; the rainbow was my Lakeland coloured pencil set, all the points beautifully sharpened, and Rosa Perry written in tiny letters along a sliver of naked wood scraped off each crayon. I was an only child. They were old and didn't quite know what to do with this unexpected gift, so they gave me paints, pastels, oil boards, brushes, all in profusion as I needed. They wanted their child to go to university, fearing art schools as dens of iniquity, but my flower studies won their hearts. Neither Mr nor Mrs Perry lived to see my watery abstract experiments much later. Kit always said they were my rebellion against the lines drawn by my parents; the excruciating niceties of thirties mock-tudor, and the immaculate flowerbeds beyond the rustic arch.

Or maybe they were a rebellion against Simon too.

I believed in you. Nobody has ever put more faith in another human being. You became my mother and my father, all family, all things, Simon. You remember the day we met, outside the library? You noticed I'd been crying;

you asked me what was the matter, but I wouldn't tell you, it was too soon. I put my head down and hurried by. Later I told you that Dad had died; he couldn't go on without her, it was no good. Why would a couple who loved each other like that want to live separately? Far better for both to be dead. They were married for thirty years, tried for ages to have a child, achieved me – and that was it.

Oh, they loved me of course, once I was there. But the truth was they had got used to just being together; the idea of a child was only that in the end – an idea. They tried as a matter of course; they had given up all hope. So I think I was a bit of a shock to them. I still remember the feeling of being the third party. No wonder. I always made such a fuss about being loved. I used to pluck at love, as a child or puppy reaches out to seize the beloved skirt as it passes. Please notice me. Please love me – and me alone. Please make everything desired become perfect, for ever and ever, happy ever after.

You used to smooth my hair and whisper that I was just a little romantic, that you loved that in me. You said you would look after me forever . . . Didn't make much of a job of that, did you? Bastard, bastard, bastard, bastard, bastard, bastard, bastard, bastard, bastard, bastard, bastard, bastard.

Twenty-two years, Rosa.

'You don't have to remind me of that. I know. I know only too well.'

I did not know if I had spoken aloud, but knew I was hearing him clearly. Maybe he was within his dressing gown, still hanging on the back of the door. Or in the clothes in the cupboard, his soul dusty and threatened by moths. Maybe he was in the dust – the idea of the dust obsessed me. Everywhere in this house he lurked, his ghost mocking me.

I began to shiver and pulled the duvet up around my ears.

What was it he had said? I closed my eyes, trying to remember. But I felt sick. It had gone, whatever it was. A justification? How would you ever know?

I slept for a while then, and dreamt I was a tiny person, living amid a mass of green. I was green too, utterly protected by this camouflage. The branches were a palisade; birdsong drowned all sounds of the outside world. Nothing was threatening: caterpillar, ladybird and fly were fellow creatures, equal-sized inhabitants of a secure universe. Even the spider did not terrify, so the tiny green creature knew she was safe even within that web.

But suddenly there was a rending and a tearing. The gauzy web in which she rocked was disturbed, and up she went, up and up, the web caught in a loop of privet, and a huge eye peering at her, struggling within. The cyclops stared. She cried for help, knowing her reedy voice could not be heard against the cacophony of birdsong. And the eye changed; it swam, it filled with tears of pity for her plight.

I caught you. I took away your freedom. I put you in a prison.
The creature recognised that voice. It belonged in the past. 'Don't let me go, don't let me fall,' she pleaded, clinging to the web with tiny, scrabbling fingers.

I can't. I must let you go free.
And suddenly the loop sprang open, and the gauze disintegrated, and she was falling, turning over and over in the air, like a leaf, down, down, down. Then the giant with Simon's eye and voice, high above and out of sight, began to weep huge tears of sorrow, dropping all around her like rain.

I'm sorry, Rosa, I'm sorry.
A voice cried out. Sweating, I shuddered awake, knowing it was my own. The room was lighter now, and the birdsong had intensified. I felt my stomach contract, acid in my mouth. Stumbling, lurching against the door frame, I ran

into the bathroom next door, and was sick. Kneeling by the lavatory, both hands gripping the seat, I inhaled the sour smell of my own vomit, and began to cry. The mess in front of my eyes seemed a perfect manifestation of the state of my own soul. In a moment of acute self-hatred I felt I should bend down and gobble it up, as a cat will eat its own sick – ingesting worthlessness, despair and rage, returning it to an endless cycle of disgust.

I know now why people inflict wounds on themselves. Raging teenagers take knives or blades and carve patterns on their skin, or burn themselves with lighted cigarettes, and their carers or jailors counsel or rebuke, according to temperament. Yet the mortification of the flesh was approved by the ancient fathers of the church: a fitting statement of unworthiness. Or sin. So the flagellants' cords scattered fragments of skin and blood, and cries of anguish were suppressed by prayers of penitence.

Yet I have not sinned, not me. It's you. You are the sinner. So why would I punish myself?

At last I pulled myself up, splashed my face with cold water, then stared at my reflection. The face I saw was gaunt and ugly, marred by alcohol, exhaustion and grief; dark brown hair in a spiky halo; purple shadows, deep furrows from nose to mouth, blotchy skin . . . Were he to see me now he would survey the epitome of ugliness. Quite natural then, to run to that other woman – the young, the beautiful, the infinitely desirable – and the world would turn a blind eye, understanding his need. Are not all men drawn irresistibly to youth and beauty?

But it was his fault.

'You made me like this, Simon,' I said.

Then, 'What does *she* look like?'

But this time there was no reply.

Since Kit and I had found the letters, I had not really considered the nature of the person to whom they were written.
My rage expressed itself in the epithets I'd used to Kit, and
within my own mind: 'Whore', 'Slag', 'Tart', 'Slut'.

Oh, we've all read articles about infidelity; I was always
mildly shocked at the violence of the words used by the
betrayed. On one of those windy television studio discussion
programmes once, there were wives one side of the studio
and mistresses the other, and the wives abused the mistresses
of other men in the very language that I was now using
myself. Whoever that woman was, who had inspired those
intimate, passionate letters, I knew for sure that she must be
at once beautiful and evil. As a child will scribble the simple,
basic elements of a face, and all faces to that child will be the
same, so my mental pencil sketched this mistress who was all
mistresses – and the lineaments were crude. An image of a
blonde siren, aged about thirty-five, bobbed before my inner
eye, and it mocked the face I saw in the mirror. I held on to
the edge of the basin, and crammed my fist into my mouth to
stifle a scream.

I put on a dressing gown, and stole past the spare-room
door, and upstairs to the landing. First I opened the door to
Kathy's room, with the little bathroom next door, and stood
for a moment contemplating the signs of my daughter's life
to date. There were two teddy bears and a doll on a shelf,
loved despite adolescence. A shelf of miniature animals dated
from childhood too. Posters of obscure (to me) singers and
film stars evoked Kathy worrying over spots and boys, while
a Greenpeace poster of a dolphin signified the anxiety of the
sixteen-year-old environmentalist. An Indian shawl on the
back of the chair, a papier mâché cat, variations on the letter
'K' in wood and plastic . . . each object reminded me with
unbearable poignancy that this was a little girl's room no

more – but worse (for that feeling had been there since Kathy left for Edinburgh for the first term) that the child and young woman who had inhabited this room had been betrayed as surely as I myself had been betrayed. On holiday with the two of us, his wife and daughter, that man had yearned to be with *her* – the slut. His slut.

What's more, he dared to reduce me to 'R'. A cipher. At least he gave his daughter the dignity of her name, while I was contracted into an initial, in case my actual name should remind that bitch that there was a real woman here, a wife at home – a whole living, breathing person, on whom *she* was cheating.

I closed the door, crossed the landing, and went into Simon's study. It was exactly as we left it, of course. Yet a part of me fantasised that terror might have roused his shade from sleep, guilt driving it back to haunt its old room, and remove all evidence of sin, during the thin blue hours of night.

No poltergeist had disturbed the furniture in Simon's study; no unquiet soul had wandered back before dawn, to sift through drawers and take away the letters I knew must be hidden. For she must have written too – the evidence was there in his own letters. There was another side to that correspondence. He must have a photograph of the two of them in Devon on that weekend, or perhaps just a small portrait, to moon over when he was forced to be with his family. How much grieving for that woman went on within these walls? How many long, clandestine telephone calls – with the receiver slammed down because he heard Kathy's foot on the stair, or my voice calling up that supper was ready? How could he have sustained such a deception for more than five whole years?

I sat in front of the computer, switched it on, listened to

its soft whine, then switched it off again. I did not trust myself to start up, and find those letters again. Yet I knew I would. I would have to study them until I knew each word by heart. Perhaps that was what I deserved – to be tortured by his loving prose forever, with no one to scream at, no one to punish, because I had failed to be the kind of wife who commands fidelity. A cipher, a nobody, a nothing, nonentity, a zero – a *wife*. That's all I was.

I felt calm now, knowing that Kit must be asleep, that Kathy was in Edinburgh – that the only two presences within this room were myself and Simon.

Apart from That Woman. She had haunted the whole house, *my* house, my home, within Simon's head, for five years. Is it possible for the living to be ghosts? In writing, a ghost is a substitute, a mistress is a substitute wife, therefore a mistress is a ghost. Of course. A polluting presence within a marriage, reminding of other worlds that are not attainable. A presence now almost as powerful in my imagination as that of my husband, but more out of reach, because unidentified.

'Who are you?' I asked aloud. 'Where are you?'

Somewhere within these books, these drawers, these papers, I knew the answer must lurk. My task would be to discover her identity; my purpose then was equally clear. I would go and find his mistress (the blonde, the floosie, the slut, the whore, the man-eater, the slag, the slapper, the tart) and TELL her.

What?

'It doesn't matter what,' I told him. 'I just want to make her suffer. I want her to know how I'm suffering now, because what she did negated the last six years of my marriage. I loved you. I cried for you. I still had you with me, even though you were dead. Maybe I loved you more in

death, because it's a permanent state – that sort of loving.
Now I hate you. And it's all because of her. That's what I
want to tell her. Just that.'

I knew I had to be systematic. Somewhere within these
papers, the desk drawers, the box files, the books lay concealed the identity of that woman. Simon had written of her
beautiful calligraphy, cleverly concealed within a business
envelope – the clever, subtle, practised, scheming bitch. He
could not have thrown her words away. Suddenly it seemed
a matter of desperate urgency to read the other half of the
dialogue, the more to get its measure.

Why are you torturing yourself?

'Because I have to. I have to.'

I opened the right-hand top desk drawer and surveyed
the assortment of pens and pencils, sorted into the compartments of a cutlery tray. All the pencils were sharpened; the
artist's rubber was clean; the ink was in its box; the drawer
and its contents looked as if the owner of this desk had tidied
it yesterday. The next drawer down contained household
bills in folders, meticulously in order – ten years' worth,
each labelled in Simon's square capitals: 'Kathy's School',
'Electricity', 'Gas', 'Telephone', and so on.

*So boring . . . all so boring. You didn't have to bother with any
of that . . .*

'God, Simon, you were so bloody neat. Everything in its
place – look.'

Yes, everything in its place. A place for everything.

The stationery was in boxed piles: large business paper,
small business paper, invoices, correspondence cards, all
bearing the logo SIROSA Garden Design. There was plain
letter-heading too, and four sizes of envelope in the next
drawer down. On the other side: padded envelopes for
reusing, gummed labels, business cards.

I dragged open each drawer in turn, surveyed its contents for a few minutes, closed it, then started again – this time shoving the things roughly around, so that each drawer was reduced to chaos by the time I closed it again. As I searched, with all the finesse of a young policeman, I was afflicted by the thought that invisible bits of Simon's skin must still lie among these inanimate things, where he had last touched, remaining in the dust of the drawers, and the whole room, forever. How could you get rid of someone, completely? All traces? You would need to strip the room, repaint the walls, recover the floor . . . but who is to say that then, even then, there might not still lurk a fragment of skin or nail or a single hair, caught beneath the skirting board, or blown on to the new paint by a draught? Remaining there forever.

Dust again. I could think only of the dust.

I slammed the last drawer with horror, almost catching my fingers. Then I leant back in his chair, and looked around. Where to look next?

'Where did you put them, Simon? Surely you couldn't have been so cold as to chuck them out – in case I found them? I bet she kept yours, all tied up with pretty pink ribbon. She probably reads them every day. She probably laughs at me still.'

Laughs?

'Women like to triumph, Simon – you're stupid if you don't know that. I want to myself – yes, I do. The only way now is to find out. I will find out! But, wait a minute, she's probably got somebody else by now. Can you see her? Do you watch her with him – your bimbo, with her new lover? Does it make you grieve, Simon, wherever you are? Does it hurt you, like you hurt me? I hope so – Oh God, I hope so!'

Why hope?

I stood up, and took the first book from the shelf, roughly turning it upside down so that, in the stillness, I could hear the spine crack and tear. But no hidden letter fluttered to the ground. Angrily I snatched the next book. And on and on . . .

Kit came in about an hour later. She looked terrible; she had been looking all over the house for me.

'You should have known I'd be in here,' I said. 'How're you feeling then?'

'Lousy. You?'

'I threw up.'

'I'm not surprised.'

'Wish I'd waited and done it in here.'

'Oh, Rosa – please!'

That note of desperate, pleading reasonableness maddened me. I could not stop myself from rocking to and fro, faster and faster – so it was hard to speak, and my words came out like the rattle of gunfire.

'I wanted to find them, Kit. Her letters – I wanted to find her letters. She wrote to him, we know that. But they're not here. I've searched everywhere. The bastard must have got rid of them. What would she think of that? That he just chucked them away without caring? Poor bitch – poor bloody bitch! Look at all this stuff . . .' I leant forward and ran my hands through the debris on the floor as if it were fallen leaves. 'And he was so neat, my Simon! He wouldn't like to see all this mess, would he? Would you now, Simon?'

I listened hard. When she started to speak I held up my hand. 'Don't say anything, or else I won't hear him, Kit!'

'Oh God, this is all I need,' she muttered, and started to move towards me.

'Don't come in! This is a sacred space now. It's an altar,' I said.

'What are you talking about?'

'The holy cow of my marriage, that's what!' I started to giggle. 'Look, Kit – can't you see blood all over the floor? If you come in you might slip in it. I've slipped in it, all right!'

'Jesus, Rosa!'

Kit bent, and began to pick up books and replace them on the shelves. I watched her for a while, resenting her presence. Then I said, 'The wrong order. He hates things being in the wrong order, especially his books. It really upsets him.'

'Rosa—'

'It does. He can't stand it.'

'Simon's dead,' she said.

'I'm glad. I'm so glad, you know that?'

'So for God's sake, let him be dead. Leave him alone now. He made his mistakes. It's too late to do anything about them now, so let him rest in peace – won't you? Please, Rosa.'

She was picking up the books mechanically and replacing them on the shelves, any old way. I watched her. My friend. Tidying his room as if she knew everything. Yet she understood nothing. I hated her almost as much as I hated him. 'Why should I?' I asked. Then, 'He doesn't deserve to rest, let alone in peace.'

Chapter Five

I sat before the computer, confronting it, as if it were the only other living thing in the hellish universe I now inhabited. Or maybe I was the only other machine.

I'm sorry, Rosa, I'm sorry.

All those letters! You must have spent so long here, writing your little loving words. My darling, my love, my darling, my love. And what did I think you were doing? Designing bloody gardens! Such a genius! God, I'm glad Kit's gone.

Why?

Because she wanted me to understand you, can you imagine? She kept telling me I had to forgive you. Six years' worth of lies and she tells me that I should forgive you. Total betrayal, but she still comes on with her liberal soft-soap, as if it could wash you clean. I asked her to go in the end. I told her I was all right. She cares about me, I know she does, but I could see how much she wanted to get out of here!

It's not her fault.

You want to protect everybody, don't you? But what about me, Simon? Nobody's protecting me, are they? Nobody cares that I cried for you, and spent hours remembering all the lovely things we did. Do you remember when we went to France with that little blow-up tent like an igloo? It was our first proper holiday; we didn't have a honeymoon but waited until the summer. We went round the camp sites and set up our tent while all those fat Germans were still unpacking their great orange ones, and we'd cook a meal on the twin camping gas stove; and I thought that every single star in the sky could see us, had to be able to see us, because we were so happy. I was remembering that, and Christmases when Kathy was small, and all the things we did, our whole life, all of it, together, and now it's spoilt. It's all spoilt.

Our whole life, all of it, all together, all.

NO, it's too easy, Simon! I won't let you get away with it! Don't you see that the time you spent with HER, the times you were in bed with HER and writing those fucking letters to HER cancels out all the rest? It's like a ripple in a lake. You threw the stone in, and the ripples spread out in circles, forwards as well as back, so I'm being rocked by them now, but so is that me who was twenty-two and thought every star in the sky had to be able to see us. Can't you understand that? It works all ways, it spreads out like poison. It pollutes. It's even in the air, now, the moment we met – when Kit introduced us, and I thought you were gorgeous – hanging in the air above us like a dark cloud, holding all the future, spoiling everything. And when Kathy was born, and you had wet eyes as you held her in your arms and told me how clever I was – well, now I think of that, and the poison's like a vein in marble or in rock, running through even a moment as precious as that, holding what was going to happen. Can't you see that? A lie calls it ALL into question; every damned thing. See? God – for an intelligent man you're really being stupid, Simon!

I listened for a minute. The house was silent. I reached forward and switched on the computer, wanting to hear its small, internal whirr. Kit's notes were on the desk: 'Foolproof Directions For Technophobes Like Rosa McKee'. It was as if they had been written in another century – when a woman, the small Rosa who had rushed back to take a last look at her husband's coffin, had entered this study with her friend, to try to start life again. Carrying on the business. Celebrating him . . .

Suddenly, as the desktop appeared on the screen, another image flickered in my memory and became clear. I looked down at myself once more, from a height, and saw the creature walking away from the grave to catch up with Kathy and the other mourners. There was a person by a tree, head bent in grief, pressing so close she could have been one with the grey-brown bark. I half closed my eyes, seeking the image, willing it to become sharper, the woman to raise her head, to show her face, to look directly at me across time, all deception gone. I knew, without doubt, that the figure by the tree had been Simon's mistress.

Then the noise at the back of the church echoed harshly in my memory: the sound of sobbing, the feet echoing, the door slamming. Simon lay in his coffin in the middle of the aisle, and the woman – SHE – could not bear it.

Ha! I could bear it, but she couldn't. I had to be brave, and so did Kathy. God, what right did she have to lose control? Sitting there, looking at the back of my head and thinking, Poor, bloody, deluded bitch, thinking her husband loved her! He was mine really, but she doesn't now that. And daring to cry for you, Simon! What bloody right?

Right to cry.

'NO!'

I had no hesitation about operating the computer. I was no longer afraid of it. I knew how to access the file. The old Rosa would have fluffed and fussed, and looked round for somebody to help her: Simon, Kit, Kathy, anybody who could liberate her back into her watercolour daydreams. This new Rosa possessed formidable concentration. Or rather, was possessed. There was no alternative, I knew that. One of the reasons I had been so keen for Kit to return to London was the suspicion that she might sneak in to delete the letters.

Well meaning, of course – but what would I be without those letters? A cipher, again, a zero. Somehow they defined me now, belonging to me and giving me a purpose. I would read them again and again, and in the end I would track HER down. Somewhere there would be clues. I would study them, and all their intimacy would be ruined. That was the first blow in the war, and I would strike it today. Again, I imagined the shadowy figure in the churchyard, and said aloud, 'I'll find you out, I will. I'll *hunt* you.'

I read from the beginning once more, taking each letter slowly. This time the pain was purer, with no shock to anaesthetise. Each individual letter, each word, each phrase, each sentence, each paragraph was like an Iron Maiden spike. Wanting respite, I showed myself no pity; I could not stop. I devoured the love letters like poison, and my self-induced death was a drawn-out agony; on and on, words scrolling before me, on and on, then back to check a detail, look for a clue to the woman's identity, then on and on.

Don't torture yourself . . . Why are you doing this?

'I haven't got a choice. God help me, but I can't help it,' I sobbed.

I heard his sigh slip into the silence.

When I reached the point I vaguely remembered (the intrusion of the stupid nickname 'Macky', which annoyed me out of all proportion, in comparison with the enormity of the whole discovery) I decided to print, and then read on. I consulted Kit's notes again, and reached for the handbook

too, to double check. What if I accidentally deleted the file?
The prospect was terrible; it was as if access to those letters
was a way of keeping Simon alive, and punishing him too, by
reading them. I was convinced he could see me. I knew he
was there with me in that room, that he would go on speaking to me too – and that I could make him suffer forever.
With that thought I changed my mind about printing. I
could not take the risk.

So back I scrolled to the beginning, again and again:

My dearest,
I have to steady myself. The unforeseen has
happened. In years to come I shall look back, like
someone staring at the sun, into the golden light of
our meeting. How can it happen? You go to see a
woman, you discuss terraces and hedges, you are as
professional as you have ever been, and yet the light is
blinding already – and you are lost . . .

Like a novice detective I seized on the first clue. Simon
and the woman had discussed terraces and hedges at their
first meeting. It might be a social encounter, of course, the
friend of a friend or something – but he used the word 'professional'. The woman was most likely a client. And if Simon
had taken on work for her, there would be a record in the
payment file. It should be easy; Simon was so efficient. My
heartbeat increased.

I'll go to see her. I'll make her suffer. I'll tell her what I
think of her.

I shall do such things . . . the terrors of the earth.

You don't think I mean it, do you, Simon? I was always
such a meek little thing. I let you organise everything: you
paid the bills, you booked the holidays, you ran the business,

you even liked to buy the food and cook it most nights. Thai, Indian, Italian – such an experimenter. Always liked to try new things my husband . . . Ha! Everybody said I was lucky, and I thought I was too. You let me make the occasional suggestion about planting: a *choisea* here, a *hedera* there. You let me be Kathy's mother. You let me daydream. You . . . *petted me*. I didn't realise that until now. You let me twine around you like a small ivy while your branches reached upwards, independent of me. And she was a bird who alighted there, carelessly.

Was she beautiful, Simon? Fine feathers to my wrennish brown? When I knock on her door, and she opens it, knowing immediately who I am, will her face be the one I see in my imagination, very early in the morning, when the air is blue and cold, and I wake sweating, thinking of you? Taller than me, and . . . what . . . about ten years younger? She's mid-thirties and divorced, maybe with her own business, and as soon as she saw you she put out her little hooks, to grasp at your love.

Did you ever hesitate? Try to walk away? Or was it instant, the passion, so that you tumbled into her bed without a thought for me, until it was too late, until you were in too deep? It was like that, after all, when *we* met. You always said you were the kind of person who made up his mind, and that was that. You made up your mind you couldn't be a great sculptor, and so you must give that up, but you'd run a good business of your own. You made up your mind to have me as your wife. You made up your mind you were bored by me and needed a mistress. Always in control, Simon McKee! And all of us around you, your creatures.

There's a poem in *Carmina Burana* where the hapless swan is singing, though roasted, and about to take its place as the centrepiece of the feast.

> Once I lived on lakes,
> once I looked beautiful,
> when I was a swan.
> Misery me!
> Now black
> and roasting fiercely!

Burning hot, wingless, it grieves. All around it, it sees bared teeth.

I play that music again and again, because only now do I understand it properly. Yet I had loved it all along, to Simon's distaste. It used to speak to me of the great cycles of existence, and of rejoicing in them. Let us live and love . . . Drinking songs . . . and beauty, and sex, and passion . . . Now I can hear only the savagery of dance and song, the torch-lit rituals that end in sacrifice, on altar and cross. Above all Orff's music sings to me of indifference, high and cold, as hard as teeth, waiting to devour the creature of the lake. *Malevolent fate*.

I miss you. I hate you.

I miss you.

Chapter Six

It was three more days before I left the house – a total of seven since the summoning-up of the spectre. The freezer was almost empty; I'd drunk all the alcohol in the house, making myself ill on the last of the brandy, which normally I would never touch. The creature was at bay, wounded in its lair, smelling the sweet damp air and leaves outside, yet unable to move for terror and pain. Rank, hair unwashed; some mornings teeth uncleaned, savouring the stale furriness of its mouth, the creature was an object of pity to itself.

Why shouldn't I hate myself, Simon, since you didn't love me?

Kit left messages on the machine, but I did not call her back. Aware of my duty, I rang Kathy to tell her I was fine – knowing such reassurances are lapped up by children because they do not seek the truth. Why should they, when it would tunnel intolerably, undermining the fabric of their own lives? All Kathy wanted now was to know that her mother was entering the various stages of bereavement and passing through them according to the book – with some tears still, of course, because that was natural. The counsellors flood small towns struck by tragedy; kindness sticks a foot in the door and whispers words of received wisdom: that this is normal, and will evolve and pass, enabling new life to begin. That is the pattern, they say. I imagined my daughter turning the pages of books from the library: Colin Murray Parkes, Lily Pincus, C S Lewis – all of them observing grief with wisdom and clarity. Poor Kathy, seeking to understand the loss of a parent, shivering in the knowledge that the line moved up, implacably, turning to the photograph of her parents she kept at the back of her address book, and crying a little, even now. Dear Dad . . .

'My father died recently,' she would say to people, just as I did when I met Simon, knowing that the noises would be sympathetic, even if routine and wishing most to deflect . . .

If she knew the truth! At first I wanted to tell her, and invite her to share my disgust for my unfaithful husband, her father, that woman's lover. But as days passed I knew I had no desire to make my child suffer too. Bad enough to lose a father, but to find a fraud? No, too cruel. Kathy loved him, and was like him. Let her carry her memories of his head bent over the snakes and ladders board, moaning in mock-horror when he was sent tumbling down a snake, letting her win.

So for the first time in my life I felt truly alone. Each day I went to the study, and could even find a bitter amusement in the fact that Simon would not have recognised me. It was not so much my appearance, or my rage, as the fact that I knew I had to take control. It was imperative to master the computer, since the machine that had led me into this misery – and mystery – might be the means by which both would be resolved. I knew my husband (but how deep the ironies of such a statement now) and respected his organisation, his logic, his method. So I knew the woman's name and address would be on file somewhere, in some guise – and to find it I had to understand the manual.

So I read it obsessively, whereas the old Rosa would have closed it after one glance. There was no choice now. It was as if my mind had suddenly cleared: a great white room into which poured the chilliest, bleakest northern light. This room was utterly empty and my footsteps echoed, small and lonely, finding a path from wall to wall, with no obstacles in the way.

Utterly alone. What surprised me was my acceptance of this condition – as if I had already experienced it, in another life or in a dream, and knew it to be fitting. One morning, very early, in the formless hour, I had a vision so vivid it made me reel. I was just born, and lying between my mother's legs (that itself obscene, to think of my grey, quiet mother thus exposed), and I was cold. I could hear panting. There were bright lights and loud voices. Yet I knew we were joined, still, and it was a comforting link with the warm red darkness that had gone forever. Then I was lifted, suspended in icy space, there was a sudden flash, and a cutting edge I felt within my belly. It was agony. Wrapped in white, laid down by a misty face which gazed in shocked tenderness then made little sounds of welcome. There was nevertheless no consolation.

I knew then that my marriage to Simon had been part of a long flight from solitude; I had allowed him to take over the role of parent, and clung to him as a child or a dog will clutch at a coat, to be sure it is there. Now that cord too had been severed, not by death but by discovery.

I looked in the mirror and saw how lank and ugly I looked. A remnant he had left behind. A cast off. A dreg. I ran a bath, poured in large quantities of the bluebell essence he had given me, and got in. My body floated out before me, white and thin, like the limbs of the damned. I scrubbed at it, then washed my hair, and when at last I towelled myself dry my flesh was red and raw, like that of the baby I had been. And the cord was cut again. I would travel outwards alone.

It was a ten-minute walk from our house to the city centre, and all downhill. I was lightheaded; there seemed a dislocation between the message my brain sent to my feet and the steps they took, so that I was weightless – a solitary ghost around which the life of the city drifted, ignorant and indifferent. I crossed George Street and entered Milsom Street, vaguely looking into shop windows, registering the fashionable pastels but as a blur – as if the world around had been transformed into the myopic drifting washes of my own watercolours.

With no destination, I wandered eastwards until I reached the weir, where I stood looking down for a very long time, mesmerised by the rush of the water. I remembered the first time we went to Dyrham Park, twenty years ago when we first moved to the city with our baby.

Simon was excited; he carried a copy of the Kip engraving, and frowned in concentration as he tried to get the locations right. 'Look, Rosie,' he said. 'It must have been extraordinary, imagine it. The idea of water was so important. Evelyn said gardens should always contain fountains and cascades, and he met Blathwayt, you know. I bet he had an influence on this . . .'

He talked his beloved garden history. Kathy blew a bubble, and I hung over her, entranced, barely hearing what he was saying.

'The cascade must have been amazing – right down that slope. God, I can almost hear it . . .'

Kathy babbled gently, those musical meaningless sounds that prefigure speech, and which I heard deep within me, experiencing love as I had never known it. I put out my finger and she grasped it tightly, smiling up at me, chirruping softly with delight and recognition.

'Look, Simon! Just look at her!' I whispered, yet required no response, my words directed not so much at him, as generally, towards the universe, asking it to marvel with me at this one child.

'The piping must have been incredibly difficult,' he muttered, squinting as if he could see the armies of workmen in rough britches and woollen stockings, digging and carrying and laying, and the owner standing nearby, fuming at the slowness of the project. 'Wouldn't it be great to find somebody rich enough to commission one just like it?'

I looked up at him vaguely, feeling the sun on my back, and hearing in the distance the hum of insects and holiday traffic. 'I think it'd be awful,' I said. Then I waved an arm to embrace the sweep of land and the distant trees. 'Look at all this.'

'But you can't prefer it now!' he protested.

'I can,' I said, 'because it started out as a deer park and it's gone back to being a deer park, and all that business of cascades is irrelevant.'

'To what?' he asked, flopping down with a grin and tickling Kathy under the chin. He never took offence.

'To what's natural,' I said.

'Rosie – if you allowed what's natural to prevail there'd be chaos – in gardens and in people,' he said. 'Why do you think the myth of the Garden of Eden is replicated in other cultures? Because people have always known that it's wild and cold and dangerous out there, beyond the wall. Nature's vicious, left to its own devices. The whole idea of a garden is about taming – imposing order. You prune, you confine—'

'Didn't stop the snake getting in,' I said.

'Ah, but he was already in there.' Simon grinned. 'He

didn't get in from outside. If you like he represented the outside – the threat. There's always a danger to Paradise. Canker. Black spot. You can't guarantee it won't be there, but you can do all you can to control it. Like this . . .'

He took my arms and pushed me back, pinioning me, as he bent to kiss me. I closed my eyes, tasted him, and smelt his skin, conscious only of my baby's gurgles and the weight of this man, and knowing in that instant that paradise would always be remade, again and again. No reptile could come near. Nothing, I thought, can ever match this happiness.

We went home that night to our flat, and cooked spaghetti with meatballs, drank cheap Spanish red, and talked of the future. We would set up our business, work together, and let nothing come between us. After making love I cried a little. 'Isn't it terrible,' I whispered, my head resting on his chest, 'to think that one of us has to die first?'

I felt him shudder. 'Don't talk about it – and then maybe it'll never happen,' he said.

'Of course it won't,' I said. And he licked my tears and we became one world.

Do we believe that, as we utter the sweet and silly words – the love, the permanence? Or do we raise our voices, and hug and kiss, and make the ultimate sublimely stupid noises of the flesh to drown the sound of silence: the chatter of the death-head's teeth? I don't know the answer. I would have known, had it not been for Simon's infidelity. I would have shouted YES: I do believe – even in the face of chaos.

But not now. Another crime you've committed, you wretch, damned forever.

I turned from the weir at last, my elbows numb from resting on the parapet. Tourist buses passed; the streets were crowded. I started to walk towards the Abbey, and found myself staring at every woman I passed who was of an age to be Simon's mistress. They were beautiful in Spring sunlight, all of them, with their legs and their breasts and their hair, celebrating their lives, with no horror waiting for them around the corner . . . Or so you think, sweet ladies, or so you think!

I imagined Her seeing me in the street, and continuing to walk towards me, knowing she was safe. I looked carefully at one woman, thirty-seven I guess, with curly red hair and faded indigo skirt and shirt. She was holding a wicker basket, and standing by the fountain as if waiting for someone. Just Simon's type, I thought, halting near her, as if I too had a rendezvous. The woman was staring towards the Guildhall, and did not notice me. She raised a hand to her cheek for a second and I noticed it was not white and manicured, but tanned – almost rough. The hands of a potter, a painter – or a gardener. I became fixated on those hands. We stood there, waiting. For a second I imagined my husband, corporeal again, walking along the High Street towards us, and hesitating for a second.

Which of us would you choose, Simon? Go on, choose!

I listened but he said nothing. I thought he must have stayed at home after all.

At last the woman became aware she was being watched – that prickle of the skin, as if eyes were like the feet of insects, crawling to make you shift and itch . . . She glanced towards me, and our eyes met. In that second I knew it was not Her. I knew I would have seen the flicker of recognition and guilt. There was nothing; just the pleasant curiosity of a stranger on a beautiful day, wondering why her friend is late. Embarrassed, I gave a half-smile and turned away.

The Abbey seemed very dark. It was a long time since I had last been inside – at least four years. Simon didn't like the building much: he said it was nineteenth-century pastiche, in effect. But I loved it. As if it were common knowledge that church services drag, the people were given something to read, and the patchwork of monuments and memorials on the walls humanised the space. In all those lofty phrases of adulation, I always found something amusing, to set death in its place. Simon called it sentimental, my fascination with graveyards and memorials. I told him it was realistic.

For it is true that death endowed my parents with a stature that they had never possessed in life. Childhood had been formal and somewhat chilly; once my mother and father were dead my imagination smoothed off the corners of memory and allowed its cracks and crevices to fill up with moss and lichen. Dullness became calmness; indifference was transformed into respect; lack of comprehension shifted to reticence. My parents' photograph sat in its silver frame on the mantelpiece, a sepia-ed in my mind's eye by the gentle action of my longings. What else is there to do?

Universal helplessness, I thought, as I walked along the north aisle, reading from habit, and it occurred to me how common, how basely common, were my old desires. The living, in the age of monuments, had wanted to tell the same half-truths. The praises of their dead were recorded for the world to read: blameless lives carved in marble and stone, slate and brass. Such 'patterns of religion'. I read of one John Wall whom 'Husbands, Fathers, Friends and Neighbours saw in Him, a Living Pattern of their duties', and found myself laughing aloud, drawing very strange stares from two Japanese tourists, who prowled the aisles, cameras ready. I imagined John Wall assaulting his maid, visiting the stews of Stall Street in the days when Bath teemed with prostitutes and down-and-outs, ignoring his wife, even when she grieved for their dead children . . . Yet there he was enshrined: the paragon of all virtue.

Yet you can't blame the dead for hypocrisy. Maybe John Wall sat down, while still in possession of his faculties, and wrote his own epitaph, instructing wife, brother, son to the letter. It's possible. But the point is surely that they wrote his epitaph for themselves. How the world saw him was how they in turn would be seen: all paragons of virtue. All. So we collude in the eternal lie, because we must, for our own sakes. Who wishes the world to know that she was married to a cheat, a liar, a sinner?

Sitting down, I stared up at the fan-vaulting, loving its serious frivolity. But now it challenged me by the very perfection of its form. Should I too seek a sort of perfection? Should I be brave, and break the collusion I had identified? Should I, for example, tell Kathy about her father – knowing that she, in distress, would inevitably tell this young man she was seeing, and thus Simon's infamy would spread? People talk to each other: gossip seeps.

('You know, I met this guy who's going out with a girl whose mother found out . . .'

'God, how awful. Imagine how you'd feel!'

'Must have been a bastard.'

'Or very clever – to keep it up.'

'An' I bet he did keep it up!'

Nudge, nod, wink – and we are all in it together.)

So many of the memorials talked of pain. Somebody died lingeringly yet bore illness 'with the cheerfulness, the firmness and the resignation of a sincere Christian'. With a sudden curl of hatred I wished Simon had died in pain. He had a good death. He just popped his clogs, like that – a snap of the fingers – with his trowel in his pocket and his sin in his heart. What an escape for you, Simon! Had you been doomed to a slow death, you might have been forced, in pain, to confess to me – and then I might have forgiven you. I might have allowed her to come to the house even, and astounded myself by my spiritual magnanimity. I would have been in control then – I who have never been in control of anything in my whole life. I would have confessed you. I would have been your priest. I might have absolved you. At least I would have taken the chance to sit and talk to you for hours and hours of the woe that is in marriage.

Oh but lucky Henry and Sarah Archbould! Surely not a lie too, though the phrases be strapped in costive diction: *Their love was disinterested, their affection mutual, and their sensibility equal, thus attached and thus bound by every tender cord which winds about the heart, their incessant prayer was never to be separated.* So in the grave is all renewed? Does the mingled dust feel love still, a flicker that will never ever be extinguished?

I got up restlessly, and walked down the aisle. In the small side chapel, reserved for private prayer, a woman was kneeling, head down on her hands so that only the nape of her neck was visible, and the grey hair above, swept into a chignon. She wore black. Something about her stopped me; I stood for a couple of minutes watching her. The woman did not move, not a shift of a foot, nor slight movement of the head to show she was alive. She might have been carved in stone or marble, a kneeling memorial – to whom? Somehow I knew she was grieving, that her black was the colour not of smartness but of grief.

Still the woman did not move. There was such a stillness in that chapel – as if the air itself stood still to allow her to meditate on the permanence of loss – that I envied her. My grief had been taken from me; there was nothing left. My soul was beaten out by tempests; I could not stop for long for fear I should be blown howling over the abyss.

So I walked on. At last, face to face with the altar, I stopped and looked up once more. There was a time when I would have contemplated the vaulting in awe, even perhaps with a tear of pure longing. I *wanted* so much – and yet it always seemed just out of reach: a light around the corner, the stillness after a note has ended. Once I went to sung evensong here (to Simon's amazement) and looked up, quivering like the notes of the great organ, willing God to speak to me, as the music soared. It was the same motivation that drove me to country churches, and led me to my flagrant disobedience over Simon's wishes. I realised that I had been seeking God, like a child looking for a refuge. My parents dead, it was Simon; now with Simon dead it could have been God. Yet the way between me and God was blocked, by Simon's sins and by my own hatred.

So he had taken that respite from me too. Simon had been my God; that was the role he played in my life – I saw it now. The dispenser of law and wisdom, the fount of all things . . .

You will tell me I am hysterical. Yet this revelation was so shocking that it made me gasp, then sit down quickly, trembling. Somewhere someone was practising runs on the organ, a maddening sound that lacked dignity. I wanted it to stop, I wanted to scream.

So did I worship you, Simon? If so, your betrayal was far more than a common infidelity, of the type that is done on desks, in parked cars, in cheap hotels, in fields – the incontinent, illicit rutting of the ages. Your infidelity was heresy, Simon McKee.

I remembered a poem by Browning that Simon had read me when we were students. It was a horror poem, the monologue of a man who loved a lady, socially his superior, so much that when she slipped out to see him he strangled her with her long yellow hair, the more to keep her with him.

The poem ends with a line Simon read with relish: 'And yet God has not said a word'.

So as I stood listening to the deafening silence of God, my mind filled instead with the demonic laughter of my husband and his mistress. I knew what I had to do. It was war. I would revenge myself on Simon, and thus declare war on God, forever. Because Christ preached forgiveness, there would be none.

I drove to Simon's grave, and stood right on it, crushing the few flowerheads that had emerged. It did not matter. His grave was a mess anyway, sweet wildness out of place amid the controlled manifestations of grief and love. So I could stamp, and uproot, and no one would care.

'Isn't it a shame,' they might say. 'She hasn't bothered.'

And, 'It's good if they keep the churchyard looking nice.'

No one was around. I knelt on the wet ground and beat it with my fists. Beyond tears, I groaned like a woman in labour. Had I a spade I swear I would have started to dig (the crone, the madwoman) to reach to him, to attack him . . . No, that's not it.

(Oh, Simon, Simon . . .)

I wanted to *warm* him.

Chapter Seven

When your husband dies, friends respond with varying degrees of embarrassed sympathy. They write, of course, because the distance is safe, and all the accustomed noises can be made with no possibility of a scream in reply. The truth was Simon and I did not have many friends at all. We had existed in a cocoon: the bubble of our little family. He had no friends left from college; I had Kit.

When we moved we slipped easily into a small circuit of what he called, with ironic acceptance, 'the Batheoisie': a gallery owner and his wife, an art teacher, a violinist, a potter, a successful journalist who chose to work from the west, a solicitor, a property man. I had briefly befriended mothers at Kathy's schools, then gradually dropped them. We hardly ever gave proper dinner parties; we liked the theatre and an occasional film, that was all. Yet Simon did know people, and we often went out for drinks with people I liked well enough. They were all well connected; they were the key to the success of SIROSA. Yet in the days after Simon's death I realised the limits of all these friendships. They had depended on him; he was the driving force in our marriage and without him I was nothing. Is that what they thought? Or was it that, after a while, if you turn down every single invitation to drinks, lunch or dinner, people sigh and give up?

I went home, picked up the telephone, and dialled three numbers. At a great distance, there were voices uttering pleased sounds: how lovely, what a surprise, glad you are feeling better, are you up to it, a dinner party would be wonderful, can we bring something? I rang Kathy too, consciously attempting to please her – which I did. The relief was audible. 'Have a lovely time, Mummy. I'm so glad.' She would go to the bar and tell her friends and lover, 'Thank God, my mother's feeling better.'

It was to be the following Saturday, so I had five days to prepare. It must be perfect, I knew that. For me. No sloppiness would be allowed; no detail ignored. I knew the men would bring wine, but I would surprise them all by offering sparkling Australian to begin with, as if in celebration. I would do it all perfectly – because Simon had, on the rare occasions when we entertained, done everything. It was my chance now. I would cap him.

I would never have done this before: choosing to spend the best part of a day studying the cookery books – all Simon's, just as the gardening books were Simon's, and the art books, and everything in this house.

Except me, Simon . . .

At last I decided on the menu, and felt excited, as if I were treading a totally unfamiliar path, at the end of which I knew was a beautiful view. When the day came I was so organised, I knew Simon would not have recognised me. I left time for a deep scented bath, and chose my clothes with care: a long green skirt and black stretchy top, scooped low in the front, quite daring for Rosa McKee. I caught my hair back with combs, and selected some malachite earrings Simon had given me years ago. I wanted to look . . . what is the word?

Suave. With an outline. That was the important thing. My clothes had become more and more shapeless in the last few years; I simply could not be bothered to hold in my stomach, Kit said. Yet I was not fat. I had as good a body as Her. I'd show him.

They all arrived within ten minutes of eight, the men clutching tissue-wrapped bottles as I had predicted. Ron and Emma Samuels ran the Equinox Gallery, near the Abbey. It specialised in modern ceramics and abstract work – most of which Simon hated. He was always less than charitable about Ron's taste – except, he said, in women. Emma Samuels was as slender as her husband was round, and her profile had an Egyptian purity.

'Rosa, my love,' she murmured, as she kissed my cheek. For a second I wondered if she could be The Woman. Then I rejected the suspicion: the look I knew I would recognise was absent from her eyes.

We were all still standing in the hall when the doorbell sounded again, and Sally Ross and Alan Grierson filled the small space with the confidence of their greetings. They were both journalists: Alan a columnist for a national broadsheet, famous for his incisive wit, and Sally a freelance feature writer specialising in interior design and profiles. We met them when Simon designed their garden.

The greetings done, I took them into the sitting room, and set Alan to open the sparkling wine. I had the glasses all ready, and a little bowl of pistachios, with an empty bowl next to it for the shells. As the doorbell rang, and I excused myself, I heard the cork pop, and Sally say to Emma, 'Thank Goodness!'

The last arrivals were Martin and Christine Larch, both teachers, both somewhat harassed, always the last to arrive at any gathering - which sometimes annoyed Simon. Martin taught art in a boys' public school, Christine was a part-time primary teacher, and also managed their three children, while Martin busied himself with various good causes within the city, from the Clean Cycle Campaign to the Counselling Centre.

There was an unspoken heirarchy among my guests. The Griersons (although Sally insisted on her maiden name, they were, in fact, married) took the most senior position, not through age (Ron Samuels was at least two years older than Alan) but through wealth and status, the cachet of small fame. It suited them (Simon once remarked) to be big fish in a small pool, that's why they had moved to Bath. After the Griersons came the Samuels, because they hosted drinks parties at the Enquinox at which all ages rubbed shoulders and the wine was better than plonk. Last came the Larches, because . . . well, it's obvious. 'The most useful, but the least interesting,' Simon said. He could be sharp and true like that.

When the second bottle of fizz had been consumed I led them all, very talkative by now, to the dining room, putting Alan Grierson at the head, in Simon's old place. I was opposite, with Sally, Martin and Emma on one side, and Ron and Christine on the other. It felt lopsided, a chillness where someone should have been. And the seating meant that Sally was next to me.

'Oh dear,' I said lightly. 'I should have invited a chap for myself.'

I felt the *frisson*. How people hate to be reminded! Eyes met briefly over the clatter of chairs. 'Oh no, darling, I'd far rather sit next to you,' said Sally, in her most gushing voice, protesting too much.

'Shall I take charge of the wine, Rosa?' boomed Ron.

'It's OK – all under control,' said Alan, exercising his right.

The first course was already on the table, and they ate quickly, with rather too many small sighs of appreciation amid talk of Bath's traffic problems. Then there was a pause, one of those moments when the tinkle of the stream ceases, and each one around the table is reminded briefly of the drought of the soul.

'I thought I'd start up the business again,' I said.

There was an effusion of approval. Then Emma contributed the first note of dissent. 'But is it really you? Is it really what you want?'

'Why do you ask?'

'Because . . .' She looked embarrassed, sorry she had begun. 'Well, wasn't it far more Simon's thing than yours?'

'Yes,' I said.

'Well,' she began again.

'Whatever Simon could do I can do better,' I said.

They stared. Then Alan Grierson laughed uncomfortably. 'That's the spirit, Rosa!'

'Shall I clear the plates?' Christine said, leaping up, so that she knocked a glass of wine with her elbow, causing general chaos. And relief.

By the time I had fetched a cloth, and Christine had mopped the wine from the oak table, and Martin had helped me carry through the casserole, my uncomfortable little remark had been forgotten. The conversation flowed easily, from local to national politics. Alan made us all laugh with his impression of the Prime Minister, and Ron held forth at great length about funding for the Arts and how the Government were a bunch of Philistines. Sally started to question his assumption, but was steamrollered, as Ron and her husband got into full stride. Martin joined in of course: he agreed with everything Ron said, and after about ten minutes I realised that none of the women were talking. It had always

been that way but I had never noticed. The conversation
was male conversation: it was about important things and
our role was to listen and make small noises of approbation
every now and then. And appreciation, naturally.

I looked at Emma Samuels, and noticed how she inclined
her head – so that the length of her neck could be fully
appreciated – and kept her eyes fixed on Alan Grierson,
laughing at each witticism, almost proudly, as if he were
hers. Sally Ross, on the other hand, looked impatient, as if
she wished to break in but lacked the proper pitch of voice to
cut across her confident husband, who irritated her. She rub-
bered her head from speaker to speaker, looking for the weak
return shot that would let her pick up the ball. Christine
Larch leant her face on her hand, and nodded each time her
husband spoke.

That is how it is for us, I thought. We are audiences. We
boost the confidence of our men: listening, nodding, smiling,
shifting our bodies so that we lean, the more easily to
listen . . .

I was shocked by the rage that rushed through me. Did I
kill you, Simon? Or did you kill me? Or are married couples
mutual murderers by collusion?

The subject had shifted to education. It generally came
up. We all had children and spent a great deal of time talking
about them and their schools, and bewailing the pressure
'society' put on 'the kids', while showing, by our nervous
obsession with standards and our disappointments, that most
of it came from us. Inevitably the conversation would turn
into reminiscence; we shored each other up with the con-
sensus that things were not as they were.

'Have you seen the GCSE English papers?' asked Alan.

'Much easier than the old O level,' said Sally.

'Well, it demands different things,' murmured Christine.

'The trouble is, half the kids move up from primary school barely literate,' said Ron.

'I don't think that's fair,' said Christine, bridling.

'Come on! They don't read, they barely think!' said Alan – whose son Mick had recently dropped out of university due to excessive use of cannabis and Ecstasy, and was currently working on a building site in Hackney deciding what to do next.

'We took on a kid in the Gallery,' said Emma, 'nineteen years old, with eight GCSEs and one A level, and honestly, he could barely spell. Unbelievable.'

'Maybe he had good social skills?' asked Christine earnestly, and looked offended when Ron and Emma threw back their heads.

'Yes, such great social skills he started an affair with the wife of one of our best clients – that American restaurateur. She was only twenty years older than him,' said Emma.

'Must have had *enormous* social skills,' said Ron knowingly, so that everybody spluttered helplessly, even Christine.

'Did the husband find out?' I asked.

'In the end, yes. There was plenty of blood on the floor,' said Ron, continuing to laugh.

'Who cleared it up?' I asked.

He looked puzzled. 'What? Oh you mean . . . ?'

'The blood,' I said.

Emma explained. 'The boy took off around the world with a backpack and a girl his own age. The woman dried her tears and stayed with her husband – who forgave her.'

'Of course!' said Sally.

'Why of course?' I asked, conscious that my voice was very flat. I had to make an effort to speak, like someone unsure of a language. They all looked at me.

'Good question,' said Alan. 'I think he'd have been well

within his rights to chuck her out. She made him look a fool.'

'Oh please! What kind of antiquated view is that?' Sally exclaimed, glaring at her husband. 'It's typically masculine to see the wife's small mistake as a sort of insult to manhood. So bloody sexist, Alan! Look a fool indeed! In front of whom?'

'Everybody who knew about it of course!' said Alan.

'What if no one knew?' I cut in. 'Would he have still looked a fool – to her and to him?'

'Good philosophical question,' smiled Alan. 'Can you look a fool if no one is looking. Like – is the table there when no one is in the room to see it?'

'Then it's not so much a question of looking a fool as being a fool,' said Sally.

'Why?' Christine asked.

'Oh, in circumstances like that, if you were the wronged person, you'd look in the mirror in the privacy of your room and know you'd been made a fool of – to yourself,' Sally said.

Martin pushed his chair back a little way. It scraped the floor. He let out his breath with irritation. 'Oh, I don't know,' he snapped. 'What is all this stuff? What's the big deal? People I know are bonking each other silly every minute of the day, and what's it matter? What age are we living in? I don't know why you have to lay all these emotions – about being made a fool of etc – on to what is basically a very simple situation.'

'OK, give us the situation,' said Sally.

'Easily. You have this man—'

'Actually it was a woman, remember?' said Emma mischievously. 'Our client's lovely wife and her toyboy. That's where we came—'

'So to speak,' said Ron.

'OK, you have this woman, and she is perfectly happily married to this guy until one day she falls for somebody else. They have a fling. Then it's over. She never stopped loving her husband, she just fancied somebody else. An itch you scratch. That's all.'

'Silly to put her marriage in danger, though,' said Christine.

'My whole point is that it shouldn't have been in danger! Marriages ought to be able to survive this stuff. If you make the act of sex matter that much you elevate it to a position it shouldn't have.'

'So to speak,' said Ron.

I watched them. Alan and Martin must certainly have had affairs, and probably Sally too. It was impossible to imagine Christine finding the time; as for Ron and Emma, it was possible to image them colluding in each other's infidelities, or at least condoning them. Something lazy and confident about them, as if to care would be too much effort, and anyway artistic people have always behaved in that way – almost an article of faith. None of this would have occurred to me before. I had known all these people for about ten years; chatted to them at dinner parties, parents' evenings, and private views, exchanged confidences about children and business, and yet I had never wondered about their sex lives. I realised I had lived in a basket with the lid on, squinting at the world through its open weave – like a pet given for Christmas, soon to be unwanted.

'Simon was unfaithful to me, you know,' I said loudly, 'but I only discovered it recently.'

It was as if someone had suddenly snapped down the sound with a remote control. They appeared to go on with the motions of talking, and yet there was no sound. I said nothing else. I waited. One of the men cleared his throat.

'Shhh, Rosa,' crooned Emma, as if I were a sick and fractious child.

'No, it is true,' I said, 'and I don't see why I shouldn't tell you. But I wonder – tell me the truth now – did any of you *know*?'

Maybe I should have felt sorry for them. They shifted in their seats and avoided my eyes, and wished – oh, how clearly you could see it! – they had not accepted this dinner invitation.

'Please tell me,' I said, sounding (I knew) frighteningly calm. 'It's all right – really, I'm fine! But I would like to know if any of you knew.'

'I didn't know anything of the kind, and I find it very hard to believe,' said Alan at last, in a voice of such dark seriousness and embarrassment I knew he was telling the truth.

The others nodded. There was a small chorus of approbation. Then a silence, which I allowed to continue.

At last Christine looked up at me with moist eyes. 'Oh God, Rosa, I'm really sorry,' she whispered.

'But it shouldn't *matter*, should it, Martin?' I asked her husband drily.

He looked down at his plate. 'Rosa, you know I wouldn't have gone into all that if I had known. I feel terrible now. I'm really sorry.'

'But it's not your fault! Why should you apologise?' I asked.

I suppose I seemed so calm and normal they all felt reassured. There was a visible slackening of the tension around the table, as if an unseen puppet master had loosened the strings. Suddenly I thought of Simon in that role: Simon the unseen, yet present in this room – like Banquo's ghost at the feast.

'Do you know . . . who?' Emma ventured, in a small voice. I thought, How bold to utter the question they all wished to ask.

'No idea,' I said, 'but I shall find out. If any of you have any thoughts or suggestions they will be gratefully received.'

'Ah, Rosa, what's the point?' asked Christine, gently.

'So I can go and see her of course!' I said. 'I want to look the bitch in the face. I want to tell her what I think of her.'

I stared around the table at each of them in turn, daring them to reproach me. They lowered their eyes; they looked away; they shifted their bodies, repelled (I was sure) by my hardness.

At last Christine spoke again. It interested me that it was she, the most tired, mild and quiet of that group, who had the courage to confront me. She even looked different as she spoke, seeming to grow.

'Rosa, I have to tell you I think you're making a mistake,' she said quietly. 'Whatever Simon did, he's dead now. He'll be dead forever, Rosa, and what's the point of you going on living, corroding your whole life by hating him?'

'And her,' I supplied.

'Yes, her too. Obviously you're hurting now, but . . . I honestly don't see the point.'

'It'll give me something to do,' I said harshly.

'Work, Rosa!' Sally said. 'Didn't you say earlier you were going to start the business up again?'

'And you can go back to your painting,' said Emma eagerly. 'I'm sure we'd give you a show, wouldn't we, Ron?'

Her husband looked very uncomfortable at a promise that could prove embarrassing later. He mumbled neutral sounds. She gave him a furious look for not playing along with her. Such is marriage, I thought.

I got up quickly to make coffee, knowing my absence from the room would be a relief, that as soon as I went through the door they would exchange glances and frowns and little rolls of the eyes. After a few minutes the women came out with piles of plates, complimented me on the food, and offered to wash up. I refused, knowing they were desperate to be gone.

So I took pity on them all. With the coffee and chocolates I sparkled. I told them animatedly of my plans, knowing that few humans can bear the bleakness of reality, of revenge, of hatred, of cruelty, of bitterness. Let us put it away, back in the box, and do not give Pandora even so much as a hint. Let her pour Armagnac for the men, like the eternal hand-maiden, smiling.

'Yes,' I said. 'It'll be very good for me. I'm going to re-establish contact with all the architects we worked with before, plus the interior designers. Do a circular in fact. Let everybody know that SIROSA's back in business. Only I won't call it that, of course.'

'Just ROSA?' prompted Emma.

'Exactly,' I said.

'Nobody would object to that . . . er . . .' said Alan, bely-ing his comment by the slight shake of the head that indicates masculine solidarity.

'Of course not!' said Sally, with a warning look.

'I mean . . .' he began.

'I know,' I said sweetly, 'but I honestly don't think Simon would mind.'

He nodded, relieved in ways he probably would not express. The men needed to feel Simon was OK, even if he was dead. That is the way they are.

After a further twenty minutes of desultory chat they all left. There were kisses on the doorstep and effusive promises to invite me round 'very soon'.

'Don't forget to ask a handsome chap for me!' I smiled at Emma.

All the women laughed. The men looked uncomfortable.

As she was kissing me on the cheek, Christine, the last to go out, whispered, 'And, Rosa, you were joking, weren't you? About . . .'

I took pity on her. 'Of course I was,' I whispered, then added in a louder voice, so the others could hear, 'but not about getting my life back on course.'

'I can't tell you how pleased I am,' she said sincerely.

I stood behind the door, listening to their cars start, rev, then drive away. I imagined their conversations. Regretting that moment's intrusion of pain, they would be relieved, nevertheless, that the old Rosa had come back to life. At least I had given them that.

They were not to know she was dead, the old Rosa. They were not to know that she listened in the silence of that house for the voice of her husband, not in grief (for that would have upset but not surprised them) but in glorious, exhilarating vindictiveness.

I sat for a long time in an armchair, staring at the dirty coffee cups on the tray, and listening to the beetles, the mice, the bats: the silent movements of those who shared this space with me.

Listening, too, for you in the emptiness.

'Are you there? Were you watching all that?' I asked.

I craned my neck. Was that you? Yes!

But all you said were the same old words, the same old bloody words.

I'm sorry, Rosa, I'm so sorry. I'm sorry I made a fool of you.

Chapter Eight

As if a precipitous valley had opened up before me, after a long climb to a chilly summit, my life began to pitch forward. First I decided that I would read just two more of Simon's letters every day, like a dose of purgative, to keep me going. I made a note of dates but not content, for in the end what was different about each separate outpouring of passion?

13th November

My angel,
I sit here wondering at my inexplicable good fortune.
I said to you not long ago (do you realise just how
short a time 'not long ago' has been packed into?) that
you still don't trust me emotionally, and you agreed.
Perhaps it is different now, but I am totally amazed at
the way you trust *yourself*. You give yourself to me,
body and soul, knowing what you feel and not
stinting – not at all. How come you are so brave?
How did they make you that way?

At first I used to think that your instant rejection of my saying how wonderful and astonishing you are was affectation, and your even more emphatic denial of your beauty likewise. I don't really care whether you think you are as hideous as a witch, because what matters is that I know you are beautiful. But it was funny when you compromised by saying that you quite like your own body – very unconvincing that was! But one day I shall go out and search the countryside, north and south, and finally buy you a magic mirror that shows your soul, and force you to look in it for an hour a day, my darling. Then there would be no competition this side of heaven. You would be contemplating the most beautiful woman in the universe.

So, are you learning to trust me emotionally? At last? I hope so, because I have made a commitment to you, within my soul, that I have never made before. I would not have entered into this thing if I had *thought*. Because I am not a masochist, and who would choose pain? But from the first we were beyond thought and problems and time and guilt.

I will see you very soon, as soon as possible.

Love, love, love, M

The next letter was written just before Christmas. I imagine they must have found plenty of chances to meet, so there was no need to write. Then, evidently, the woman went away.

17th December 1988

Dearest,

Which would be worse, I wonder? Having you just
down the road (well, you know what I mean) over
Christmas, so near and yet so far? Or you being five
hundred miles away? Both put me on a rack of
frustration . . . in any case, this is academic because
you are going to your friends' and there is nothing I
can do about it. How lucky they are! At least if you
were at home I could telephone you and maybe slip
out and see you. That is what I wanted and you told
me I was selfish and of course you were right. It's not
the first time you have reproached me, but somehow
it was the most serious. You accused me of being
ready to let you spend Christmas totally alone, just so
that I could have the pleasure of knowing you were
there, and that I could make contact as and when I
had the chance. You were right, and I groan with
shame, my only love. Please forgive me.

My only defence is this terrible, deep dark need for
you. You have gone abroad for four weeks, and I do
not know what I will do – without the phone calls,
and the visits. Rosa and Kathy have put up the tree
already and it twinkles at me, telling me to be brave.
All that garish tinsel and those baubles mock me. Last
night I felt such a head of steam inside me, at the
thought that you would be making your holiday lists
already (so organised! Just like me!) that I wanted to
leap on it, and tear it down, sending all those old
decorations flying to the four corners of the room.

God, I will miss you so much. But believe me, I do
want you to have a wonderful time, and the only

thing I beg is that from time to time you spare a
thought for me, stuck here. (I can hear you laugh
deep in your throat, and say, 'Of course, silly boy!') I
have the little parcel you gave me, and you have
mine, and we have made a pact to open them at
exactly the same time on Christmas morning. I feel as
excited as a child when I look at the blue starry paper
and golden ribbon.

Have a wonderful Christmas, my love, this our first
together, even though apart . . . Together in spirit,
now and always.

All my love, Simon

Christmas was always an important day for me. I know
Simon had wanted more children: his response to being an
only child. But I was an only child too, and I only wanted
Kathy. I stayed on the pill. For a while I even lied to him,
pretending I was off it, and that the miracle simply did not
happen. He was disappointed, I know that. He must have
had a vision of a Christmas full of people; family and
friends around the table, music, fires, drink, laughter. But
my desire was to tuck in the flap at the end of our little box,
so that it was just the three of us and no one could come
near to spoil it. We always did the same things, which
amounted to little (salmon on Christmas Eve, bucks fizz on
Christmas morning, goose not turkey because Simon pre-
ferred it) but they had for me a cumulative value that was
awe-inspiring.

Yet he felt 'stuck here'. He wished to destroy our garish
tree. And when did he sneak off and open her present, com-
muning with her spirit?

For a few moments, after reading those letters, I had
to lean back in the chair and breathe with concentrated

slowness. My heartbeat had increased; pain made me dizzy. Still, as I felt my lungs expand and contract, expand and contract, and stilled my own shaking, I knew I was right to read on, despite the torture. And that I would until the end. It would prevent me from forgiving.

My next task was to take on the client list. I roughed out a letter to the effect that since Simon's death I had been wondering what to do, but that the business would continue under the old name. I would be in a position to offer clients a full service of design, consultation and maintenance. And so on. I informed them that I would be taking advertisements in the obvious places, and hoped that I could be assured of their continuing support as well as their recommendation. I said that I would follow up the letter with a phone call, just to check that all was well with their garden; also to discover if they could perhaps suggest names of others to contact.

My sudden impulse to keep the name unchanged took me by surprise. It slipped out, but I knew it was right. To remove Simon's name from the logo he had created seemed petty somehow, and I was beyond pettiness. The van, the letter-heading – all could stay the same, only now I would be in charge, and to keep Simon's name there was, in a way, to mock him. So that's what I would do.

It was easy to find the client and contact lists, but doing the mail merge defeated me, so I sat and wrote every envelope by hand, a task I quite enjoyed because of its tedium. I was not so lacking in self-knowledge that I could not see how self-punishment went hand in hand with my desire to 'punish' Simon. The point is: in life I had thought us indivisible, and yet I had been wrong. We had been divided by our family routines, by Kathy's homework, by the branches of the Christmas tree, as surely as by his great passion for that woman. Now in death we would not be divided. Whatever I did to him I did to myself; hurting myself was the means by which I would fuel myself to go on and on, until I found her, and brought retribution to both living and dead.

I thought of women who find out that their living husbands are having affairs. We have all read the anecdotes, and perhaps taken pleasure in the naked fury which hell cannot match, they say. That woman, married to a peacock of a man, cut the right sleeves off all his suits. That one, married to a bon viveur, took his finest wines and distributed them around the village, a bottle on every doorstep. Another angry female paid for an announcement in the newspaper, to say her boyfriend was not only a lying shit, he stole from his office as well. All the crying alone at night, all the tearful scrutiny in the mirror, all the pain and the self-disgust . . . and yet they had the courage to do such things, the terrors of the earth. Remembering such stories, I loved them for it.

But they were rich in good fortune, such women. They had someone to scream at. They had living flesh to rake with fingernails, if it should come to that. And a beloved face to show guilt and terror in the face of female rage. I had nothing. I had a pillow to pummel, and a shade to talk to, that's all.

The urgent task now was to find out the identity of the bitch and my starting point was that client list. If indeed she had been a client (and I was sure that was the case) then her name would be on the list. Also, I could cross-refer with the diaries (he kept the loose pages of previous years filed in a box) and discover which female name cropped up at about the time the letters began, or just before. He could not have been so cunning as to use a false name for her, not at the

beginning, for how could he have known? Then too, my
follow-up phone calls would surely give me the final answer.
If I found a likely name, and she was one of the ones I rang,
I knew I would sense her reserve. Then I would have it, I was
sure. And I would go to see her.

She was beautiful, he said so in that letter, although she
did not believe it. I went to the mirror, and stared at myself.
Was I beautiful? At least, had he ever told me so? I couldn't
remember, although surely he must have done.

A memory. He came into the bedroom one day, about
eight years ago, when I had just washed my hair, and towelled it roughly, but without combing through, so that it
stood out around my face. I was wearing a white towelling
robe. My face was pink, and he took it between his hands,
and said, 'How come I love the sight of you so much?'

That's all. But in that moment I felt so loved, so much
loved, I wanted to rush out into the streets, just as I was, and
tell everyone I met that it was the case. Out there were
countless millions less blessed than I, yet perhaps the knowledge that such love is possible might give them some
consolation. I smiled back at him, and whispered, 'Maybe it's
because you love me, Simon.'

Then he smiled and said, 'Well, you could be right!' We
stared at each other for a second, with the tender complicity
of married people who know that nothing more needs to be
said, and that the swift turning away into domesticity will
enhance, not mar the quiet beauty of what has just happened.

Now I thought: Why didn't he come out with it properly,
like he did to Her? Why didn't he say, 'I love you Rosa, and
you are beautiful.' That was what I needed. I needed to be
told. I needed the torrent of WORDS she got.

I told you.

Yes, Simon, but not in the right way.

Should there be a script, Rosa? Why could you not listen to what I was saying in the way I chose to say it?

Oh but I did, and it pleased me then. It made me so happy, it was as if I was surrounded by frills. But what matters now? The fact that the simplest of fond memories, like that one, is sullied by what I know you went on to, a couple of years later. She was waiting in the wings, even then, casting her shadow over our room and the privacy of that small exchange between husband and wife. And you were looking in my face, expressing – what? Not passion, for that came later with Her – but deep affection . . .

Which is more valuable?

Which indeed?

I heard him clearly, and it made me even more angry. How dare he be dry and answer back? I knew what I wanted, and that I could never have it. I needed someone to write me letters like that, so that you could imagine the paper itself catching light. I wanted to meet the man who felt like that, and wrote it down. I yearned to be called beautiful, to be adored. It was not enough to have been loved as a wife – if indeed I was.

Of course I was. Not even my rage would deny myself that.

BUT IT WASN'T ENOUGH.

She took what was mine. For who is not to know that in a marriage the couple might fall in love all over again? If Simon was ripe for passion (how easily those clichés slide out!) then he might just have taken my face between his hands one day, and felt the flame leap within him. He might. If it had not been for the fact of meeting her.

The telephone rang. It was Alan Grierson. He said hallo, he was ringing to thank me for the dinner party which they had very much enjoyed, and how was I feeling, and we must all get together soon. But those polite formalities did not deceive me. There was an interest in his voice I had never heard before. After an inconsequential chat, elation crept through my veins, because I knew what he wanted.

'Er, I was wondering, Rosa – would you like to meet up? For a drink or a meal or something.'

'That would be lovely,' I said, deliberately adding, 'It's always nice to see you both.'

'Well, actually, Sal's gone to Scotland. She's interviewing Billy Connolly on location,' he said without altering his tone, 'so – you know – I hate cooking for myself . . .'

'So do I,' I said.

'Well, let's have a slap-up meal and masses to drink,' he laughed.

'Sounds perfect,' I said sweetly.

'Well – tonight?'

No wasting time, I thought. Or Simon spoke – I'm not sure . . .

We fixed the time and the place, and when I put down the phone I was smiling. I went from room to room in the house, triumphant, feeling my own reflection glitter off walls and windows, hard and dazzling.

She had been a victim, poor Rosa McKee. She had been the one in the kitchen while the phone calls were made, the one who dressed the garish, despised tree, the one who planned the holiday in France that would cause such stress and grief to the deprived lovers. She had been the one to find the letters. She was set on the rack – pitiable. She had suffered grief in so many forms. Oh, poor Rosa! Poor creature in its den!

But not any more.

There was something else at the back of my mind bothering me. Something I needed to do, but which eluded me.

I glanced around the sitting room, frowning. Then, in the corner by the television, I saw it and remembered.

Simon 'bought' my watercolour of columbines, just before we married. He paid me with my single diamond ring, because I did not like to call it an engagement ring, disliking the idea. 'Sounds like a lavatory, to be "engaged" ,' I said, and he agreed. We talked so much about ownership in those days, the beginning of the seventies when it was all right to live together, commitment unfashionable. Simon and I were drawn together for many reasons, but one was (we agreed much later) the need to be committed. He called me his 'little orphan', but he was an orphan too. His parents divorced when he was ten. Both remarried soon afterwards, his father going to live in Hong Kong, and his mother to Edinburgh, where her second husband owned a department store. Gradually Simon lost touch with his father, a hard man (he said) interested only in making money. His mother had a son, Tom, by her second husband, and Simon felt superfluous to her life. As soon as he could he moved south; in the early years of our marriage his mother died of cancer, and Simon saw no reason to keep in touch with his step-father. But his half-brother Tom might visit us once a year, and was clearly moved at Simon's funeral.

So, yes Simon, you were an orphan too, and that is why we needed each other. No slipping accidentally into shared domesticity for us, no experiments with freedom. And no 'engagement to be married' either. We went to the register office and we signed the paper: no ceremony, no fuss, but total commitment. To mark that, you gave me a simple wedding ring, and in payment for the columbines a tiny diamond on a gold band.

Band of gold.

I'd forgotten that! You called yourself my band of gold,

playing on hus-band. You smiled and called yourself 'Band', saying you would play my tune. Such silly little things become the language of a marriage, defying meaning. Silly language, like the language of the letters. I had forgotten . . .

Yet we called each other by our proper names, like adult people.

I plucked the small picture from the wall, recalling that Simon had gone to the trouble of having it reframed about ten years ago, because he suddenly disliked the gold frame, and wanted something simpler. So he chose limed oak, the pale colour setting off the creamy pinks and purples of the flowers perfectly.

I examined it closely. It was good. There was technique there. Once I used a brush with four hairs, my idea of perfection to achieve the smallest of strokes, the finest detail, like a miniaturist. Looking now at Simon's favourite picture, I wanted to throw it across the room, watching the glass smash, and tear the paper. What did it say about the flower? Nothing. Simon loved my flower painting, I thought now, because of the fact that it said little. It could be contained. It was like all his paths and walls – only the wall was around my personality. No wonder he was disappointed when I started to mess about again in the abstract. But what did he know about me or my painting?

What would I do now? What could I ever do?

The picture was still in my hand. I looked at it for a long time, not knowing why. My impulse to destroy it had gone; it could remain as a memorial to Simon and to the wife he had fancied he knew. Replacing it at last, I turned and found myself going up the stairs to the spare room Kit had last used. I fancied I could smell Dioressence. I looked around and wondered why we keep a room for visitors, and deprive ourselves of that space – oh, good little wives and hostesses!

Why did I feel I had to play about with my watercolours at the kitchen table? Why did I not annexe territory? And all the while he was sitting in his cosy little office, listening for my foot on the stair, then safely picking up the telephone to ring his mistress . . .

Rage gave me the strength to push the bed into the corner, then pull up the green carpet, rolling it clumsily and dragging it out on the landing. I took down the flowered curtains. Then I shoved the chest of drawers up hard by the bed, and covered both with a sheet. The large marble-topped bedside table I pulled to the middle of the floor   and it was done. The once-pretty guest room was a mess. Now it could be mine.

Sometimes our bodies move as automata, obeying a programme of which we are not even aware. There was no plan to any of this. In a daze I opened up the cupboard under the stairs where, at the back among dust and spiders, I found my easel, as well as an old haversack full of painting materials: two palettes, oil holders, two palette knives. There was also a box of oil paints, bought for Kathy, I remembered, and (since she was as meticulous as her father) with all the tops screwed on very carefully. I knew there were brushes too, and found them at last. They were scrubby, and would not do for long.

No matter, I thought; this was the start.

Chapter Nine

'I started to paint today,' I told him, holding out my right hand, with its traces of ultramarine.

He held my fingers very lightly for a second, on a pretext of inspection, then asked, 'Why did you stop?'

The conversation so far had had that slightly stilted quality of a first read-through, when the actors are seeking to define their parts though they may be familiar with the classic text. Alan Grierson and I had never been alone together. Social life is conducted within sets of couples, and at a distance. Face to face with each other, in this new intimacy, we both felt embarrassed.

His way of hiding it was to be flashy. He had chosen one of the best restaurants in the city, and ordered a half bottle of Moët and Chandon to start. I drank too quickly, needing to feel that loosening buzz, so that I could go on with this. With what? Of course we all know. It has been enacted before.

I looked at Alan as if for the first time. He was Simon's age, but smaller and more heavily built, like a boxer. He had that rumpled, ragged look of most journalists, which speaks of physical and intellectual self-indulgence over too many years, and with the veneer of world-weary sophistication which is self-consciously attractive. As a young man he'd been a 'fireman' for the *Sunday Times*, and had a wealth of anecdotes about wars and disasters to captivate admiring dinner parties. His whole demeanour said 'been there, done that'; women loved his battered and majestic face, and imagined tidying the greying hair, worn a touch too long at his neck. At least, I imagined that to be true - because it was what I was feeling, as I held out my hand to show the paint.

'I didn't ever really start.' I shrugged. 'Oh, when we were students doesn't count, now. It's too long ago. At that time I was going to be an illustrator, and my special thing was botany. Simon loved my flower paintings.'

'I know,' Alan said, 'he told me.'

'I was a water-colour person,' I said, drily, 'watery in technique, watery by nature.'

'I don't know about that. I was thinking . . . a miniaturist,' he said. 'I always thought of you as like a miniature yourself: someone who, looked at through a magnifying glass, would show a terrifying complexity. Yet on the surface . . .'

'Simple!' I laughed.

'Deceptive,' he said. 'Don't put yourself down. You're too quick to do that, you know.' He paused, before going on, 'By the way, Rosa, you look really beautiful tonight. Quite . . . different.'

'Ah,' I said. 'Thank you, Alan.'

I had taken a long time deciding what to wear. All my clothes seemed trailing and frumpy, and I wanted to look slicker. Sexy. Finally I had gone to Kathy's wardrobe, knowing she had left some clothes behind. I found a purple body with a low neck and a short, straight skirt. To my amazement they fitted. I had some black hold-up stockings, and wore my one pair of black heeled shoes. I tried the tailored jacket

Simon had bought me, and it looked exactly right. I looked like someone who meant business. The face in the mirror smiled. Much more make-up than I normally wore completed me. Thus masked and costumed, I felt like an alien. Yet the reflection in the mirror was what I wanted. Simon would not have known me.

My reward was the open admiration of this man I had known at a social distance for ten years, and who was looking at me now as if seeing me for the first time. I knew that whatever movements I made would be echoed by his; this dance had its patterns; what was amazing was that I, Rosa McKee, seemed to know them so well in advance.

'I want to be different,' I added. 'I feel as if I've just walked through a door, and left my old skin hanging on the other side. That's why I've started painting, I suppose. The kind of things that are in my mind – they're new. I think people might find them shocking.'

'Even me?' he asked, with a grin which defied anything in the world to shock him.

'Even you,' I said.

The food was excellent. We drank a Meursault with the first course, because we had both chosen seafood, then he ordered a bottle of claret.

'I'll be drunk,' I laughed.

'Good!' he said, then looked embarrassed. 'I don't mean—'

'No, it's all right Alan, I'm not thinking you're trying to get me drunk because you've got wicked designs on me,' I said archly, feeling flirtatious and frivolous. I did not know this woman.

'Even if it might be true?' he said softly, not taking his eyes from my face.

'If it is true then I don't think we should talk about it,' I said. 'At least not yet.'

He raised his eyebrows and grinned. 'Deal,' he said. 'But I can't make any promises about later.'

We talked about the break up of Fleet Street, and he told me stories about Rupert Murdoch and the Gulf and the BBC. He was witty; I laughed a lot, offering him the perfect audience, just as – by the way I looked and leant on the table – I was offering him myself. He knew it, and I knew he did. The space between us shifted and contracted according to ancient patterns. It gave our conversation, for all its wine-filled ease, the slow, deliberate formality of a gavotte.

Then, as if he wished to become serious, he asked, 'What exactly is it you're starting to paint? Go on, it interests me.'

'Destruction is what I want to come on to,' I said, 'but I'm starting with growth. The two things are preoccupying me at the moment. I've got this thing – I wonder if you can possibly understand it – that there's something extraordinarily beautiful in destruction. It's like . . . I want to walk out into the desert, for the first time in my life. Nothing green. Just bare emptiness, under a burning sun. Nowhere to hide. Utterly pitiless. Do you see?'

'Not really,' he said, frowning.

'Have you never wanted to destroy the structure of your own life?' I asked.

'I've put it under threat – from time to time,' he said, with a wry smile. 'Work, friendships, marriage, the lot. But that was in my wild youth. Now – I want to consolidate. I like it like it is. It's easy. I certainly don't want to destroy it.'

'Then why are you having dinner with me?' I asked.

His expression did not change. I liked that. I had intended to jolt him into embarrassment, but did not succeed.

'I don't see having dinner with you as an act of destruction, Rosa,' he smiled.

'Ah, but you don't know,' I said.

'More an act of creation – maybe,' he said. 'But who can ever know? These things happen.'

'Nothing just happens,' I countered. 'All of us, we know what is going to happen. We know what we're doing. We may not plan it, but it isn't accidental. To say that absolves us from all responsibility. It's much too easy, don't you think?'

'Don't fight it, Rosa. There's nothing wrong with things being a bit easy,' he drawled lazily, reaching forward and just touching the back of my hand with his forefinger.

'Me – I'm in the process of moving from what's easy to what's utterly, terrifyingly difficult,' I said. 'I've got to take a sledgehammer to a whole lot of things in my mind and clear a space.'

'Then you can start to build again?' he said.

'Too easy as well!' I replied. 'Maybe I'll decide I like the bomb site. Maybe I'll go on living in it just like that. Keep it clear. Keep it hard.'

The waiter had brought coffee, and mint chocolates. Alan was chewing one, and fiddling with the piece of gold foil, forming it into a small roll. I took a chocolate, smoothed the foil, and wrapped it around the tip of my left forefinger, twisting its tail to form a little golden goblet.

'I always did this when I was little,' I said, dipping the miniature vessel quickly into what was left of my wine, and drinking from it.

Then I held it out to him. 'Here,' I said. But instead of taking the thing he looked at it for a second, then picked up the little golden roll he had made, and put it, slowly and carefully, into the narrow bowl of the cup. There was something so clearly sexual about this insertion, I felt a loosening inside me.

'What were you like when you were little?' he asked.

'Afraid of things. I used to have a nightlight until I was about eleven. And I used to imagine that I heard voices in the rustle of the curtains, and saw faces in the patterns of the wallpaper and the crack in the ceiling. When my parents took me to see *Snow White* I had nightmares for months. All I wanted was to feel tucked in, secure. My father used to tuck the blankets in so tight around me, and I used to say "Tighter, Daddy, tighter!" Then I used to burrow down so I could hardly breathe, because I thought that if I was hidden they wouldn't know I was there.'

'Who?'

'The ghosts, of course!'

'Poor little Rosa,' he murmured. 'Do you still believe in ghosts?'

'Definitely,' I said.

'Is that frightening?' he asked.

'No, just challenging,' I said.

'You look fierce.'

'I am fierce. Now. I think I just discovered fierceness.'

'Should I be scared?'

'Oh, I think so – maybe,' I smiled, turning it into a swift baring of teeth. Alan laughed, holding my gaze.

There was a long silence. Alan called the waiter, and when the bill came he just tossed down his credit card with a nod for the boy to take it away. He looked impatient, and drummed his fingers on the table.

A death rattle, I thought.

'I really like you, Alan,' I said quietly.

'Shall we go?' he asked, when he had signed.

We walked out into the night. It was warm. The street was empty. I was reminded of the ache you feel when you are young, on summer nights, alone and knowing the rest of the world is engaged with itself, with its own love. You smell food and flowers in the darkness, as a voice somewhere in the distance laughs, and you know you must be excluded from that private experience forever.

'I don't feel like going home,' he said, as we walked towards his car.

'Don't then,' I said. 'You shouldn't drive anyway. Come and have a drink at my house; it's walking distance.'

It felt odd, this walking by the side of a man, without taking his arm, as I always did with Simon. We did not belong together; we did not fit. Yet I was determined that we should fit, just as the tiny foil baton had fitted into the minia-ture golden cup. There was already such an intimacy between Alan and I that I hesitated and took his arm at last. He made a tiny noise of satisfaction, like a grunt.

As I opened the door, and stood for a second looking down my dark hall before snapping on the light, it seemed to me that something white flitted across the corner of my eye, a fluttering thing, like a moth. I thought of Alan's question about ghosts, and as I walked ahead I wondered if Simon's spirit, caught out there, was haunting the home he had so thoroughly betrayed. Fanciful, yes – but I wanted it to be true. I wanted Simon to see.

No, the truth was, I *knew* he would see.

'What would you like?' I asked, pausing by the sideboard.

'Oh, Rosa,' he said.

The air was still and warm between us, as thick as the silence in which were buried the names of my dead husband and his living wife. Alan stood with his arms at his sides, watching me.

'I don't think I need another drink, Rosa,' he whispered, 'I need . . .'

I knew it was important for me to be in charge. It would negate the whole thing if I were to allow things to happen, as

I had always done. So I stepped towards him, and put my hands on his shoulders.

'What is it you need, Alan?' I whispered, moving my face close to his.

He kissed me with a ferocity that took me by surprise. I suppose I expected diffident tenderness, even some shyness. But Alan Grierson was like a man falling on a pool of water in the desert, scrabbling on his stomach for the last drop. I felt my body respond, despite myself, and was glad to be held. I saw how a man might gain comfort from a prostitute; nothing whatsoever to do with love or even affection, merely the rasp of flesh on flesh for momentary oblivion.

Yet I was more fortunate. Here there was, at least, some affection.

It was all as I had foretold. Even his gasp of adolescent delight as his hand met the strip of flesh above the stockings was as I had known it would be, when I chose to wear them. I moved away from him then and said, 'Not here.'

Leading him upstairs to my bedroom, I wanted to laugh aloud and turn to him and shout, 'Don't you understand, you stupid man? It's got to be in our bed, Simon's bed. I want him to see. I want him to watch. I want him to suffer for ever and ever!'

Alan's lovemaking was expert and sensual. He gave me more pleasure than I had known for years. Simon and I had become like brother and sister, a normal state in marriage. It was enough to curl in bed at night, holding each other briefly, before settling comfortably into the spoons position. My body had forgotten its own crevices and their needs. It was all right. I did not mind.

But since reading Simon's intimate letters I had been conscious of longings that could not be fulfilled. My own hand had begun to seek out those declivities, although usually I sighed with frustration. That would not do either.

But this did. His hands and his tongue touched me every-where, so that I cried out, again and again. When at last he came he gave a short sigh, and whispered, 'Rosa, oh lovely little Rosa,' then lay heavily across me, wetness between our legs.

Soon he was asleep. I lay there in the darkness, listening to his breathing and trying to ease my leg free. Absent-mindedly I stroked the back of his neck, wondering where such instinc-tive tenderness came from, and whether it could survive until the day. The silence of the house was so deep and the room itself so dark, that I could imagine I had died and was myself in the grave.

And so, who was this dead stranger with me? Where had he come from? Where was he going? He had as little to do with me as a night bird in the sky, out there, alone, and hunt-ing. The spasm finished, there was nothing.

Yet, I decided, I must make him love me. It had to be achieved, the sex was not enough. He must sleep with his head on Simon's pillow, again and again, and yearn for me when in bed with Sally, his wife. He must sneak to the tele-phone to speak to me, listening over his shoulder for her footstep on the stair. He must write me a letter to flame off the page. He *would* love me.

Possibly then I would be satisfied in my mind as I was now in my body. Because I knew Simon would be with me, observing, always. *Was* with me.

'Your bed, Simon,' I whispered. 'Are you watching?'

I thought I heard someone crying somewhere, in the still-ness, a soul in anguish, which would never find repose.

Chapter Ten

14th February 1989

My darling,
You are amazing. Here I am, at two in the afternoon,
when I had expected to be holding you in my arms,
and I know that it doesn't matter that I'm not. I'm
sad of course that you had to cancel our 'lunch', on
today of all days. But I understand your family
obligations: illness is illness, and you had to go – and
yet love is like an illness too, isn't it, so why aren't
you here?

No – no more of that. I'm not even thinking,
Never mind, I'll see her next week, or even, When
I saw her last week it was stupendous – so what AM
I thinking? I am thinking that loving you is
independent of our being together, that our being
together is an expression of that love, not the thing
itself; that thinking of you is to feel love flowing
through me – mine for you *and* yours for me. I am
holding my breath so as not to break the spell.

But how could this spell be broken? What could

stop our love except death? And in truth, my dearest one, I feel that death itself would be too feeble for us. Today on Valentine's Day I think of love as all-powerful, perpetual, invincible. The snowdrops are nodding their heads and laughing at death. I can hear birds in the garden and their chirruping is a passionate song in the face of death. My own breath, quickening always when I think of you, defies death. Your pretty Valentine card (so tiny, handmade too) in my shirt pocket is a testimony to the life force of the universe, expressed in human love.

Sometimes when we have made love, and I am lying next to you in your beautiful bedroom in a state of suspended ecstasy such as I have never known, it seems to me that I can hear the shared rhythm of our hearts marking out the passage of time, and of our lives. And then I feel how beautiful to die there and then, with you, but knowing in that instant that I would not die, I would be with you forever in spirit, as I had just been in the flesh.

I take out the little paper heart and I kiss it. It will burn, of course, because I take your things and I love them for a while, and then I burn them. Yes, I have to be so careful, and we agreed that. But there is also something sublime in the solemn, loving act of destruction. They have had their life, and every word becomes engraved like pokerwork on my memory, before they twist into grey ash, and I think of how the Chinese burn things for the dead to take with them into eternity. So the pretty heart with its feather will catch light, and flare –

just as my love for you will do, even after I am
dead.

    Believe your . . . Mackie-Valentino (Oh sorry! The
babblings of lovers . . .)

So, I thought, what a waste of time for me to search for
her letters. He burnt them all, like a criminal trying to cover
his traces. And succeeding. The next letter was much shorter,
and bore no date.

Sunday evening

    Darling heart,
A very quick word, because I have just spoken to you
on the phone. It seems to me that every letter and
phone conversation now goes deeper than the one
before. The phone is the most dreadful instrument, or
so I always thought. It was for business, that's all. I
detest it and have always found it impossible to
convey feeling through it, or to hear feeling from it.
And yet you turn it into a thing of tenderness and
love; somehow your voice on it is more tentative,
softer, the shyness that sometimes leads to
brittleness gone, to be replaced by a kind of gentle
wonderment, which is what I feel for you, though I
cannot express it on the damn thing. But always now I
am suffused with elation after every call, long or
short, nonsense or deep seriousness. Our love
becomes ever more amazing to me as it becomes ever
more real and precious. How long is it now? Nearly a
year? Or a lifetime?
    Please don't say that I 'make sacrifices' for you. We

make sacrifices for each other, and that is all part of
our love. What is important for you to know is that
you don't even have to need me, although until now I
have wanted you to. After our mini-crisis, I had what
amounts to a revelation; the outcome is that there are
no conditions attached to my love, and you don't have
to do anything to have it and keep it.

All shall be well. THANK YOU for being there
when I phone.

All my love, S

Two weeks had passed since my night with Alan Grierson. In
the morning he had woken with a start, and looked at me for
a second as if he could not remember who I was or why he
was there. Then he blinked and kissed me. Then he said, 'Oh
God, I hope Sally didn't phone me. She always sounds irritated on the machine if I'm not there and she expects me to
be. How will I wriggle out of that one?'

Lie, like you men always do, I thought.

I said, 'You must tell her you took me out for a meal, and
that I was very upset about Simon, so it was a late night. Tell
her how sorry you feel for me. Then – if she rang this morning, say you got up very early and felt like going out for a
walk.'

'Just like that!' he laughed, reaching for me.

More so than the night before, when we had both had a
lot to drink, I found this sex with Alan exquisite. He was a
good lover; he waited at the right moments, tantalisingly,
so that I had to work a little, and understood the balance
between gentleness and determination. For me it was like
waking after a long, long sleep; the brother-and-sister
affection of my marriage had lulled me. I had forgotten

about selfish sensuality. Now I wanted it. Not love, but pleasure.

In the event, it turned out his wife had not telephoned, so he was, as he put it, 'in the clear'. He telephoned me each day, to ask if he could 'drop by'. Sally came back, but had to have days in London; their lives were separate; I teased him that he was a practised adulterer. Unsure whether compliment or indictment was intended, he decided on the former and smiled. As if some hidden pact had been reached we settled into a pattern. I decided that every other day was enough, and allowed him to visit at four when my day's painting was done. So we would lie down with my hands smelling of paint and turpentine, and I remembered the Christopher Logue poem I'd loved, set to jazz, when I was young, 'Drunk as drunk on turpentine, from your open kisses . . .' The dreamy sensuality of the saxophone echoed in my memory, with its melancholy yearning for impossibilities. All lovemaking with Alan was tinged with that, like a vein running beneath the surface of the skin.

I would look at him as he dozed after he had finished and always ask the same questions: who was this man, this stranger, here in my marriage bed? He was Simon's friend – sort of; he was my friend too – in a way; he was Sally's husband – certainly. It all added up to a central mystery, a sort of universal grief.

I understood nothing. My life with Simon, Kathy's childhood, Simon's death, my discovery of his deceit – and now this relationship melded together in eternal transition, flitting past the corner of my eye like (the image came back again and again, almost tangible) a white moth in evening gloom.

The old Rosa might have wept sentimentally, as she did when her daughter left home and she was left with the photograph albums. She might have cried, 'I can't bear it.' The recent Rosa knew that when she drew breath, the air that hit her lungs would be icy and raw; what's more, that there is no escaping it. Anything can be borne, if enough resilience is granted to the bearer.

When Alan and I made love with the keen skill of grown-up adulterers and the affection of friends, it seemed to me that this was a paradigm of human life itself: the slow start, followed by the long, frenetic seeking after new experience and sensation, until the moment of brief and terminal ecstasy. Then, last: the descent into oblivion. I recalled reading that in the sixteenth or seventeenth century people used to write of orgasm as 'dying'. The accuracy of this astounded me – the more so because I had never thought of these things before. Sometimes I would fancy, as I looked at Alan, that I could see the planes of his skull, and that the shadows of sockets replaced his eyes. And there was the dark, damp smell of soil beneath the fishy smell of sex.

After two weeks he laughed that his real rival was my painting. Playfully, he tried to enter my studio room, but I took his arm and told him seriously that it was forbidden.

'Nobody will go in there until I've finished,' I said.

'Finished what? One painting?' he asked.

I shook my head. 'No, what I've set myself to do,' I said slowly, realising that so often nowadays I said things before I had thought of them and was disturbed afterwards to find I had uttered a truth.

For I had set myself to paint without knowing what I would be painting. I wanted it to be like automatic writing; I wanted something to take me over and choose both palette and forms. The strange thing was I had no doubt that this would be the case.

From the day I had squeezed out a range of greens and blues and raised my brush to the canvas, I felt consumed. It was as if there was a sooty blackness at the corners of my eyes, focusing vision with an intensity that was at once thrilling, terrifying, like a high fairground ride. I allowed myself to make a few marks, then found my hand sketching out the whole in broad strokes of palest sepia. The geometry came. I could not stop it. The first painting was finished. It was a knot garden under an invisibly stormy sky, grey sombre upon greens.

Where did it come from, that pattern of low hedges, in a complex geometry of curves and corners, with its central silvery fountain, low and dry? Paradise was a garden, divided into four by its rivers, flowing outwards to the four corners from the central fountain, the Spring of Life. Yet I had not painted paradise, nor was there much evidence of growth in my knot garden. The box hedges were dark. The beds were empty. It hung there, static and brooding. It frightened me.

I sat on my stool and contemplated my work for a long time. (This was the pattern of my new life too. The long emptiness that could only be filled by me. The silence of the house. The delight of it, yes, the delight of my grief.) It pleased me. And it was inevitable that I thought of Simon, because I knew he would have liked it too.

I hadn't spoken to him for a while. There seemed no rush. His voice had receded, but I knew this was temporary. He was disgusted at what I was doing with Alan. Maybe he was jealous, maybe he was morally disapproving because of Sally – such hypocrisy being normal. Whatever – he was not speaking to me, and that was good. I had no wish, for a while, to hear him.

I haven't told you about Simon's voice. It is the gentlest

voice, so that sometimes people have to crane their neck a fraction, to catch what he is saying. It lends intimacy and respect, that small action. It gives his words weight. People have always listened to him, although he lacks the kind of blustering confidence that leads men like Alan Grierson through a conversation like a horse cantering along a track. The thing that makes people defer to my husband is his stability, I think. He is centred, he could be rooted; he inhabits his corner of earth with perfect weight and balance, so that no unexpected gust of wind could budge him. Oh, he might be threatened, his arms might wave with momentary disturbance, but he will settle again. That's what must have happened when he met Her. But then he settled back into his allotted place, living here, seeing her when he could, loving her. Loving me?

One afternoon I was in bed with Alan, and after he had slept a while, and I had disentangled myself from our mutual stickiness, feeling that languor in the limbs Blake called 'the lineaments of gratified desire', I asked him outright.

'Did you suspect Simon was having an affair? Come on, Alan – the truth.'

'On my word of honour, I didn't,' he said. 'Look, Simon wouldn't have known if I had been having it off with Martin's wife, would he? We keep each other in compartments. Why should anyone have known?'

'It's such a small town,' I murmured.

'Anyway, love – why don't you leave it? What the fuck's it matter – now? He's dead and you've no idea who she is; it won't do you any good to keep on about it.'

'Do I keep on about it?' I asked, feeling annoyed and crossing the room for my robe. 'I think this is probably the second time I've mentioned it to you.'

'Don't get all iffy, Rosa,' said Alan. I liked the fact that he refused to be rattled by me. 'You don't have to say things for me to know that they're going on and on in your sweet little brain. And on and on! Take my advice, love, and leave it. Live your life – let poor bloody old Simon rest in peace.'

'How would you feel if you found out Sally had been unfaithful to you? How do you think she'd feel if she knew about us?'

He got up, shaking his head, and wrapped a towel round his middle. I liked his body rather more than Simon's – compact where Simon was rangy. It fitted mine. We were in proportion.

'Listen, Rosa, you and I inhabit very different worlds, you know. You can't imagine this is the first time I've broken what we laughingly call the marriage vows. It doesn't shock me, about Simon. Do you hear me?'

'It went on for about six years,' I said.

'So what?'

He was smiling but his eyes challenged me.

'Don't you think it matters?' I said, sullenly.

'What the fuck's any of it matter? We'll all be dead soon enough,' he shrugged.

'So I could pick up this phone right now and tell your wife that you've just been in my bed, making love to me? And it wouldn't matter?'

'Rosa, don't be a bloody fool,' he said, disappearing into the bathroom.

'I told you I was into destruction!' I yelled after him.

I didn't see him for a week after that, and I was unsure whether to be glad or sorry. I liked the space, but missed the afternoon sex. Yet I knew he would come back. He liked it too. We were playing this game according to strict rules, and in each predictable action we, the middle-aged adulterers, were coupled with the long-dead. I exulted in my music: *an ineffable game begins / in their limbs, arms and lips* . . . YES!

Meanwhile I began to hear from SIROSA's old clients. Several phoned to say that they were glad that I was back in business, and that they would pass on the name to friends. One or two invited me to come and design a new corner of their gardens. Several more sent postcards with similar messages. There were various gardening jobs I had to arrange, using Simon's old list of names. Suddenly there were things to do, and I was glad, even though the tasks were mundane. But I drove out to Shepton Mallett where a photographer, a friend of a friend, had bought a rectory and wished for a cottage garden to indulge his urban craving for rusticity – even though the existing garden, laid out formally with lawn and shrubs, was far more in keeping with the proportion of the place. No matter, I thought. Then I had an appointment in North Stoke, where a solicitor wanted a *potagère*, and was happy with my fairly obvious sketch of six beds separated by brick paths. In my heart I knew I was playing at this. It was just a means to an end. Then I would think again.

I read more and more of the love letters, each morning, with my coffee, going up religiously for a daily fix of poison. I was obsessed, looking forward to the moment when I would see his words on the screen, and be able to follow the progress of his great love. The truth was that it just went on – and on. Passion settles into acceptance; the wildest flights of poetic fancy contract into normal expressions of affection. There were subtle shifts of moods in the letters, of course, and long gaps of many months when clearly they had seen each other so often Simon had not felt the need to write. But there were days when I found the letter I was reading tedious. I had read it all before.

So what did She think? I wondered. Did she yearn for her lover to return to the old hyperbole of passion? Or was she easy too, the affair becoming as familiar and essential as an old pair of gardening gloves? To me, it was disappointing, as if I had bought a book, believing it to be a thriller, then found myself reading cheap romance. Or had expected poetry and found advice on soil types. Since my life had come to depend on the drama, giving it momentum, I had no wish to be cheated. What really bothered me, I realised one day, was that she and Simon had settled into what was clearly for him another form of marriage. That was almost as shocking as the naked adoration.

I say that my life was steered by obsession, yet that became less true as the weeks drifted past. My relationship with Alan resumed its uncomplicated sensuality, and the garden design work picked up. I realised two things. First: I needed very little money to live on, as Simon had left me perfectly well off. (The appointments with the solicitor were tedious, because I had taken no interest in our finances, but Simon had made investments and was well insured. He had been sensible in that at least.) So I was free. I didn't have to cook if I chose not to; there were more hours in the day than I had ever known.

I filled them. After the knot garden came a dark arbour, leading into blackness. Then an empty stone pool, surrounded by topiary: balls and cones, like guards around the edge. I painted a maze from above, yet with all its angles curving, like so many tangled scrolls. I filled canvases with ochre gravel and tumbling ivy; I set individual flowers as if spotlit, against a background as dark and lush as a rainforest. I invented a savagery of leaves. There was never any sky.

The second realisation was the important one. Hand in hand with the conviction that some day, when I made the effort, I would come face to face with Simon's mistress was the awareness that my real impetus was towards another revelation. At last, in the action of brush on palette, in the flick of paint at the edge of the knife, in the trance of composition, I came face to face with Simon's wife.

Chapter Eleven

She said, 'You're doing so well, Mum!'

I had let Kathy into the studio only after much persuasion, but felt I had to justify my days. Now the face she turned to me was excited, but puzzled, even daunted, as if she was not sure how to respond. So 'You're doing so well' is easy, what one might say to an invalid on the road to recovery.

'It's different, isn't it?' she added.

I nodded and told her I felt I had to move on from anything I had painted before. As if there was a decision involved. As if this was part of a life plan, instead of a crisis I'd been catapulted into, and within which I had grown used to living. 'I'm really proud of you,' she said.

I looked at my daughter. She was so like Simon, the same nose, the same cheekbones, the same soft voice: so much his daughter that when she was five she liked to 'file' her things, making little piles of this and that, and searching for boxes to label and put them in. She was a quiet child, who took things seriously; easy to hurt by a teasing smile which appeared to patronise one of her schemes, when in fact you were simply adoring it. She expected life to be manageable, and made it so, experiencing none of the real turmoils of adolescence. She had her crazes and her friendships, she went to school and did her homework; she was still worrying about the environment when her classmates had moved on to hanging round clubs, lying about their age. People said we were lucky: our daughter was 'no trouble'. She got her grades and her place at Edinburgh; we opened champagne, and later Simon and I whispered that we hadn't done badly. 'Nobody tells you how to do it, after all,' he added thoughtfully.

Of course he was right. Being a parent is a series of accidents; if you're lucky a prize bloom grows, despite the odds, in your small patch of garden. I think I was a good mother, and know exactly how the world would define that quality: I didn't leave my child in the care of au pairs; I didn't stay out drinking and smoking until four in the morning (like Kit, although she had no children so it didn't matter anyway); I didn't even think about a career; I gave my child my time as well as my love. I read to her, I played with her, I taught her to sew, I took her shopping, I went on a 'Greenpeace' demonstration with her, I tested her on her French verbs and history dates, I gave her cookery skills, and took her to art galleries too. And I adored her. Yes, the perfect mother.

And it paid off. The bargain was kept.

Yet what if Kathy had rebelled, done drugs, dropped out? Would it have been my fault? Maybe blame and credit are equally irrelevant; maybe it is all as random as death. Looking back over the years of Kathy's life, I was conscious only of a thin, tired aching for her to know me not as the mother who had done all those things with her and loved her, but as this lost and lonely soul who suddenly found love itself called into question.

'Why proud?' I asked.

'Because of the way – you know – you're coping. Getting on with things.'

'Oh, you have to,' I said.

'Yes, but . . . well, I read that some widows sort of . . . give up,' she said.

For some reason that amused me, so that I laughed aloud, and Kathy looked slightly shocked. 'What do they give up – the ghost? Good thing, I should say!' I said.

'Oh, you know what I mean, Mum,' she said reproachfully.

Of course I knew what she meant, just as I had known she would get the right books, and read them, the more to know what she was talking about. So like her father: such certainties, such order. How could she possibly approach my chaos?

'Do you . . . miss Dad a lot?' she asked.

I shivered then, and was silent for a few minutes, not trusting myself to speak, while she stared at me, half expecting me to cry, anxious at what she might have triggered.

Do I miss you, Simon?

I haven't left you. I am with you all the time.

'I think about him all the time,' I said at last.

'So do I,' she whispered. 'I'll be in a pub with Greg, or just going to a lecture, or whatever, and suddenly Dad will pop into my mind. Nothing particular. Just – him. And then I can't believe he isn't here, and that I won't be able to tell him what I'm doing. It makes me feel like I'm in a wood or something, and I'm scared and I reach out to hold his hand, and it isn't there, and won't be there ever again.'

'Lost,' I said.

'Like that,' she nodded, pointing at a canvas about a metre square that was propped by the window.

We both stared at my maze painting, the first of many mazes that subdivided my retina when I drifted off to sleep, dark and brooding geometries of box, with no discernible way out, except for the smallest of wild creatures. I wanted to paint a stone one too, a labyrinth with, at its centre, some suffering, savage thing, head thrown back in an eternal rictus . . .

'I suppose that's why I painted it,' I said.

'I wonder what he'd have thought of all this,' she said. 'I mean, do you think he'd have expected . . . ?'

Her voice tailed off. Once more she looked puzzled, narrowing her eyes a fraction as if trying to imagine her father looking at my work.

'He didn't expect me to do anything,' I said.

We went downstairs in silence, and when we were at the kitchen table, mugs of coffee in front of us, just as in the old days, I could feel her relax. My studio had intimidated her. Those dark paintings on canvas and board, the studies in charcoal stuck up with masking tape all over the walls, the utter confusion of painting materials (my natural untidiness grown far worse), the mess on the floor . . . Kathy could make no sense of it all. It spoke no language she understood. But the grammar of the kitchen was perfectly clear to her: subject and object in proper place; structure and meaning indivisible. It was part of her education. Not her fault, mine.

We talked about her boyfriend, Greg, and she blushed and said she wanted me to meet him. I teased her a little about settling down, then we chatted about her course, her friends, the flat, the cost of electricity, her need for a decent jacket, the way Quorn makes a good shepherd's pie if you add finely chopped mushrooms and some pinenuts for texture. She made more coffee. She complimented me on the windowsill herbs: basil, coriander, tarragon, marjoram. Then the talk subsided into a moment's easy silence.

'Anyway, Mum, I want you to tell me why you're painting all these gardens,' she said then, giving the last word a peculiar emphasis.

'I like gardens,' I said.

'Yes but . . . not like that,' she said dubiously. 'I mean, the paintings are marvellous, it's just that they're so . . . dark. You used to paint *light* things.'

I nodded agreement, without saying anything.

'Is it because of Dad?' she asked.

'What do you mean – the darkness?' I replied.

She sat opposite me, cradling her coffee, and when I looked at her directly she lowered her eyes. Perhaps our children don't want to know us. Perhaps they run in terror from the knowledge that we are as lost as they are, and as afraid of the night.

'No, I meant the subject. I mean, you're painting his kind of garden, aren't you? I remember when you used to quarrel about gardens.'

'Not quarrel, discuss,' I said.

'But you used to get quite angry with each other.' She smiled. 'I remember once listening at this door and you got seriously irritated and called him Dutch Willy.'

'What? I don't remember that!' I said, smiling at the absurdity of the phrase.

But I did remember. Strangely, if you had asked me if Simon and I ever quarrelled I'd have said an unequivocal No. I was right to reject the idea of these discussions as quarrels – they were mere differences of emphasis in a settled universe, that's all. Yet sometimes they upset us, as if analysing the detail of garden design could, suddenly, open a chasm at our feet – and there we were, standing on opposite sides, shouting at each other, while cold winds blew all around.

'I suppose you could say this is your father's way of getting at me,' I said lightly. 'I wanted to paint wilderness, and he's got me painting Dutch and Italian gardens. These men always get their own way, even when they're dead.'

I know my tone jarred; again she dropped her eyes, turning down her mouth a fraction at the corners as though she might burst into tears.

'Don't talk like that, Mum,' she said.

'I'm sorry,' I said, out of habit.

The truth was that I had been partly dreading the beginning of Kathy's vacation. I loved her, I telephoned her twice a week, I wanted to know every detail of the relationship with the tiresome-sounding vegetarian Greg, but I did not actually want her living with me for the summer. There was the work, there was the painting, there was Alan, there was my private obsession, there was no room for mothers and daughters. My guilt gave me a stomach pain; I blamed Simon for that too. Had I not become this creature, had I been allowed to remain as mourning mother, I would have longed for my daughter's arrival. When she told me (nervous, apologetic) that in fact she would only come down for two weeks, before setting off for four weeks in France and Italy with Greg and two other friends, I was able to be understanding and magnanimous.

'You've made me a liar, just like yourself,' I had told him.

I didn't lie to you, Rosa.

'Well, what's lying by omission but lying? You lived a lie with me, for all those six years. Don't tell me you didn't lie to me, Simon!'

Our life together wasn't a lie. It was its own truth. Don't you understand that? Why do you want to destroy it all, Rosa?

'That's the most astounding, ridiculous, sickening thing I've ever heard! Me – destroy? It was you, Simon! You did it, not me!'

Not me . . .

How I hated that echo, despised his excuses, wished my

hands could reach out to slap and stroke, instead of the voice, the bloody *voice*.

Can you quarrel with the dead? Maybe that's what hauntings are: a perpetual argument, unquiet spirit with unquiet spirit, eternity not long enough to get it all said. Simon was frequenting me because of his sin, of that I was certain; on the other hand I was refusing to let him lie in peace; in the end both are the same, it does not matter. *Why sittest thou all on my grave, And will not let me sleep?* ran through my mind: the old idea that too much grieving is unfair on the beloved dead, keeping them awake.

Kathy was looking at me, with the petulant, reproachful expression of a disappointed child. I was not saying what she wanted me to say.

'Mum, you're in such a strange mood,' she said.

'I'm sorry,' I said again.

How many times do women apologise to their husbands, parents and children? Why should I not tell Kathy the truth, and stop apologising? Everything would be put in context then; she would understand. I looked at her, taking in the particular reddish-sandy colour of her hair, curling just above her shoulders, the grey-blue eyes, the straight nose she dislikes, the delicate planes of her cheeks – so like Simon.

I thought: Simon, I'm going to tell her the truth about you – about France, Christmas, the lot! She can't go on idealising you. It's not fair on me, Simon, do you hear me, on ME!

I said, 'Kathy, there's something I want to tell you. I wasn't going to, but . . .'

My tone of voice obviously alarmed her. She leant back in her chair and folded her arms tightly across her chest for protection. We spoke at once.

'Is it . . . ?'

'You're not going . . .'

We stopped, and smiled. The moment relaxed us, making possible what was about to happen, perhaps. I nodded with mock-graciousness and said, 'You go first, love.'

'Is it . . . a new man?' she asked.

'Oh *that*,' I said. 'No . . . well, I have been seeing someone. You don't mind, do you?'

'No, course not,' she said, with a grimace that belied the words. 'I think you should get out, and be with . . . people. Life has to go on, doesn't it?'

I told her to say what she really meant.

'Oh, Mum, it's hard, you know? It's like when you're little you think your mum and dad are there forever, a pair, solid. That's why divorce must be so horrible for most kids. Whatever happens you want your parents to be there together, making that wall.'

'A windbreak,' I said.

'Well . . . anyway, with you – when Dad died I kept thinking, She'll never find anybody to match up to Dad, and I didn't want you to. You know? And that made me feel really bad, because it was so mean of me – like I was con-demning you to be alone for the rest of your life. But it's hard, Mum! I don't want you to replace Dad. I can't help feeling that!'

Her voice had risen to a pitch almost like panic. Her lips were parted and her eyes were bright; she looked as though she had just done a sprint. Her hands twisted within the baggy sleeves of her sweatshirt.

'Do you think I'm selfish?' she asked, quieter now.

'Of course not,' I said, making it right for my child, clos-ing the curtains and keeping the bad things at bay.

When she was little and had frightening dreams, Simon discovered a foolproof method of coping with her fear. We would both go to her room, and while I sat on the bed and stroked her head, crooning, 'Shh now, shhh now,' he strode about the room like a herdsman, gathering up the bad dreams.

'Come on, come on now, all of you,' he would say in a voice that brooked no rebellion, flapping his arms to drive the invisible nasties towards the door. Then he would flap some more and bark the command, 'Come on! Out you go, out you go – all of you! Out!', stride out on to the landing, noisily open the door of the lavatory, and flush 'them' away. Then he would come back rubbing his hands and saying, 'Well, that's them all gone!'

It worked. She trusted him utterly, and believed the bad dreams were washed away down the pipes, never to return. Maybe there would be new ones next week, but Daddy would drive them out and drown them. Always. We would both kiss Kathy then, and whisper a soft goodnight, and go downstairs exchanging the self-satisfied, loving glances of parents who know how to handle even the terrors of nightmare. We knew we were unassailable.

'You couldn't, could you, Mum? Nobody could be like Dad. Be like you two were . . . I just can't imagine it. Girls at school used to be jealous of me, you know? Either their parents were divorced or separated or else rowing all the time. Do you remember that girl Amy in the fifth year, the redheaded girl who was good at drama? She came home from school one day to find her Dad packing his cases, moving out. She had absolutely no idea her parents hadn't been getting on. She was really messed up by that – really missed him. She got bulimic. She blamed her mum . . .'

'Why?'

'Oh, that probably wasn't fair. She just felt that her mum, sort of, *let* him go.'

I felt angry. 'Oh, you mean she thought her mother should have worn stockings and suspenders and dyed her hair blonde, anything to keep her man? Why on earth is it that *we* always get the blame?'

'Nobody's blaming you, Mum,' said Kathy. 'I didn't agree with Amy at the time. She was a pretty neurotic girl, and I felt sorry for her. No – the point I was making was that I always felt so lucky because you and Dad had such a fabulous marriage. I remember when we went on holiday, like to France, and I would always feel happy because you and he talked and were so close – so that sometimes I felt you'd like to have been on your own! Really romantic. I liked that.'

'Did you?'

'It's still like that, you know, Mum. Most of the people I know in Edinburgh have divorced parents. It's awful. You think there's nothing *settled* any more – and the thing is, they say they think they'll probably divorce too, because it just goes on. You learn from what you've seen. Whereas me – I won't marry unless it's for life. Like you and Dad.'

She was very bright-eyed now, and I knew she could cry easily. The look on her face reminded me of when she was about seven, and she would stand in front of the Christmas tree, eyes bright, gazing upwards to wonder and joy. In her mind's eye she was gazing at the spectacle of her parents' love, with the same emotions.

'So – do you understand, Mum?' she asked softly. 'Why I just said what I said? It's not that I mind you seeing this bloke – and I'm really glad that you wanted to tell me about it. It's just that I'd rather leave it there, for a while. I mean, you aren't thinking of marrying him, are you?'

That was said with a grin, and a deliberately light tone, but it didn't fool me. She was anxious; her voice pleaded for a negative.

'Bit soon,' I said. 'Anyway, he's spoken for.'

'What?'

'Oh, never mind. It's a long story – all of it. We'll save it for another time.'

'Yes,' she said, with relief.

For a second Kathy looked at me with that dubious, side-long expression I had seen upstairs in the studio. Then it switched off, as she added, 'Mum, can you find me a really nice photo of Dad, one I can put in a frame? I really miss him. I know it must be twice as bad for you – but he was my dad. I never realised . . . Oh, I wanted him to know how I did in my degree. I wanted him to give me away when I got married. I wanted him to go on being there . . .'

Then she began to cry, as I knew she would. It was not the racking, tearing grief of the sobs that echoed from her room after Simon's death, like my own. This was a quiet keening, like a small dog waiting for its master, who gradually realises that he will not come.

What could I do?

I comforted my daughter, putting my arms around her to rock her and murmur a repetitive 'I know, I know', just as I did when she was ten or eleven and had quarrelled with one of the swiftly changing 'best friends' whose random sadism blights the life of all young girls, and later when she thought she was plain and would never get a boyfriend. The power of comfort is the consolation of motherhood, beyond words or reason, residing in touches and sounds that have their origin in the cradle.

'I know, darling, shhh, I know,' I crooned.

But my real knowledge was that I could tell her nothing. My isolation was made complete.

Chapter Twelve

It continued to amaze me that not once in the letters did Simon ever refer to his mistress by name. The omission seemed abnormal for, although the Valentine pages in newspapers reveal the range of private petnames people have for each other, you know that in life and on paper Bunnykins must become Bill – sometimes, at least. Since Simon can't have imagined that his letters would be found, the utter anonymity of the woman can't have been a covering of traces. No, she lived for him as endearment incarnate: my dearest, my love, my darling, my light, my life. It had the effect of turning her, for me, into the universal mistress, the great passionate abstract which has threatened the stability of the universe since Troy.

Most of the clients had got back to me one way or another. Most phoned in acknowledgement of my letter, some sent cards or letters, all welcomed my return to 'life' – although of course they didn't put it that way. In addition, there were one or two fresh enquiries; clearly my name had been passed on. I went on site meetings, and realised how easily I could do this: design the garden knowing what they wanted, simply adding one or two ideas of my own, meet the contractors, oversee the landscaping, then the planting. I began to carry Simon's old trowel in my bag, like a badge of office. The point was that the business impinged on my life very little. The person who drove out in the van was an actress. She played her part with skill, but in the pleasantries of daily encounters and the businesslike arrangements, she knew she barely existed. It would be so satisfying to be able to say that this new, busy Rosa gradually banished the quietly malevolent spirit who inhabited the studio and who sat in front of the computer, reading and re-reading Simon's letters, but it would be false. Rosa McKee was false, in as much as the world still saw her as Simon's wife, Simon's partner, the bearer of his name and his standard.

'Do you really like all this garden stuff?' Alan Grierson asked one day, after Kathy had left for France, and I was liberated to welcome him to my bed in the afternoons.

'It's what we've always done,' I shrugged, 'and therefore it's something to do.'

'I can think of better things to do!' he said, rolling towards me. He usually wanted to make love twice, but sometimes I couldn't be bothered. It made my legs ache, and my mind was elsewhere.

I sat up, absent-mindedly stroking his head. He groaned and buried his face in my side. I heard a muffled, 'Rosa, you're driving me mad.'

This power was new to me. It amazed me that this man, this journalist who had been round the world and slept with untold women (he said), was telling me that I was the best ever. With him I made my body work by instinct – raw and predatory where once I had been reticent, even shy. Sometimes when I came I thought of Simon, and screamed, 'Look at me! Look at me!' inside my head, my triumph almost complete. Waiting then for Alan to work himself to his own climax, and hearing his groan as he finished, I felt as if I straddled the universe, nerves aflame, blood singing in my veins, owning all, being all, *living* for the first time for years – while *he* was dead, eaten by worms within his neglected grave.

Lucky Rosa.

Yes, I am lucky, and I deserve it. I'm no longer your cipher, so stupid as not to see what was going on.

As stupid as Sally is now?

Don't try to make me feel guilty, Simon – to make yourself feel better! It simply won't work. The truth is I don't care about Alan's wife any more than that woman cared about your wife.

But she didn't know you. Sally knows you . . .

So what, Simon! You've taught me such a lot. I'm grateful to you!

Lying listening to Alan's deep breathing, as he dozed, I could fancy there was another breath in the room, light and shallow, constantly sighing out its grief. It was the same each time. I loved the invisible witness to my sin (and how I liked to use that word to myself, the forbidden word, the modern taboo) and the fact that he too was on the rack.

'I'd love to go away with you,' said Alan, as he was dressing.

'Simon took Her to Devon,' I said, 'and to La Mortola. They had a wonderful time, wouldn't you know.'

'I don't give a fuck about them, Rosa,' he said, exasperated. Already I had the power to banish his habitual light cynicism and make him angry and frustrated. 'I'm talking about us! Let's go to Paris, Venice, wherever. I want to wake up with you. I want to spend whole days with you. I want some time – don't you? Proper time!'

I stared at him, amazed. This man was almost pleading with me. Alan Grierson, with his stories of wars and politicians, the man I had been rather in awe of for years as he regaled dinner tables with his opinions and anecdotes and flirted shamelessly with women – this man was begging me to want to spend time with him.

'Well, don't you, Rosa?' he repeated.

I imagined us in Cipriani or the George V, drinking champagne, revelling in the secrecy of being away. It must have been like that for Simon and his woman, and for illicit lovers since Lancelot and Guinevere. Then I imagined myself at home, with Kathy, when Simon was uncorking the champagne on Dartmoor, and the rage curdled once more. Sally would be at home as I had been, having believed (probably) her husband's tale about the foreign trip.

'I've got too much painting to do,' I said shortly. 'I'm building up to an exhibition at Equinox.'

'Really? Ron didn't tell me,' he said in a huffy voice, turning his back and looking out of the window.

'That's because he doesn't know yet,' I said.

'So the painting comes before me?' he asked, turning and looking at me bleakly. I was doubly surprised then. My announcement about the exhibition hung before me in the air as being exactly right, if unexpected. And now I saw in Alan's face the astonishing truth of his feelings. He expected me to put him first.

'I'm afraid it does,' I said quietly.

We stood on opposite sides of the bedroom, gazing at each other. The gulf between us was huge; it was as if we had never touched.

'Does all this mean anything to you?' he asked at last, making a short stabbing movement with his right hand, to embrace the room, the bed.

'Yes, it does, Alan,' I said. 'I like being with you, I like making love, I miss you when you can't come round. Is that OK?'

'Sometimes I look at you and don't know who you are,' he said.

'Join the club!' I replied, sitting down in front of the mirror and pulling the brush through my hair.

My reflection pleased me these days. I had started to wear a little more make-up, my hair was growing longer than I had worn it in years, and my face had a glow about it I put down to fresh air and sex. Alan called me beautiful. When he did so I always thought, in a flash, that I wished I could be as beautiful as Her, because she had to be more beautiful than anyone, for Simon to love her as he did.

I leant forward, thinking I saw the beginning of a blemish on my cheek. But it was just a shadow of a line. As I inspected this tiny indication of my own mortality, I thought I saw Simon's reflection, crossing the room behind me, but not looking in my direction. I froze, my hand in mid-air by my chin. I thought I felt a current of cool air too – and turned quickly. Alan was by the window, still looking at me. All was as it had been.

'What's the matter?' he asked.

'I thought I saw Simon just then, behind me, in the mirror,' I said, seeing no reason to lie.

'Jesus!'

'No, not him – Simon,' I said drily. I like Alan, but sometimes thought I liked making him angry even more.

'What's wrong with you, Rosa?' he asked, a note of despair in his voice that had not been there before.

I got up, crossed the room, and put my arms around him for a minute. I liked this man, I really liked him, but knew I would never love him. As if he read my mind he whispered, 'I think I love you, Rosa,' leaning against me briefly, and groaning, just as he had when he came. I held him there, then stepped back, my hands on his shoulders, looking up at him. I wanted, in that instant, to throw back my head and howl to the heavens. I had wanted to be loved, and now I was loved – and yet it was not right. It was not like the love in those letters. That was rare and precious and unique – according to Simon. This felt like any old affair, where both are in it for sex and affection, yet one slides fatally into love. Another mess, tedious in its ordinariness.

'What's wrong with me?' I repeated. How could I begin to tell him, when I didn't fully understand the extent of my own malady? What would you call it – retrospective jealousy? Or unrequited love?

'For God's sake, talk to me,' he pleaded.

'Alan, I can't talk to you properly, because I'm talking to Simon. All the time, in my mind, and sometimes out loud. I'm asking why he did it to me. I'm trying to understand.'

'No, you're not, you're wallowing in it. Look, Rosa, millions of men have been unfaithful to their wives, and millions of wives have done the same. There's nothing special about it, can't you see that? Nothing! Why can't you just bury it – with Simon? Like I've told you a hundred times. If you don't you'll drive yourself mad. And drive me away.'

'Oh, Alan – is that a threat?' I asked playfully, turning away. Why should I worry about this man? He thought he loved me, but he would cease to love me. The only permanent love in the universe was Simon's love for Her – and mine for Simon.

When Alan had gone I went to the study and opened the file again. I had reached a point – two years after the affair began – of great crisis. Or rather, they had reached it.

2nd February 1990

Dearest,

Yesterday afternoon was so utterly painful I feel as if
I have been to hell and back, and barely lived to tell
the tale. I can't believe that you said what you said,
and that our amazing, miraculous relationship is
over, ending as the most ordinary ones do – when
the girl gives the boy his marching orders and he
goes away hurt, to play old records and lick his
wounds in his room. I've got no memory of driving
home; it's a wonder I didn't have an accident. And
when I got into the house I had to hear all about
things I had no interest in – Rosa and Kathy around
me expecting me to be husband and father, when all
the time I wanted to run down the street screaming
your name and begging the world to make you come
back to me.

DON'T LEAVE ME DON'T LEAVE ME
DON'T LEAVE ME DON'T LEAVE ME

That's the trouble, isn't it? I am a husband and a
father and suddenly you've had enough. Oh yes, you
said you wouldn't make demands on me, and that in
our time together we had one hundred per cent of
happiness, and that was all that mattered. You were so
good, so tolerant, so reasonable . . . no wonder it
couldn't last. You said all those things, but in the end
you were as weak as any other woman – you who I
thought above mere jealousy. Because that's what it is,
isn't it? You're jealous of my wife, aren't you? It seems
such a common emotion . . .

Oh, forgive me. I'm hurt and I don't mean what I
say. You aren't ordinary. You're extraordinary. People

like R and I are the ordinary ones, in our little
domestic cocoon with our little business, worrying
occasionally about the size of bills and whether
Kathy will get her grades. How small we must seem
to you, from your lofty tower! And now you've
locked the door and pulled up the ladder and say I
can't come near you any more. To protect me you
said. Or are you fibbing? Isn't it really all about
saving yourself?

I can't breathe, darling. Please don't do this to me.
I beg you.

3rd February

Oh my love,
I didn't mean anything of what I wrote yesterday.
Please forgive me and let me start again. I took a deep
breath before I sat down, willing you to be kind and
listen to me. I tried your number ten times and got
your lovely voice on the bloody machine. Yet I knew
you were there. God, this frustration will kill me! I
feel a sort of tightening in my chest. Last night R was
worried about me, and insisted I went to bed early.
She said I was pale. If your heart is breaking, does it
show so easily on your face? Poor R, she fluttered
around me, and gave me some painkiller, because I
had to tell her I had a headache. If only one could
cure heartache so easily. I wanted to cry on her
shoulder and tell her that I am dying of grief because
the love of my life has told me we cannot go on. But

could I do that to my wife - who is, after all, the cause
of all this? Of course not. So I was snappy with her, as
if it were her fault. She looked hurt and went away.
Poor R.

Can we go through it, one last time? When we had
been together about two months I told you, in deep
seriousness, that I would never leave my wife. You
were wonderful and told me it didn't matter, that we
would carve out our own life within the confines of
your house and garden. And so we did.

Now you've changed. You met that man and
actually have the nerve to tell me that since it's
obvious I will never leave, and since you are tired of
being alone, you think it might be better for you to
have the time and space to let another relationship
grow, if that is what is fated.

1. If that is what you want to do, you must do it.

2. If you are trying to hurt me so much that I
break, finally, and tell R the truth, then you will
not succeed. I made my vows to her and I will not
leave her. She isn't fitted to stand alone. I HAVE to
stay! Quite apart from the matter of Kathy's exams
etc.

3. Whatever happens, you must know that I will
always, always, want you.

So there you have it. Go your way. I will stay here,
as always. I will wait for you to come back. I know
you will come back.

Simon

I admired his confidence. He knew he had her exactly
where he wanted her, though she obviously tried like mad to
break from his grasp. For a few minutes after reading, I almost

felt sorry for her. Her bid for freedom didn't work, so much
was obvious. The next letter was predictably triumphant.

                                    23rd February 1990

    Sweetheart,
This will be very quick as I've promised to go with R
to Sainsbury's. Will the ladies on the checkout glance
up at this middle-aged man with greying hair and
notice he's the happiest lover in the universe?
    To be serious – thank you, *thank you* for yesterday.
Those four hours transported me and I am still dizzy.
Too much for one body to take, too much for one
mind to contain. I always said I knew your other
relationship wouldn't work and that you would come
back to me, but in many dark nights of the soul I
doubted it. Now I am proved right – and all other
human loves fall away: small and pathetic beside ours.
Poor David! I can afford to pity him a little now you
have sent him packing, although I have wanted to kill
him myself. I accused you of jealousy! God, it's eaten
me up and spat me out!
    Enough. All I want to say is I ADORE YOU. And
we will go on for eternity.
    With all my love,
    Simon (the Believer)

I closed my eyes, and could remember that time quite
clearly. Simon had seemed ill, complaining about his head
when I asked him, and locking himself away for hours. Kathy
and I were worried; she made him a beautiful get-well card,
a collage of scraps and cut-out paper doily, just as she might

have done when she was little. I had theatre tickets but he would not come, insisting I take Kathy instead. I remember how we fussed over him before we left . . .

Anger was a habit now, so much so that it had begun to bore me. I found myself thinking instead how lonely Simon must have felt, suffering like that but able to tell no one. Grief places you within a ring of flames, flickering all around your body, so that no one else can approach unless already burnt. I knew. And suddenly I also knew that the pain he had felt then was not so very different to the pain of bereavement. When he thought he wouldn't see Her again he *was* bereaved. He must have woken each day in the long, grey hours of early morning, when the room, like your life, is indistinct yet your misery is clear and sharp as a scalpel, probing away at the gut with clinical precision. You lie there, eyes wide open, as your blood and bones unite to whine, *Please please please please* . . . And you think it will never end. *Don't leave me don't leave me*, you whisper into the darkness.

Abject and alone: I had been that and so had my husband. I pitied him, and for a strange second wished I had been able to comfort him.

I sifted through the cards and notes from clients, and my list of names. The old diary pages were already out. I knew that if I started to go through and collate I might find the identity of the woman who had so wounded my husband. Yet I held back. Perhaps I was afraid of my own promise that I would go and confront her. Perhaps I needed this drawn-out preparation – if not, why hadn't I completed the search a long time ago? I needed her ghost just as I needed his; they were both presences in this quiet house, and I did not want them exorcised. Not yet.

What are these ghosts for? I wondered, as I went up the stairs. I paused on the landing and stared down at my wild garden, imagining him walking there. I squinted, but there was nothing. Would I see through him to the bushes, the trees, Simon's apparition transparent, as his soul never was? Might he be clanking chains, symbolically fettered by his own deception? Such are the images of ghosts we inherit, from the quivering white sheet with black holes for eyes calling 'Whoo-hoo!' to the disembodied footfall above our heads, when midnight shuts down the world but the floorboards still creak. Ghosts warn, admonish, threaten, terrify, beg forgiveness. They return once a year, on All Souls' Night, or the Mexican Day of the Dead, to join the beloved living and say, 'Don't forget me, please.' They nibble at the essence of our lives, for sustenance. They do not go away; on the contrary, they go on telling us that it never ends.

'Are you ever going to show yourself to me, Simon?' I asked.

But there was no footfall, and no figure in the garden, nor even that voice. I went to the studio and began another painting, losing myself in the sensuality of green. In a few hours yet another maze had formed itself, this one with a wisp of ghostly white at the centre.

Chapter Thirteen

One day Kit telephoned me, asking 'How are you?' in the voice of someone who does not really want to know the truth. Her phone calls had been sparse, and I thought I knew why. I told my friend what she wanted to hear, that I was painting, that business was picking up, that I was going to ask Ron and Emma to consider giving me a show. I knew there was a direct correlation between the relief she felt and her decision to 'whiz down' and see me, just for lunch.

'It's been too long. We'll go somewhere decent,' she said.

I picked her up from the station, and could see immediately that she was impressed. She had looked at me, for a second, as though I were a stranger: another woman to appraise.

'You look wonderful,' she said, taking my arm as we walked to the car. 'I can't tell you how much good it does me to see you!'

Once we had ordered our meals she reached across and rested her hand on mine for a few seconds. 'I've been neglecting you,' she said.

'It takes two,' I replied, 'I've been neglecting you too.'

'What's the news? I want to hear everything. I tell you what, I can guess something – I bet you've got a lover.'

'How do you know?' I asked.

Kit cackled her barmaid's laugh so loudly one or two people turned round. I grinned at her, feeling such fondness for this woman that I couldn't speak. A life force – that's what coursed through Kit, and for as long as I had known her it had swept me along too, perhaps because I had lacked my own.

'Cos you look so marvellous! I know it doesn't sound particularly liberated but there's nothing like good sex to put a sparkle in a girl's eye! Go for it, Rosa!'

The laugh cracked the air again. I shushed her, glancing around. The waiter, hovering nearby, was trying to control a smile.

'I already did,' I whispered.

'So who is he? Come on!'

I told her about Alan, whom she knew of course. Kit knew everybody. You couldn't go out with her, to cinema, theatre or restaurant, without a voice crying 'Kit!' Many times she would kiss and make bland noises of enthusiasm, then say, when the person had gone, 'I haven't the faintest idea who that was. Let me think . . .' Yet you knew the unknown 'friend' walked on feeling warm and flattered by her attention.

'I've always thought he was really sexy,' she said. 'You know he had a big affair with Liz Evans – oh, about ten years ago.'

'Really!' I smiled. 'Well, I'll be able to tease him about it.' Liz Evans was a well-known columnist who dealt in comment to a degree of low malice and stupidity matched only by the height of her reward. The information diminished Alan in my eyes.

'Always a taste for married women. No demands possible, you see.'

'Ah, but I'm not a married woman – not any more,' I said.

'Probably scares him,' she said.

'He says he's in love with me.'

Kit groaned. 'Oh, they all say that at some stage, especially if they think they haven't got you just where they want. I suppose it's sweet – really.'

'What about . . . what was his name . . . Mark?' I asked.

Her face changed, as an ice cube dropped into alcohol will change its form immediately, softening at the edges.

'That's different. That's utterly real,' she said.

For a second I felt irritated by her assumption that her relationship, Mark's feelings for her, were 'real', whereas Alan's expressed love for me was a sham. Then I squashed the feeling as soon as it had begun. For although I did not know her lover, I knew she was right. Alan and I were passing some time together, that's all. It was not a great love. It could not match Simon's – or hers.

'He's been in America for ages,' she said, resting her face on her hand and looking sad. 'I've been missing him like I had a kidney cut out or something. But he's been writing. I pick up the letters at the office.'

'What do you do?' I asked, and when she looked puzzled, added, 'When you get a letter – what do you do?'

'I open it and read it of course!'

'How many times?'

'Oh, I see . . . OK, well, I snatch it up, and rip it open, and read it about four times, and kiss it sometimes, then carry it around in my Filofax pocket for a while, then finally put it in the envelope with all the others. He writes so well. Wonderful letters . . . I told you, didn't I? He quotes me poems, extracts of something he's been reading . . .'

'Will you keep them forever?' I asked.

Kit frowned, and chewed a mouthful of chicken before replying. When she finished, and looked up at me again, her eyes were bleak, as if she had looked into the future and seen why the fortune-teller looked surprised. 'What's forever?

We've made a pact, he and I, never to talk about next month, never mind next year. You know, I used to fantasise about leaving Paul and spending the rest of my life with Mark. I'd design our whole flat in my mind, choose the colour of the bedlinen, plan our holidays – everything. I was determined to do it at one point. I thought, well, I've got one life and this is *it*. Then I started doing sums – when I'm seventy he'll still be only fifty-six, and so on. It was so depressing I couldn't bear it. So I never think about it, and nor does he. We just lurch from meeting to meeting.'

'And Paul's still got no idea?' I asked.

She shook her head. 'Not an inkling. I invited Mark to a drinks party at our house, and there they were talking – but not for long. They couldn't have much to say to each other, they're so different . . .'

'God, Kit – didn't you feel horribly guilty? To see them talking?'

She nodded. 'Of course! But so what? Life's just so bloody complicated and I can't get myself off that hook.'

'So why keep the letters? Paul might find them.'

'I've thought about that so much since . . . You know. That day. I went home and took the packet, and thought of dumping it somewhere. I can't burn them because we don't have a fire. Do you remember the end of that Moreau film *Les Liasons Dangereuses*? She goes to burn all the letters, and the flames roar up and burn her face, so she's horribly disfigured. Poetic justice, I suppose. Anyway, I'll tell you something, Rosa – if anything ever happens to me I want you to promise to go to our house and get Mark's letters. Will you?'

She was smiling as she said it, so I laughed lightly. 'Oh yes, search about and tell Paul what? Very likely, Kit!'

'No, I mean it! I've thought about it. You know, I've got to go to Paris next week and the plane could crash. So – listen, really! In my study there's a small cupboard by the window, sort of distressed grey paintwork. It's full of stuff I need to store. Well, on the bottom shelf on the right-hand side there's a big jiffy bag sealed with two huge bulldog clips. It's got "VAT" on it in red marker-pen, crossed out, then your name and "GARDENS" in black.'

'What?' I exclaimed. Suddenly I felt cold.

'I thought the VAT thing was too obvious. So I've photocopied a few pages from garden design books and put in a few cuttings from garden design columns in the Saturday papers, then all Mark's letters are underneath. If . . . well, you never know . . . You'd go and tell Paul we've been working on a book idea, and say you have to get the plans, find the envelope, burn the letters. Paul would never know. And that's it. I already vaguely mentioned to him a book about the Gardens of Britain, you words, me pictures.'

'Very clever,' I said thoughtfully.

'Look, let's face it – under the circumstances he wouldn't be asking too many questions, because I'd have popped my clogs!' She grinned.

'It's not funny,' I said.

'Believe me, I know.'

'But you've really worked this out, haven't you?'

'Of course! Infidelity and ingenuity are two sides of the same coin.'

'But – it's a horrible thought,' I said.

'Yeah, well, I'm not too keen on the thought of dying myself!'

'I don't mean that. I mean it's a horrible thought having to do your dirty work for you, Kit.'

'It wouldn't be dirty work. You'd be protecting Paul. And you know all about that, Rosa.'

'That's why it makes me feel bad.'

'Oh look, sweetie, just forget I ever mentioned it, OK?'

She order another half bottle of white. Unused to drinking at lunch time, I already felt that softening at the edges of reality which made Kit's scenario seem vivid. In that second the room's edges faded into black, and each person within it – restaurant staff, customers – was transformed into a death's head, eyes gaping, mouth mewing in the face of eternity that it wanted to live, wanted to live. We can't afford to think of it, and yet we do. Kit had done so.

I shivered and gulped the last of the old bottle, remembering how Simon had burnt the woman's letters. I told Kit. She looked uncomfortable, as if she didn't want to be reminded of that day in Simon's study.

'And I hope by now you've got rid of all his,' she said quietly.

'Yes, I deleted them all,' I lied.

'I'm so glad, love. I guessed as much. You *look* like someone who's living in the present, not raking over the past. Now, tell me about the painting . . .'

I talked to her as I had when we were students, about ideas and form and colour. Soon we moved on (which I wanted) from my work to art in general, and the Turner prize, and about the pretentious nonsense that is written about conceptual art. We laughed in mutual complicity – teasing each other for sounding so conservative yet both knowing we were absolutely right.

'They can't *draw*,' Kit said with disgust. 'I mean, you're a superb draughtswoman, but these kids get a bloody degree in Fine Art without so much as being able to paint an apple on a table in mock Cezanne. As for the photographers . . . God! Every year hundreds and hundreds of the poor little buggers graduate with poor seconds, having written essays about the politics of photography, and taken a few crap snaps of people's toes and God knows what, then they want jobs in the real world. Forget it! The thing is – it's all about hate, isn't it?'

'What is?' I asked, feeling fuzzy and not following – but suddenly feeling I had been found out.

'The art and the photography these kids produce. It's kind of *meagre* – like that's what they think constitutes the human soul. They hate people. They hate to think what people are capable of, if stretched. Reaching up, looking at the stars, like Wilde said. But just look at Rembrandt or look at Avedon, say, and that work's about understanding and truth – *and* it's about love. Don't you think?'

'Maybe the others are right, though,' I said. 'Maybe we should accept the fact that we're all small and miserable, with petty little desires – and not pretend. Crappy people who deserve crappy art.'

She looked almost angry then. 'No way!' she said in a loud voice. 'The point about Rembrandt or Picasso or Goya is they KNOW how bad people can be, and how they'll lie and cheat, how so often the soul shows in the face and I'm afraid it's bloody ugly . . . but that doesn't matter. Out of the shit they grow flowers. They're tolerant. They don't say, "Look how crappy we all are." They say, "This is how people are, and we have to tolerate it, because, my God, we're capable of such great things too!" Have you ever seen the Avedon portraits of drifters?' I shook my head. 'Well, it's all there. These people are standing there, really crisp in black and white, and huge, and you see in the lines of their faces what they've been through, and their eyes are sort of blank but challenging too . . . And they're a . . . a testimony to *respect*. He's about tolerance, just as much as Cezanne, when he painted those lumpen country people.'

I heard what she said, and loved her for her fire; the enthusiasm that drew me to her when we were students had not diminished, even though her trade was largely tired and cynical. She had once told me that when she went to each new job, whether it was a picture of a young fêted novelist or an old maestro, she always felt the excitement of not quite knowing what the accident of light and shadow would shape within the lens. And I thought wistfully that I would love to believe, as she did. I said so.

'But you do!' she protested. 'You should have seen your face when you started to talk about your painting. You're doing it each day, proving it.'

'What?'

'That it's worth making your mark on the universe.' I grinned at the over-dramatic statement, and shook my head, but she was not to be put off. 'I mean it, Rosa. The fact that you're painting again says something—'

'Like I can do a daub or two,' I interrupted.

'No, you eejit – it says that you've come out of that terrible pit you were plunged into. Why would you make your daubs if you didn't believe in them?'

'Therapy,' I said.

'Bullshit,' she said.

'Well, I'd wait and see before you get so confident,' I told her, 'because looked at all together it's a pretty dark set of paintings. God knows what you'll make of it.'

'What do *you* make of it?' she asked.

I thought for a moment. The strange thing was I had never asked myself the question. I knew that my paintings were a silent expression of my dialogue with Simon, but I could not interpret the whole – not just like that. Perhaps in time it would become clear. But meanwhile Kit was waiting for me to speak.

'Each one is a section of a huge whole,' I said slowly, 'like those little plastic puzzles you'd hold and try to move round the little squares to make the picture. So I suppose I've got this vision of a garden, a big estate like the sort Simon used to love and I hated, and I'm creating it slowly. Like a sort of present to him. Like the garden he can rest in forever. It's got all the elements: bits of topiary, pools, dark corners, mazes, parterres, geometry . . . And it's his. But no one else will know that.'

As I was speaking I felt surprised, like someone suddenly startled out of sleep, blinking and wondering where on earth she is. I suppose the wine was speaking, and yet I knew, once the words were out, that they were true. Kit was staring at me; for once she did not know what to say.

'In a way I hate it. I hate the fact that he's bloody well making me do this!' Kit gave her head an almost imperceptible shake, and looked worried. 'But the next part of the project is for me.' I went on, 'I'm going to paint my own inner landscape.'

'What's that like?'

'Not what you'd expect,' I said. 'Nowhere I've been . . . I can't talk about it now. But the whole thing's called The Desert in the Garden.'

Why did I say that? Until that moment, I swear, I had not thought of what I was doing as a whole, let alone named the exhibition. Yet there it was, called into being once and for all by the act of naming, and reassuring me that it was *right*. I sat back, suddenly exhausted, and felt rather drunk.

She began to talk about Mark again, telling me he was planning to write a novel, talking about how brilliant and creative he was, this man she loved. Then she made a tight ball of her hands. 'Something I want to tell you, Rosa. I've said it to him, but only once. It's something that makes me so sad.'

'What?' I asked.

'A child. I dream of having Mark's child. Oh, I know, I was the one who never wanted children. And I really didn't! But now I dream of holding a baby, my baby, the baby I never had, and it's his and mine, a part of us both. But I know it will never happen, and sometimes that makes me cry and cry. If I'd met him years ago . . . but then, that wouldn't have worked either. It's so sad, Rosa!'

'Yes, it's sad,' I whispered.

We were both quiet for a few minutes. Words were intolerable. Wine greased the lock, but when finally the door creaked open the land outside was too cold and bleak to bear. The door had to be pulled back and sealed shut again.

'I'll tell you what,' Kit grinned, making a visible effort. 'there's one problem about getting old, especially if your bloke is younger. I don't know if you have it.' She looked around her with a conspiratorial air, and leant forward, dropping her voice. 'Pubic hair,' she hissed.

'What?'

'Yes – it starts to go grey. Has yours?'

I started to giggle, and shook my head. Kit put up a hand to ruffle her wild mane of hair, and looked mock-tragic. 'No, seriously, it's awful! I mean, I can put a colour on this lot, but down there . . . I mean, think about it! Think of the implications, Rosie! Not very sexy, is it, to go down on a greying muff?'

We were leaning, heads together like schoolgirls. I snorted. She was trying to retain an unsmiling face, but it began to crack. 'Dear Claire Rayner, What shall I do? Yours sincerely, Worried Greymuff of Islington.'

I was almost out of control now. She began to laugh too. I saw the waiter looking at us, with an indulgent grin. Schoolgirls.

'So what's the answer?' I spluttered. 'Knowing you, you've got to've come up with one . . .'

'Henna sample packs from the Body Shop,' she grinned. 'You get them to try out on your hair, and it's just enough.

Got to be careful not to let it go inside you, though – ouch! Anyway – you make a paste, smear it on, cover it with cling film, let it dry, and hey presto!'

'What's it look like? I mean when it's done?' I asked.

'Fox-y!' she drawled, and set us off again.

When at last she called for the bill the restaurant was empty. My stomach had the stretched and sated feel of too much food and too much laughter. I don't think I had ever felt closer to Kit in my life.

'Who needs men?' she asked, sticking her arm in mine as we walked from the restaurant. 'I tell you what! Why don't we go on holiday together – in the autumn? We could do a package. Like Shirley Valentine without the Greek fisherman!'

'I'd love that,' I smiled.

When I had put Kit on the train, I went home and slept for an hour. I was woken by the telephone, but when I picked it up there was a moment's silence before the receiver at the other end was replaced with a soft click.

'Hallo?' I repeated, fruitlessly. Then I said, 'Simon?'

Why did my woolly, disconnected brain think even for a fraction of a second that it might have been Simon on the telephone. The old Simon was dead. The new Simon lived in this house with me, and since he spoke to me every now and then he had no need to use the telephone.

'Am I going mad, Simon?' I asked.

You're making sense today, Rosa. But perhaps that's a part of your being mad. I know all this, because I went mad, did you realise that? If you torture a man for six years he will go mad in the end. Before he dies.

'I didn't torture you!' I protested.

But you did. Innocent little torturer in your black mask! Oh, none of it was your fault! You were just there, and every time I looked at you I knew I was doomed to be stretched between two points, until my joints split. Agony, my little torturer – to be on the rack for six years, like that . . .

'Oh, why didn't you go then? If it was so bloody awful for you. Why didn't you have the courage to leave me, and go and live with her?' I was crying now, and rubbed furiously at my eyes.

No, it takes more courage to stay.

'I wish you hadn't stayed! I wish you'd gone. Then I might have got on with my life much sooner. The things I'm doing now, the person I've become . . . I wouldn't have started to paint with you around. You got in my way, Simon!'

Twenty-two years, Rosa.

'Yes I know! And was each one torture? Maybe it was for me. Maybe that's what I'm just discovering! Maybe that's what's making me insane – knowing that I wasted all that time being your wife! How many widows discover they can live only when their husbands are dead? How many go on to take courses, run businesses, be free – for the first time? Oh, they wouldn't put it that way, of course – it would be too shocking. But they're so much more lucky than the other ones with nothing left to live for once the man is dead. They might as well go right out and perform suttee – much more honest than simply fading away.'

I felt so angry with him. He knew it and did not reply. So I paced from room to room, picking up small objects we had bought through the years of our marriage, putting them down again, and wondering where it all came from and what it signified – these pictures, plates, ashtrays, pieces of pottery, books, cushions, rugs.

These fragments I have shored against my ruins.

'But they didn't prevent your ruin, did they, Simon? Your ruin was inside you, ticking away, day after day, month after month, until finally the explosion occurred and I was left to pick up all the pieces. And I'm still picking them up.'

Stop feeling sorry for yourself, Rosa. You're alive.

He was right of course. He was always right. I stopped at the window and looked down at my neglected garden. Cow parsley was rampant, the roses lolled over the path that led nowhere, long suckers waved insolently: all anarchic, everything collapsing into everything else. It looked a mess – like the grave I had not visited since that day.

Chapter Fourteen

I decided it was time. So I sat at Simon's desk with the letter file open on the screen, and the client file open on the desk, and my list of names.

ζζζζζζζ

My Darling,
What's the date? I haven't the faintest idea. I'm snatching fifteen minutes alone with you, and so it doesn't matter. It's midnight and R has gone to bed at last. We spent tonight watching *Dr Zhivago* – R's idea, because she said she felt tired and not up to anything. But the film! I saw it when it first came out, and liked it very much then. But now to watch it was a sort of agony, so much did I identify with poor Zhivago and his doomed secret love for Lara. He loved his wife, of course, and his duty was to her and his children – of course. But in the 'of course' is the tragedy of the world, because the really great loves, the really grand passions, the really profound needs are all excluded from its parameters.

Anyway, R cried at the film, but I sat there, my stomach clenched tight, and my eyes dry – too moved for easy tears. Then we said goodnight, and I pulled out our paperback of the novel and came up here, to turn the pages and think of you. I kept coming across things that made me think of us.

'He realised, more vividly than ever before, that art has two constant, two unending preoccupations: it is always meditating upon death and it is always thereby creating life.'

That's not so much because of us, but because it reminds me of my work. You remember we were talking about gardens in winter? It strikes me that the secret of creating a beautiful garden is to always visualise it in its hour of death. That way you reach the structure. Equally, the secret of creating a beautiful life is always to meditate on your own death – to *live* it if you like. Each day. Sometimes I feel that leaving you is like dying . . . And so by loving you so much, and by having to leave you so much (because of our circumstances) I am placed on the interface between death and life. Should I mind that? Or should I rejoice?

Enough. Back to Boris. Page 353: 'They loved each other greatly. Most people experience love without noticing that there is anything remarkable about it. To them – and this made them unusual – the moments when passion visited their doomed human existence like a breath of timelessness, were moments of revelation, of ever-greater understanding of life and of themselves.'

There it is, my darling. He knew! And what about this. Page 371: 'As you know, the word passion in Church Slavonic means, in the first place, suffering, the passion of Christ.'

That's made such an impression on me. As you

know, I'm an old atheist – but that's got nothing to do
with it. Suddenly I'm faced with the equation between
passion and suffering, and it helps me to make sense of
my own life. That's how it is. That's what I have
chosen. SO! I want to throw back my head and fling
my arms in the air and howl my defiance at
conventional life, and the little rules that hem us in. I
want to shout from the rooftops that desire is as
important as duty. I want to spit in the face of death
and jeer, 'Do your worst, you skinny old bastard,
because you can eat up my flesh but you can't touch my
love!'

Isn't it odd that we live in a world where passion is
frowned on – or at least, the naked expression of it?
Sex is fine – all those awful little comic newspapers
are obsessed with it, and it seems anyone can bed
anyone else and no one will worry. Yet at the same
time married people are pilloried if they're caught
having an affair. But sex and affairs is not what we are
about. The passion and the suffering are flames too
bright for the world. That's why it turns away.

When he was dead his Lara cried by his coffin, and
when I read that chapter, just now, I couldn't stop the
tears, at last. She says, 'Your going, that's the end of
me. Again something big, inescapable. The riddle of
life, the riddle of death, the beauty in genius, the
beauty of loving – that, yes, we understood. As for
such petty trifles as reshaping the world – these
things, no thank you, they are not for us.'

So all lovers withdraw into their community of
suffering and of joy, so selfish and yet so sublime.
Why should you and I be different? Impossible.
Like giving up. I send you kisses through the night,

wondering if you are asleep in your wonderful
room, or if you are lying awake now, in the silence,
listening to the owls, and thinking of me. Please be
awake! Please don't let me be alone here. Please let
out a breath – NOW – so that I can breathe in, and
in that second take something of your life, your
soul.

You'll read this and say I'm sweet and silly. Just
blame Pasternak, my love. No, no! Blame yourself,
for initiating me.

With all my love,
S

There were tears in my eyes, but they were not tears of
rage – not this time. I remembered that night when we
watched *Zhivago*, and I teased Simon for fancying Julie
Christie. He hadn't wanted to watch the film at first, then sat
like a statue, not responding to odd comments I made about
a particular sccnc. It was odd, his silence; with something
implacable about it, as if he were about to sit in judgement
and knew no alternative. When the film had finished, and I
was snuffling quietly, he said he was going upstairs to do
some work. I asked him not to; I wanted him to come to bed
with me. I think that film must have such an effect on anyone
with an ounce of human feeling, making you want to reach
out and cling to the human creature who you've been cast up
with (for better for worse) because you know that out there
it's cold and lonely. So cold, with no one beside you at night.
So lonely with the pillow smooth next to you. So perpetual,
this longing for the measured breathing beside you in the
darkness: the little sounds of a humanity that may be small,
weak and fallible, but which is nevertheless set beside you for
the long march into the darkness. And so to be treasured . . .

Then, in the room I still thought of as my husband's study, I cried aloud, despite myself, 'Oh Simon, Simon, Simon, Simon. Why did you die? Why did you leave me here alone, to struggle on without you? Even if you were still loving Her, I wish you were here . . .'

But he didn't reply this time. I expect he could not bear to watch me reading his letters, and especially that one. For it was beautiful and it was private. I knew I had no business to read it. He was right to take offence.

I imagined the woman who owned it, reading that letter, and was afflicted by such an envious ache I had to lean forward, as if I had a stitch. I saw her walking to her bookcase and finding *Doctor Zhivago*, and sitting down to read, sharing with Simon. I heard her sigh, then cry, as the text moved her, and she thought of Lara, and Yury, and herself. I watched her walk outside in the morning, into the beautiful garden he sometimes mentioned in the letters, and see his hand in the low box hedges, the terraces, the imaginative plantings of white and purple in misty corners. Then she would go indoors again, and telephone him and they would plan their next meeting.

Yet – what if 'poor R' were to answer the phone? Swiftly it would be replaced, or else she would run her fingers over the buttons to make a confusion of sounds the other end. I did remember such instances, but in my innocence put them down to error somewhere else in the universe, not in my own home. As vividly as I had imagined the previous scenes I saw myself picking up the phone to hear the click the other end, then shrug my shoulders and think no more about it. Then – God! – I felt such pity for Rosa, for the poor deceived wife, the innocent, the victim, that once again acid flowed into my mouth.

I snatched the list of client names, and my own list of

replies, by telephone and card. I had avoided this confrontation, but it would be delayed no longer. I took a good few
minutes to run down the lists, and cross-refer. In the end it
was as I had expected – or almost. Only one name on Simon's
list was not on my own – but it was a man's name: *Charlie
Fitzgerald, Winter House, Winterstoke, Somerset.*

I frowned and thought hard. The name Fitzgerald was
familiar, yet I could not remember why. I presumed it was
because he had mentioned this client to me, and rested my
forehead in my hands, as if willing my brain to function.
The truth was I had expected a Miss. Nowhere in the letters
was any mention made of a husband: the woman was
youngish and unattached – she had to be. This Fitzgerald
person was a red herring.

Then I remembered the diaries. I found the pages for
1988, the first year of the affair. I scrolled back to the beginning of the letters and noted the date, then found May in the
diary. It was very difficult to read Simon's spidery hiero-
glyphics, bad enough at full size but almost impossible in
miniature. He had many abbreviations that took me a few
minutes to work out, before I could interpret them as
suppliers, architects, and so on – names familiar to me. But
no 'Charlie Fitzgerald'.

I was almost ready to cry with frustration when it occurred
to me that the little device I had read as 'GC', and thought to
mean 'Garden Centre', was equally capable of being inter-
preted as CF. The entry came on April 26th. An
appointment at 2 pm. There was another one on April 30th.

Turning the pages slowly, scrutinising each day, I found no
more entries that might help me. It was a waste of time.
Whoever this man was Simon had met him once, and pre-
sumably gained no work. Fitzgerald had not replied to my
circular because he was busy or rude or merely indifferent.

He might even have moved away. My simplistic notion that I would find the woman's name so easily mocked me now.

I hesitated before picking up the telephone. There was the maddening click, then a woman's voice on the answerphone; 'Hallo, I'm sorry there's no one here to take your call. Please leave a message after the tone. Thanks a lot. Goodbye.' I put the phone down, then dialled again, to hear that voice twice. It was soft and warm, and utterly confident; it made my scalp prickle. But the second's instinctive feeling that this was the voice of Simon's mistress was banished immediately. It must be Mrs Fitzgerald. It was impossible that his affair had been with a married woman because it would certainly have come up in the letters. The guilt of adultery was all his, not hers.

I decided to leave a message. 'Hallo, this is Rosa McKee of Sirosa Garden Design, wondering if you received my note. It would be very nice to hear from you at your convenience.' Then I gave my number and slammed down the phone, feeling angry although I could not say why. After five minutes I gave into temptation and called Alan Grierson. I confess I wanted to be held, wanted sheer sexual release just as much as I wanted him. But the voice that uttered an impatient 'Hallo' was Sally's. I hung up.

Chapter Fifteen

When I walked through the churchyard gate I saw, even at that distance, that something was different. I shook my head slightly and blinked, as if I were imagining. Yet the sight remained the same, all the more shocking to me as I drew nearer.

Simon's grave was beautifully tended. There was a proper, old-fashioned headstone carved with traditional skill – a weeping tree spreading across the top. Beneath, in finely chiselled lettering, it read simply, SIMON JAMES MCKEE, 1948–1993. Beneath the name the stone mason had chiselled a small trowel. The velvet turf was bordered by white and purple alpines, and in the centre a single jasmine trailed up and over the stone. The effect was beautiful in its controlled simplicity. Nothing I could do would destroy it, I realised. She would return again and again and make good. It was hers, not mine.

I stood for a long time looking down at this creation. There were no weeds. She must come every few days, or perhaps each day. For a wild moment I fantasised about waiting there until she came, but immediately dismissed the thought as absurd. Even I quailed before the imaginary self-inflicted humiliation of haunting the churchyard to frighten my husband's mistress. In this, as in all other things, she had won. The grave would remain as testimony both to her taste and her victory.

But how dare she! I turned away at last, helpless, and my indignation grew as I drove home. In the house, I seized the directory and found the vicar's number. He was clearly shocked by my brusqueness as I demanded to know who had erected the stone.

'Well . . . ah . . . I assumed it was you, Mrs McKee . . .' he said.

'Well, it wasn't me!' I replied, incapacitated by anger, not caring what he thought.

I thought of telephoning likely stone masons, then slammed the Yellow Pages shut. What was the point? I wasn't going to hang around that churchyard waiting for her to come and trim the turf with her little shears. Let her play at weeping widow at the grave. I had better things to do.

I switched from paint to pastels and oil sticks for more speed, although I could not have explained the sense of urgency. The palette changed too – from the tones of an English dusk to the colours of the sun: cruel and implacable. I closed my eyes and took some paper, and the first thing my hand sketched was an animal skull against red earth. Its outline was crude and jagged, its eye sockets black daubs. There was no finesse in this pastel, and I knew Simon would have loathed it. So I sprayed the fixative and contemplated my work, wondering what it meant.

When I was alone, sometimes in bed, sometimes in the bath, I found my mind moving among images of the desert, and I was a baked, desiccated creature, clinging to survival in an alien landscape. I could watch this person from my great height: Rosa McKee alone, face to face with imminent destruction. Yet I was elated by the prospect of that destruction and wanted to push the creature to her utmost limits. I knew that deep down I was attracted to the chaos that lies concealed beneath the ordered universe. I daydreamed of Bath in the dark ages, described in the Anglo Saxon fragment we had pinnned up on the kitchen noticeboard, and imagined it destroyed again now: the dry earth heaving and cracking beneath the crescents and squares, the Georgian stones toppling into chasms, as unspeakable creatures of darkness crawled from the earth's centre, to scorch elegance with their fire.

So my desert series began. In one, a corner of an English garden, a terrace with an urn on it – from which golden sand poured unstoppably, silting the foreground. A row of English yews grew impossibly from soil the colour of Australia's red centre. There were more skulls among bleached rocks on harsh, pale earth, and strange hybrid creatures lurking in the shadows of vermilion rocks. In my imagination I saw dry river beds, and the purple shadows of dunes. Foliage, where it existed, was silvery grey to brown. I painted a confusion of forms: dune becoming cliff face, or perhaps deep gorge. The earth blazed or shivered in the desert night. Mica glittered. Trees raised bare stubs asking for mercy. There was no sky, never any sky.

I freed my wrist as I had never done, to trace big curves with the oil sticks, enjoying the absense of the brush, so that the medium was an extension of my hand, responding to the smallest nervous spasm. As days passed, and I retreated to my studio whenever possible, the work became more and more abstract. I mixed pastel and oil stick to create a flat, matted texture, as dead as my heart. The ochres and sienas and reds were blank and pitiless; even the rocks lost their shadows, as if this world of my inner eye was locked into a perpetual noon.

I was reminded of something I had read, a long time ago. It teased me, until one day, as I caked oil on one spot to resemble a small rock seen from on high, a small plane maybe over the desert . . . I remembered. That evening I found the book easily (Simon believed in alphabetical order), and flicked through. It must have been ten years since I read *The End of the Affair*, but I remembered how much it moved me, and angered me at the same time. I rejected the idea of rejection, of sacrifice. I did not believe it. Now, as I turned the pages, letting my eyes skim read here and there, I felt a spurt of sympathy with Bendrix's terrible hatred. I knew about that warping of love; it had poisoned me too.

For some reason an image had come to me through yellow ochre and scarlet lake, through the desert of my own vision: it was from Sarah's diary at the core of the novel. I quickly found it. Perhaps the pages fell open at that point, I can't say. But to my astonishment the passage was marked with a pencil line in the margin, faint and straight. Who had done it? Perhaps it was Simon, perhaps me, or why should I recall it? But I had no recollection of doing so, and felt unsettled. I read:

I know he is afraid of that desert which would be around him if our love were to end, but he can't realize that I feel exactly the same. What he says aloud, I say to myself silently and write it here. What can one build in the desert? Sometimes, after a day when we have made love many times, I wonder whether it isn't possible to come to an end of sex, and I know he is wondering too and is afraid of that point where the desert begins. What do we do in the desert if we lose each other? How does one go on living after that?

He is jealous of the past and the present and the future. His love is like a medieval chastity belt: only when he is there, with me, in me, does he feel safe. If only I could make him feel secure, then we could love peacefully, happily, not savagely, inordinately, and the desert would recede out of sight. For a lifetime perhaps.

If one could believe in God, would he fill the desert?

I have always wanted to be liked or admired. I feel a terrible insecurity if a man turns on me, if I lose a friend. I don't even want to lose a husband. I want everything, all the time, everywhere. I'm afraid of the desert. God loves you, they say in the churches, God is everything. People who believe that don't need admiration, they don't need to sleep with a man, they feel safe. But I can't invent a belief.

There was a pencilled asterisk at the end of the marked passage. I closed the book and sat perfectly still for a few moments, then flicked through the pages again. This time the back flyleaf fell open, to reveal handwriting – Simon's handwriting, even more minute and faint than usual. There was an asterisk, then this:

I will approach the desert – light scouring the eyeballs, arid heat shrivelling the skin, the emptiness of the wasteland searing the mind, the very soul. What choice is there now? Long ago I dreamt of deserts, looking at images in books and longing for the ugliness of sweat and steam. Why? To cast off the refinements that have entrapped me. Ah, but that was a dream of obvious desertion. (There's a word for you!) It was too obvious. What need is there to travel towards pitilessness? For now I see the desert in the green of my own garden, the plants in my room, the flowers on my desk. I am parched. I am invaded by sand.

My own mouth was dry. When could he have written that? I assumed it was during his affair – although in a moment of terrifying uncertainty I wondered if he had written it during the last week, while I was painting. I knew the thought was utter nonsense, and yet the notion that my husband's ghost had watched me painting, and deliberately described my work, was preferable to the idea that years ago he had prefigured it.

Were you so unhappy, Simon? I asked. Why didn't you give me any indication? Was I going to the shops, and chatting to Kathy about school, and sitting down to supper with you both, and fretting quietly about whether or not I should go back to my flower paintings . . . and all the time you were hiding behind the mark of the perfect husband, the perfect father? You were in despair and I hadn't the slightest idea . . .

Rosa, you knew all the time. You just didn't allow yourself to understand. I used to catch you looking at me sometimes, as if you were puzzled. You wanted to know more about me, yet you stopped asking. You do that in marriage, don't you? It's as if you live in a room with all the doors closed, and locked, and you are afraid to open any one of them, in a version of Russian roulette, in case that is the one that falls off into the void of eternity. Rosa, I was in despair for six years. Do you hear me, Rosa? Can you imagine what that does to a person, especially when it must be hidden? Much of the time I didn't want to live. You see, I couldn't leave you—

I hate it when you say that – it makes it my fault again! So I killed you, did I? That's what I've been thinking. But for God's sake WHY couldn't you leave me? I don't understand that at all. You were so much in love with her – why didn't that overcome everything else?

Because it couldn't.

You disappoint me, Simon! What's the point of experiencing a great passion – one which puts you on a level with

Pasternak and Greene and Shakespeare and all of them – if you still stay inside your room, too scared to leave it forever? If that had been me I'd have broken down the walls. I'd have let the wilderness in. I'd have thought, I've got one life and I must lead it to the full, no matter what gets destroyed in the process.

The romantic agony, Rosa – the permanent adolescent fantasy of poets. I had no time for that chaos. God, if we obeyed all those instincts the jungle and its beasts would be at the door.

So? Aren't they there anyway?

The door is so strong. We fortified it through the centuries. I believe in that. It's all there is. The wolves can howl outside, in the black and stormy night, and we hear them and shiver; we don't open the door and let them in, Rosa. That would be mad. We have to keep the madness out.

But you didn't succeed! You were driven mad. She and I – between us, we drove you mad so that, in the end, your heart gave out, like Zhivago's. What did you see before you died? Did you see Her across the street, and call out, but maybe not be able to get to her? Did you think of her in your last few seconds, and call her name? Or was it me you wanted? Tell me, Simon, I beg you to tell me!

What would you say if I told you it was neither of you? What would you say if I told you I simply saw a whiteness of light, or maybe – of God.

I wouldn't bloody well believe you.

It all comes down to a matter of faith, Rosa. But then, you had faith in me.

I thought I heard a long, shuddering sigh, and realised I was sighing myself, defeated. The book slipped off my lap and fell to the floor, making me jump. I called his name again, twice, but heard nothing. I was left feeling angry that he should suddenly invoke God when in life he had always denied him. It was typical of that man, to want everything both ways, in death as in life.

I rose, picked up the novel, and went back to the studio. I looked at the picture on the drawing board, then, without thinking, grasped *The End of the Affair* by the spine and tore it in two, feeling a rush of elation at the destruction that contradicted everything I had been taught.

Look after your books, Rosa, and never turn down the corners; you must always keep yourself neat and tidy, Rosa; a gentleman always walks on the outside, Rosa, I don't care what people say; you mustn't ever leave the washing-up until the next morning, Rosa, because it is so slovenly; take your shoes off at the door so's not to dirty the new carpet, Rosa; have you done a drawing, dear, let me see, oh that is nice; take your father a cup of tea, Rosa; go upstairs and do your homework like a good girl; cover your school books with brown paper to keep them clean . . . This was another voice. In my memory. My mother.

All that echoed from my childhood, setting me surely on the path of submission that would lead me to Simon's altar. My mother dressed me neatly in clean white clothes and held me there while the high priest husband raised his knife. Poor Rosa McKee, poor victim. But now the creature sat up on the altar, risen from the dead, and terrified them all. She grew her hair. She bared her breast. She raved as she seized the holy book and tore its pages scattering them to the winds . . . Yes, I did know I was driving myself mad.

I picked up the butchered book, and ripped out the page with the marked passage, and Simon's written note at the end.

These fragments I have shored against my ruins.

What else is there? I would keep them forever. So I tore around the edges to make the pieces smaller, then sprayed them and stuck them to my picture of red rocks against a background of brittle green water. I scraped a little pastel across the stuck fragments and was pleased by the way the texts fitted. They were part of my painting: stuck there for the world to see – and to understand, if it possessed enough vision, and enough mercy.

Alan telephoned, and when he arrived I could not stop myself. There were no preliminaries. My whole body was an open mouth, starving and scrabbling for sustenance. Raising myself above him, it was as if my head inhabited some chilly, thin height, while my thighs heaved in sweating, sterile hell-fire. With fingers still dirty with oil and pastel, fingernails caked, I stroked my hands over Alan's body and streaked his skin with red and yellow and brown, like sacred warpaint, so that it was as if he too became part of my work. Mine.

While he was still asleep I went across and flicked the button on the stereo, turning up the volume. Alan woke in panic, realised where he was, then settled back against the pillows, complaining. 'What the fuck're you doing, you crazy woman?'

'Don't you like it?' I shouted.

'What is it?'

'Carl Orff.'

'Well, he can piss orff! Come back here and sleep. Come on . . .'

'No,' I laughed, as I started to dance.

I felt the rhythms of that music deep within my pelvis, where I had felt my lover only minutes before. I revelled in my own sweat, in the smell of me. Around the room I gyrated, as Alan watched – and as Simon watched too. Neither of them could touch me. All that could reach my soul was the sound.

Chapter Sixteen

'I have to tell you, Rosa, I'm amazed.'

Ron Samuels was telling the truth; his astonishment pleased me but was so profound as to be faintly insulting.

He had spent only about fifteen minutes inspecting the canvases and boards standing against the walls, and the works on paper laid out in piles on an old decorator's trestle, but it had felt like an hour to me – my entrails removed and laid out steaming for inspection.

The face he turned towards me was puzzled beneath the superficial admiration. I knew what he was thinking: Little Rosa McKee, poor Simon's wife; we've known her for a while, and she's very nice and all that, but how come she's done this? Where did it come from?

'You like it?' I asked, disguising my instinctive triumph with acceptable humility.

'Like it? I think it's bloody brilliant!' he said. 'You must have a show – and quickly. I mean with us. You must be with Equinox. See this, and one of the other galleries'll snap you up. Tell you what, Rosa – because of my bookings I'd have to wait a few months before I could give you a one-woman show. But we've got the New Talent mixed show coming up in three weeks' time. There's a couple of critics coming down from London – people who owe me. You wouldn't have as much space, but I could give you that back room to yourself, and at least you'd be launched. I'll put out a special additional mailing, if you'll help me cobble together a few thoughts . . .'

'I want it called "The Desert in the Garden",' I said.

'You see it all as a sequence?' He looked around the room again, thought for a while, then nodded. 'God, I feel really excited by this stuff, Rosa! And I do reckon it's better to show sooner, not later. What do you think?'

I thought: SEE, Simon? See how well I'm doing without you?

I said, 'I think I'd like that, Ron.'

'Fantastic!' he said, throwing an arm around me. 'Emma's going to be so thrilled! She always used to say there was more to you than meets the eye!'

'Well, she was right!' I laughed.

I always do that. That little light laugh tinkles in the air by my face, and irritates me like nails scraping a board. Nothing that has happened to me has changed that tendency. There have been times when I have heard myself do it, and hated the cowardice that quails from the implicit statement – Look at me; listen to me; I am a serious person. Once at a dinner party, a couple of years ago, it was Alan Grierson who asked me, in his conversational-chit-chat tone, if I'd been reading anything interesting lately. 'Just the usual rubbish!' I said lightly, which was his cue for an anecdote about Kingsley and Martin Amis. In fact, I had just finished *Anna Karenina*, and had been profoundly moved by the novel, haunted especially by the thought of Anna's son. To give up even your child for love, I had thought, how could it be possible? Maybe I didn't mention it because I knew that all conversations are reduced by social pressure to exchanges of banter, or pugnacity – and therefore wanted to protect Tolstoy. Maybe it was because I wanted to protect myself. So I chose to be light, to be malleable, to present a face to the world that it expects to see. Women are like that: afraid of conflict, we need to be liked. I sometimes look back and think that, like a Labrador bitch with an indulgent master, I have wagged my way through my life, and would have gone on doing so until my incisors fell out, unused.

If Simon hadn't died.

'Do you mind if I ask you something, Rosa?' Ron was saying.

'Ask away!'

'This work . . .' he waved a hand around, 'it's not like anything I'd have expected from you. You used to do flower studies, didn't you? And I saw one watercolour – semi-abstract. Bit wishy-washy, I thought – nothing like this. This has got real . . . er . . .'

'Muscle?' I offered.

He nodded, looking at me again with that vaguely puzzled expression. I felt he needed my help. Maybe it's unfair to do as we do, to go on deceiving the world, to persist in wearing the mask of Little Red Riding Hood when the face we see in the mirror is that of the wolf . . .

Ah, but it wasn't the case, Rosa. Not until Simon died. Correction. Not until you found the letters.

'I know what you're thinking, Ron,' I said firmly. 'You're wondering where all this is coming from, aren't you? You're thinking that the person you thought you knew couldn't have painted like this. Am I right?'

'To be frank, yes,' he said.

'You see, it's all to do with a view of reality,' I said. 'I never used to want to know too much about it. I couldn't bear it.

Painting stamens was one way of avoiding it – and wishy-washy abstraction another. But this – this is my equivalent of kitchen-sink drama, Ron.'

'So you call it realism?' He sounded dubious. 'The technique's there, OK – but some of these are more surreal. No – I'd say *hyper*-real. Look at that . . . and that . . . Reminds me a bit of Magritte.'

'Realism's what you know about the world,' I said, 'but that isn't necessarily what it looks like. What's more realistic – a Constable landscape or one by Max Ernst?'

'It's very *dark*, Rosa,' Ron said, ignoring my question.

'That's what I said – it's what I know about the world,' I replied.

Ron was looking thoughtful. 'Yes, but the thing is I've seen plenty of painting-as-therapy in my time, and this isn't it. You're not just painting the inside of your own head, Rosa.'

'Maybe I'm painting the inside of yours?'

'Whatever – I just know in my gut you're *saying* something most people will read. Even if it frightens the hell out of them. What I'm wondering is, was it always inside you?'

'Maybe it was, but I couldn't read it. Like it was in a foreign language I just learnt. Or maybe that's not true. Maybe I've just been reborn.'

Ron roared with laughter, as if I had made a joke. I joined in, although I was perfectly serious. But I was feeling light-headed; his response to my work had been so genuine as to be almost unwilling: he hadn't expected to like it, probably planned on being patronising and kind – but would go away now knowing that he had been mistaken in me. I could paint – really paint. What I saw on his face confirmed what I already knew.

In fact my feelings went beyond something as simple as

happiness, or pleasure, or even a sense of achievement. I felt as if I had jumped off a precipice, to lie shattered at the bottom, and that all the broken parts of my body had crawled around in the darkness, feeling for each other, trying to reconstruct – and managed it finally, but all in the wrong order, to create a grotesque like the ghastly female that poor nameless monster urges Frankenstein to create as his companion.

And this monster knew that in fact she was beautiful. She raised her head to the stars, like an Ayrton Minotaur, and let out a long mooing cry, not of anguish but of triumph. That was the nature of my survival: the final dominance of the deformed.

When Ron had left I called Alan, and when Sally answered the phone I told her my news. She was as excited as you would wish a friend to be, and said she would tell Alan to phone me when he got in. She must have congratulated me about four times. When I put the phone down I sat looking at it for about ten minutes, thinking how sad it is that people go on trusting each other, still believing in a sort of muzzy general good, despite all the proofs to the contrary that keep coming in every day.

Did I feel guilty? Alan had counselled me against guilt, and indeed I felt that what Simon had done to me gave me *carte blanche*. I simply wished that Sally was a stranger to me, as I was to Simon's woman. All the time, everywhere in the world, strangers are hurt, physically and mentally, and there is nothing you can do about it. But if someone is suffering next door, then you do have responsibility, like it or not. How many woman, falling for a married man, say, 'Look, I love you, and I want to have an affair with you, but because you are married I am sending you away and will never see you again'? Such renunciation is no longer part of our culture, if indeed it ever was. Of course that is what Simon's woman would have said. But could I blame her for not doing so? It was worse for me, or should I say, it was worse *of* me? My lover's wife said warm things to me on the telephone.

About ten minutes later the doorbell rang, and there was Alan. He hadn't been home. He had rung me from a callbox to find my phone engaged, and had decided to stop by anyway. I explained that I had been on the phone to Sally, and told him why. Then Alan Grierson, the cool one, who once intimidated me, the tough journalist who'd been everywhere and done everything, grabbed me and whirled me round the room.

'It's brilliant news! Old Ron knows talent when he sees it. God, I feel so proud of you, Rosie.'

He hugged me until I was fighting for breath, then demanded to see my work. I told him I would prefer him to wait for the show, but he begged, then insisted.

'If I don't deserve a preview, then who does?' he said.

I watched him as he looked at the paintings and leafed through the works on paper. I had grown to love his stocky build, and how his hair, worn slightly too long even though heavily streaked with grey, curled over the collar of his denim shirt. He had a way of hunching his shoulders that drew attention both to his build and his authority; whereas Simon was slimly, even elegantly built, this man had a massive stillness about him that I found sexual in a way I had never known before. I loved his broad torso bearing down on me. I loved the way he could hold me beneath my hips and hoist up the weight of both of us.

But I didn't love him.

'Talk me through,' he demanded, turning to face me. He was grinning.

I shook my head.

'Jesus, Rosie – you're a bloody genius, you know that? I'd never have thought you could produce stuff like this. It's fucking brilliant!'

'You're not very original, Alan,' I retorted. 'Ron said that; I'm sure everyone will say it. What I want is one person to say, "Rosa, at last you're painting like I knew you would!"'

He looked offended. 'OK, OK – but talk to me. Explain them to me. I mean, they say plenty as they stand there, but I want you to talk to me. You know, sometimes I'm in bed with you and I haven't the faintest idea what you're thinking. I tell you I love you and you whisper "Me too", and it means Jack shit. Then I come in here and I look at what this woman of mine's been producing, and I want to know where it's coming from. I want to get inside your head, Rosa, as easily as I can get inside your beautiful body!'

But the thought of *that* precipitated meltdown. I said nothing, just crossed the room, put my arms around him, pressed my mouth against his, forcing it wide and running my tongue slowly all around his teeth, into every single crevice. I even found the trace of nicotine narcotic. It seemed, after a few seconds, that we could sway there forever, mingling saliva, conscious of nothing except the urge for each other's flesh. I pressed my stomach and thighs hard against him.

At last Alan broke away, took my hand and pulled me to my bedroom. Our love making was more rapacious than ever; I sensed that he was rougher than usual because of the frustration he had just expressed, as if by splitting me in two he could penetrate the real person, whose soul would spill out on to the bed. When he came, a long time after me, so that my legs were aching and in truth I longed for him to finish, he cried out, 'I love you, oh I love you,' as if in agony.

'Me too,' I whispered, and wondered what it meant. The

grammar was certainly suspect: did I love Alan or myself?
Neither.

The head that was buried face down, exhausted, in the pillow next to me was not the right head. It slept. I put out a hand and touched it gently, then quickly covered my own mouth to stifle a cry that welled up suddenly, and threatened to burst its banks, wash through the room and drown us both. He cried with me, as well, within my head, like a song.

Oh Rosa, poor Rosa, poor Rosa McKee.

Nothing that had happened, not the rage nor the triumph, could compensate for what was missing – for the simple fact that the head face down on the pillow was not my husband's head.

Chapter Seventeen

Kit telephoned to ask if she could bring her boyfriend Mark to the private view. Her excitement at the prospect touched me; she was almost inarticulate in her enthusiasm, both at the idea that my work would be exhibited and that she would see if for the first time with Mark.

'It's the coming together of so many things, do you see?' she said. 'I've known you for so long and I honestly never thought you'd reach this point. God, it's exciting! I'm going to buy a painting, you know!'

'You might not like the stuff, Kit,' I laughed.

'I will, I know I will,' she bubbled, 'and so will Mark. Oh, Rosa, you'll fall in love with him yourself!'

'Er, I don't think that would help matters,' I said drily.

The prospect of the exhibition had consumed me. There were frames to be arranged, and notes to write, and a guest list to be supplied to Ron. I was so busy I stopped my daily reading of Simon's letters. They had receded, and although I knew this was healthy (or rather that the world would judge it so) the essential inner part of me that had grown to depend on them missed the reading. Simon himself receded too. I ceased to hear him, and the silence was so vast I was glad of the activity that filled it.

To my delight, Kathy phoned from Provence, and agreed

to return a couple of days sooner than she planned, to be there for the show.

'I wouldn't miss it, Mum; I'll feel so proud of you,' she said.

We worked out the timing, and it turned out that the best plan was for Kit and Mark to collect her at Heathrow on their way down. Kit brushed aside my gratitude.

'My first thought was that we'd come by train, and stay the night in some grand, romantic hotel. But now we've both got to go back the same night anyway.'

'What about Paul?' I dared ask.

'Oh . . . well, he did want to come himself, but as luck would have it he has to see a client at six that evening. So it works.'

It works. Infidelity works and there are sighs of relief from the lovers. The amount of energy that is put into arranging secret meetings, and ensuring alibis, would light the universe all the way to hell.

On the day before the show, when I had finally delivered everything to Ron and Emma, I went back home and sat in the study. Still on the desk was my futile list, and the name and address of the Charlie Fitzgerald who lived in Winterstoke – and who was the only one of Simon's old contacts who had not replied to my letter. I stared at it for a while, then switched on the computer, heard it whirr, then switched it off again. I was like one sated, who suddenly sickens at the thought of more.

I went upstairs to a studio that was in complete disorder but could not face doing anything about it. Outside birds were carolling wildly in my overgrown garden. It was very warm and I felt restless. I needed to get out.

In a discontented reverie I found myself driving to Winterstoke, not knowing why. There was something about this name Charlie Fitzgerald that bothered me, but it was impossible to say why I was drawn to look at the house.

I turned off the main road and guided my car slowly down deep lanes towards the village. Hedgerows drifted by, foaming with cow parsley. I pulled over into a gate entrance and stood for a moment watching a kestrel hovering, hovering – before giving up to soar away, leaving some tiny life spared for a while. This part of the countryside was quite rare, in that it epitomised a perfect vision of England, with fields and hedges and small copses laid out as they might have been a hundred years ago. Only a heap of black plastic bales in the distance testified to modern farming techniques. No wilderness of the romantic imagination, this was nature tamed by the hand of man, according to the requirements of need. Years ago I would not have responded to it, for my mind hankered after moorland and mountain or lowering forest, not necessarily as I had experienced, but as surely a part of my mind's landscape and language as the poetry of Wordsworth.

Now I looked at this gentle patchwork with a feeling close to love. The greens were so soft and various, the outlines blurred by wild flowers and grasses, the horizon so domestic and unthreatening that it reminded me suddenly of something in my childhood. I must have been about four, or maybe five. My parents were keen cyclists, although they were also the proud possessors of a mushroom-coloured Vauxhall. On this day they strapped a child's seat to the back of my father's bicycle and we went for a picnic in the countryside, just a couple of miles from Lichfield. They chose a field, and we walked to the centre to sit and eat our sandwiches. I can remember (with the vividness of technicolour) the thick carpet of buttercups and daisies, in such profusion that I was afraid to put my small feet on the earth but trotted on tip-toe after my mother and father, crying out that they must be careful not to step on the flowers, not to kill them. My parents walked ahead, carrying the shopping bag that contained our simple picnic, and called back at me, 'Come on, Rosa, it's all right! They'll grow up again if you tread on them. It won't matter at all.'

I remembered the three of us sitting in that field with the richness of flowers, bees, fields and hedges stretching out for miles around, just like the ones I was looking at now, and realised that perhaps for the first and last time in my life I had felt an utter oneness with the world around me, so that I knew (with the absolute wisdom of childhood) that to tread on a single daisy was to do harm to my own small head. But my mother suggested I make a daisy chain, reassuring me that for each one I picked two or three would grow, and so the field would be even more pretty. I knew it was simply because she wanted me occupied, and so I didn't want to pick the flowers. Still, they took out their books, as usual, but I didn't mind, never expecting games because my elderly parents were not like that. The heat and silence was a blanket, wrapping us round, and as I looked up at the clear blue sky, I tried to see it as a bedspread, and beyond it the chilly darkness of a bedroom on a winter night. I lay back and stretched one leg up, kicking at the air, imagining kicking at the sky, kicking off the warmth, making a hole, letting the void pour in . . . Imagine it! The most terrifying, yet utterly exciting thought . . . But so cold.

'Oh, keep your legs still, Rosa dear,' sighed my mother, turning a page.

I watched a bee skimming the surface of the flowers, almost too laden to fly, and a tiny spider make its way up a blade of grass just by my foot, only to launch itself off, hanging from a web invisible to my eye. I reached for a buttercup, and held it against my chin for the invisible golden semi-circle of its reflection; then at last took it apart, examining each petal and stamen with minute attention, destroying the flower, I realised with a shock, but only to look, only to learn.

At last, with nothing else to do, I made the daisy chain. So many flowers had to be ruined in its creation because my clumsy, stubby nail could not target the slits, and so the stems were mashed not pierced. And it was so hard to thread the heads that sometimes petals fluttered down in my frustration. But gradually, flower by flopping flower it lengthened, until at last I put it over my head and cried, 'Look, look!'

'Very nice, dear,' my mother said.

'Why don't you make a crown as well?' said my father.

'No, it's time we went home,' said my mother.

The day seemed chillier then. Perhaps that's why she wanted to move, or perhaps the sun was still as hot as before. But it is impossible to know what I wanted from them – what level of adult response was needed to match my wonder, my achievement, and my sudden new awareness of the minutiae that add to the vastness of the whole. Attention, fussing, petting, praise? I can still remember disappointment free-falling through my body.

They were packing up. They placed bookmarks carefully between pages, folded greaseproof paper and brown paper bags to use again, and shook the last drops from the thermos out on to the grass. They were perfectionists, my parents, they could achieve an immaculateness of detail in their life, but what of me?

Nothing was right. The grass was flattened. The daisy chain around my neck was already sad and wilted. I tore it off and threw it away.

'Oh, that's a shame,' said my father.

'Nothing lasts forever, dear,' said my mother, with such complacency I wanted to stamp and scream, raging against the impermanence of things – and the imperfection at odds with the structure of a single flower.

I got back in the car, disturbed by my memory. No day is safe from the visitations of the dead; they come to you, not at night as in childish nightmare, but into the brightest, warmest moments, reminding you of what is lost.

Winterstoke is approached by a long lane which narrows into a bend, then dips suddenly, the hedges almost meeting above the road, so that you have a still, dark sense of slipping into the earth. I had never been to the village before, and yet I felt I knew it. The stone house with dormer windows was succeeded by a farm advertising lamb for the freezer, and then, much further along the lane, a row of cottages, willow-herb growing profusely from the stone wall bordering the lane. All was in its place, just as I had known.

At the top I came to a crossroads and hesitated for a moment before deciding on a right turn. It led to a small village green, with three or four houses of medium size overlooking it. All was still. Nobody was around. Glimpsing a squat Norman tower, I parked the car, guessing that my destination may have been the old Manor House, and would therefore lie near the church.

I walked along a lane, smelling roses and honeysuckle. Before I reached the church I found myself passing a pair of tall stone gateposts, surmounted by weathered balls. Carved into one of them was the name, 'Winter House'. The iron gates were shut, but through them I could see a perfect small Queen Anne house, with wisteria growing round its dark green front door. The path was gravel, bordered by a low box hedge; the lawns had the viridian perfection of a bowling green. I could sense that there were large gardens stretching back behind the house. Were they designed by Simon?

Now I had reached my destination I was unsure what to do. It was impossible to imagine ringing the brass doorbell, for what excuse would I have for an unsolicited visit? Self-consciously, I stepped back, feeling that perhaps a member of the Fitzgerald family might glance from a window and be suspicious of the strange woman at the gate. As I did so, I saw an elderly woman coming along the lane towards me, wearing gardening gloves and carrying a trug. She smiled and said 'Afternoon', with that expectant air of village people who want you to explain your presence. Her accent was local but not broad.

'What lovely flowers,' I commented, indicating her trug.

'I've put the best in the church,' she said, 'but these don't fit the arrangement.'

'Ah – always the way,' I replied, inanely.

'Are you just visiting Winterstoke?' she enquired politely, looking me up and down.

I knew I had to say something, so half turned to point at the silent house, and asked her if that was where the Fitzgeralds lived.

She looked dubious. 'Fitzgeralds?' she said with a query, stressing the sibilant. 'Well . . . no . . .'

'I'm sorry, I thought it was the home of a . . . Charlie Fitzgerald? He was a sort of business connection of my late husband's, and as I was passing the village I thought I'd introduce myself.'

At that she frowned, and gave me a very strange look indeed. I wondered what I had said to offend her, and smiled ingratiatingly. All the time I wondered what on earth I was doing there. This wasn't even a wild-goose chase, I thought. This was utter nonsense.

'He?' she said. 'A business connection? That's a bit funny, if you don't mind my saying so.'

I was embarrassed and said, 'I'm sorry?'

'You must have made a mistake somewhere along the way – because there's no Mr Fitzgerald at Winter House. Mrs Fitzgerald was already widowed when she moved here . . . Oh . . . it must be six or seven years ago.'

'Oh, I see . . . *Mrs* Fitzgerald. I must have made a mistake . . . I'm so sorry.'

Clearly she had decided I could not possibly be a burglar, and that I did not even pose the generalised threat of the stranger. So she nodded, before shifting the basket to the other arm as a prelude to moving on.

'Yes, it's Mrs Charlotte Fitzgerald, but you won't find her in at the moment. She's gone away for two weeks, I think it is. To France.'

Clearly I was expected to respond to the last, gratuitous piece of information, and yet I found it hard even to murmur a polite 'Really? How lovely' before nodding to her and walking on towards the church.

My nerve endings quivered. Now I felt convinced I had arrived at the right place. That garden behind the wall was Simon's garden, and the woman who owned it was Simon's mistress. I hadn't expected her to be a widow . . . and yet, no matter. You can be widowed, after all, at any age. That she was rich as well as beautiful was evidenced by the fine house behind me. I sat down on a low table tomb in the church-yard, and closed my eyes, imagining my husband driving to this village for six years. He must have been at home here. The soft insistence of wood pigeons, drowned now and then by the clatter of rooks, must have been the music he heard when he awoke in the softness of her bedroom, after they had made love. Maybe that woman I had spoken to knew his car – people in villages always know cars – and whispered to her neighbours how nice it was that poor Mrs F had a boyfriend now.

I was sweating. My hands were shaking. I realised how gossamer was the web of calm self-absorption I had spun around myself in the last couple of weeks. Once again I found myself whispering 'How could you?' but Simon was not here, and the dead beneath these gravestones were deaf strangers to me.

I rose and paced around the church, noticing nothing until I reached the north wall. There I stopped. Two things caught my eye, and made me stand, trembling as I was, and stare at the church. There was a small locked door, its paint peeling, in the wall of the church, with a carved tympanum above it. Though the stone was worn with age, I could clearly make out the spreading shape of the Tree of Life, with an angel each side of it, blowing the horn of judgement. Then, above and to the left as I looked, was a tiny monstrous carving of almost indescribable ugliness. It was a female; you could tell that from the crude breasts, even if it were not for her blatant display. For, bald and crudely carved, she was sitting with her knees drawn up, her hands passing round and beneath them to grasp her vulva and yank it open, like an enormous bag. She was disgusting.

I tried to wrench my gaze away and look at the Tree of Life again, the tree of Paradise, but that offered no consolation. For those angels were trumpeting their judgement on sin, since there was a worm in Paradise, as I always reminded Simon: our human inheritance, the serpent causing shame and grief as surely as this grotesque. What hope was there?

Her frog eyes stared at me and yanked my gaze. They

seemed to mock me with their unwavering conviction that this is what it is reduced to in the end, all human life and love diminished, the fecundity of the soil triumphing, the coupling of people and of beasts, the smell, desire, panting, greedy, grasping, unfaithful unto death. The effigy laughed at me. I heard her reedy voice inside my head, supplanting Simon's voice.

You and your pathetic human love will be dust and ashes, crowed the frog face and the stick legs and the slack pouch of her sex, while I . . . Hah! I shall remain here forever, my genitalia gaping across the centuries to devour other husbands, other wives.

Chapter Eighteen

The insert Ron Samuels had written for the catalogue was almost embarrassing. 'The art of Rosa McKee is that of the miniaturist suddenly writ large, working her pictures to an astonishing, meticulous degree, and yet not shrinking from the grandest overview which can only be summed up by one word: transcendent. The stark figurative detail of the "garden" series, followed by the sweeping, looser strokes of the "desert" sequence (almost verging on the abstract), shows a stylistic scope that is rare. The bravery of the artist must be applauded no less than her command of technique. To look on this work is to experience a spiritual shrivening which leaves the spectator in a state of astonished awe. Rosa McKee's paintings and works on paper – unpeopled as they are, harsh and uncompromising though their vision might be – force a re-evaluation of humankind and its place in the universe.'

I smiled. What was all that about? Again I was two people: Rosa McKee being flattered, and Rosa floating high above and seeing all this as utterly absurd. Did the gallery owner really mean all that? And if so, what did his words themselves mean? The 'true' Rosa was beyond flattery. All that mattered was what she had produced, and also the simple face that she had produced. What it *said* to anyone else was irrelevant. This Rosa was the inhabitant of those dark gardens and desiccated wastes; there, in the chill of evening and the blaze of midday, she sought to talk with the dead, and knew that the dialogue would go on forever. And that it was all that could possibly matter.

But here on earth I was excited and flattered and triumphant. I wanted the work to sell; I needed praise, I was tempted to photocopy Ron's words a hundredfold and leave them lying around in shops and cafés all over the town.

I went to the gallery at six, and stood with Ron and Emma, admiring the hanging. Equinox was spread over six rooms – the first two floors of a Georgian town house. The Samuels lived above, and stored work in the basement. The space they had allotted to me was generous: a large square room in which they normally displayed modern ceramics. Now the display tables had gone, and my paintings were hung around the walls, and the total wall space was greater than that given to any of the other four artists in the exhibition.

As I stood there I thought first how proud my parents would have been, and then, how disconcerted. Simon I pushed from my mind. I did not want him there in the gallery with me. He could haunt a Queen Anne house for a change. This was *mine*.

Ron and Emma were congratulating me. I felt shy suddenly, unable to respond. A sudden noise at the main entrance to the gallery distracted us, and we went to greet the early arrivals. As I hoped, it was Kathy, looking suntanned and fit - and followed by Kit and a man. There was so much fuss of kisses and exclamation, as I was reunited with my daughter, while Kit made sardonic comments about the chaos at Heathrow, that I barely glanced at Kit's companion, until suddenly she herself realised that he was being neglected.

'Rosa – I want you to meet my friend Mark. Mark Parsons – Rosa McKee.'

I shook his hand, murmuring how pleased I was to meet him, and, as Kit introduced him to the Samuels, and Kathy wandered through, impatient to see my exhibition, I quietly studied my friend's lover.

Mark Parsons was, I knew, in his mid-thirties, but looked younger. He was pale, with sandy, curly hair, and a broad smile, and a disposition of nose and eyes that most people would have agreed on as handsome. The crumpled cream linen suit, worn over a green T-shirt, had a loose elegance I found very attractive. In fact, I was aware I was staring, and dropped my gaze, only to find him talking to me.

'Kit's told me so much about you,' he said. 'You've been friends for ages, haven't you?'

'Oh, years and years,' I agreed, then wished I had said something else, since the notion of years and years conjured up age, and although Kit looked younger than hers, the discrepancy between them was still obvious.

'She's very excited about your show.'

'Yes, it's wonderful. I mean – I don't mean the work's wonderful, you'll have to see for yourself. But I hope you like it. And I hope she likes it. No, the whole thing is wonderful. I haven't been painting long, not this time round anyway, and so I didn't expect this. So I'm very excited. Yes.'

I was babbling, and felt embarrassed for myself. Why is it that social occasions and one glass of wine turn you into a gibbering fool? I wanted to take Mark into a quiet corner and tell him that I could see exactly why my friend was so much in love with him, because given half a chance I would fall in love with him myself.

'Can I go and see?' he asked. His voice was low, with a hint of amusement in it, and reminded me of Simon's.

I was showing him the way when Kathy came out of the alcove and flung her arms around my neck. 'It's brilliant! I don't know where it's all coming from, little Mum, but I'm really proud of you.'

The smell of her hair and skin reminded me of her childhood, and for a moment I felt weak with love. It was not so different from sexual desire, this swoop of feeling for my child, because it was both intensely physical and inevitably frustrated at the same time. You cannot return your child to the womb, yet that is the essential craving of your flesh, when you inhale the memory of infancy. I clung briefly to my daughter, not wanting her to see the wetness of my eyes.

Mark Parsons had gone through. I wanted to follow him, but by now the gallery was beginning to fill up, and there were more greetings and introductions. Martin and Christine Larch arrived, then shortly after them Alan and Sally. Sally rushed to kiss me with real excitement and affection as Alan watched. His greeting, on the other hand, was so constrained I felt people would realise we were lovers. I kissed him effusively, and felt him flinch – as if my touch were unbearable, here in a public place. Alan looked self-consciously louche in a blue denim suit, worn with an unnecessarily smart shirt and silk tie. I decided he needed a haircut.

I showed them to my pictures, then moved away, murmuring an excuse about more wine. In reality I wished not to be present as they sought words to describe either their enthusiasm for my work, or their confusion, and came out (inevitably) with gallery platitudes, like 'interesting' or 'powerful'. My eyes found Mark, standing close to Kit, immersed in conversation yet making gestures towards one of the paintings, clearly the subject of their discussion. I was glad. For a second, jealously, I had imagined them to be talking about personal things. I wanted to be at the centre of their stage, even if only for a couple of hours.

The rest of the gallery was buzzing now. Ron introduced me to the other artists, all of them much younger than me. Sarah-Jane Crowther worked in collage, with two intricate box constructions on display as well; David Fisher and Jez Wright showed what I thought of as soulless brush gestures; and Adrian Askew was showing beautifully executed pencil portraits, together with some etchings which incorporated text. I had already inspected their exhibits and made the obligatory artist's noises of fellow-feeling masked as appro-bation. No matter what we might think of each other's work we shared the same dislike of private view chatter, and people standing with their backs to the work - or even (as I saw) leaning on it.

I returned to 'my' space, and was pleased to see that already it was crowded with strangers from Ron's mailing list, and that most of them were actually looking at what was on the walls. Suddenly I felt afraid. What if I were to be revealed as a charlatan? What if my new confidence was the sham I sometimes suspected?

'I like it – very much,' said a voice at my elbow.

Mark Parsons was offering me a glass of champagne. He held his own in his other hand, and smiled at my look of sur-prise, lowering his voice in a mock-conspiratorial manner. 'Kit and I smuggled it in. The plonk they serve at these things is always so disgusting. So go on – take it and drink to a magnificent show!'

We raised our glasses, and drank. He was smiling at me. In truth, I could not take my eyes off him. There was some-thing about Mark that made me want to put down my glass, take his arm, and walk out – to find a hiding place and talk to him for eternity.

'I bought one,' he said.

'Oh - which?'

'The one that looks like the ocean's boiled up to burnt sienna, and each little rock has a black shadow. Do you ever read T S Eliot?'

I shrugged. 'A bit.'

'Oh, well, it's hard to explain, but there are these lines in "The Waste Land" and also in "Four Quartets" that kept coming into my mind as I walked round.'

'Tell me one,' I said.

'Oh . . . "Come in under the shadow of this red rock" – that's one. And "I will show you fear in a handful of dust". God, your stuff's so full of fear! Don't you think? Anyway – then there's lots in the Quartets about the rose garden, and unseen voices, and so on. I'll tell you what. I'll send you some extracts, to see if you see what I mean. Would you like that?'

'I'd like it very much,' I said, momentarily thrilled at the thought of getting a letter from this man – a letter to *me*. 'But I have to say . . . uh . . . I don't think this is all about fear. There may be fear in it, but it's only the fear of knowledge and that's not really fear, it's acceptance.'

'OK, granted. But if I was to do the meanest thing, and ask you to sum up for me what you think the central drive is, what would you say?'

'Oh God . . . all right . . . Exposure, I suppose.' When I had said it I wondered what I meant. And yet it seemed somehow accurate.

'You mean in the sense of helplessness?'

'More like a sort of pitilessness. Like when . . . Oh God, I hate analysis. What's the point?'

He nodded, never taking his grey eyes from my face. 'I know. But there *is* a point when someone really wants to know. Not just small talk. That painting's going to be hanging in my flat, and every time I look at it I'll think of you. 'That's my excuse.'

I was so absurdly pleased by that thought I could barely speak. So I simply shrugged, as if nothing mattered to me less, and said flippantly, 'Oh, let it mean whatever *you* like,' when Kit joined us. I noticed she went instinctively to link her arm through Mark's, in that gesture which is one third affection and two thirds possession, when she remembered they were in public and stopped.

'I'm so happy you two've met at last,' she whispered. 'Two of my favourite people in the whole world.'

'I'm glad too,' I said.

Kit winked at me, and jerked her head back to where Alan Grierson was standing talking to Christine Larch. 'He looks sexy tonight, Rosa – what've you done to him?'

I hated that. Mark was smiling, and I suddenly could not bear him to know about me – not that sort of thing, only about the world of the paintings. I did not want him to meet Alan – who was already glancing towards us curiously. I did not want him to meet anyone. I wished at that moment not to have met him.

Is this how it happens? I wondered. The accidental meeting, after which you know as surely as you know the lines on your own hand that you will have no choice but to pursue another meeting, and follow every event to its source? My relationship with Alan was different; there was nothing accidental about that, but a deliberate seeking out, and a satisfaction of mutual needs. Mark Parsons shone within that crowded, smoky, noisy room; there was something infinitely gentle about him, and sensitive, and intelligent, something so *fresh*, I wanted to lay his head on my breast and stroke it for an infinity of tenderness.

I shushed Kit with a look. Embarrassed, she retreated into

'art talk', praising my pictures, and comparing the garden sequence with the desert sequence in language that bordered on pretension. I heard it and so did Mark. He caught my eye and smiled.

'I've bought that one, sweetie,' Kit was saying, jerking her thumb, 'and it's cheap at the price.'

'Why did you choose it?' asked Mark.

'I've always thought of myself as at the centre of a maze, congratulating myself on finding my way there, and feeling really clever – until the moment I realise I can't find my way out. So the picture . . . that's the moment.' She paused then put an arm around my shoulders in a way far removed from her usual jokey manner. 'You're a clever old thing, you know that, Rosa? You've seen right into the heart of things, haven't you?'

The two hours of the private view passed by quickly. I drank much more wine than I should, and was amazed to see the red dots proliferate on my paintings. I expected Alan to buy, and maybe even the Larches, and certainly Kit; but the gratifying thing was that so much was bought by people I did not know. Ron introduced me to John Reilly, the critic, who was full of praise for my work. Kathy stayed at my elbow like a reminder, as if she knew that I was in a dream, and needed someone to pin me to the earth. Dazed and silly, standing with Kit, Mark and Kathy, I thought for a second that it was impossible to be so happy again.

Yet I was mistaking triumph for happiness, I realise now. My self was so fragmented I did not know which part was the most true. There was the Rosa McKee of these paintings, who might burst into flames were you to strike a match near her. There was the Rosa who stood watching her own achievement, with the normal human response to it: pride, pleasure, disbelief, excitement. Somewhere else was the Rosa who was the wife of Simon, who had believed in her husband and her marriage until the day she called up the intimate letters on the computer and was destroyed forever. Would it be right to construct three separate narratives for those women? Or would that be to impose the borders, boundaries and banks, the division so essential to Simon's designs, on the actual wilderness of the mind?

Kit announced she was taking us all out to dinner, although it was unclear who the 'all' included. There was a momentary wrangling between Alan and Ron, each of whom offered to treat. Kit was adamant, but only until Mark suggested gently they split the bill three ways, and then she conceded with no more fuss. Before we left, she took me aside and whispered that she 'didn't really want the others', because she wanted me to have more time to get to know Mark, but that we had no choice. I agreed. Then Ron came up to me quietly and whispered that he felt bad about not including the Larches, who hovered by the gallery door. As I passed Alan to invite them, he took the chance to whisper that he had hoped we might be able to make an excuse to slip off for a private celebration. I told him not to be absurd.

There was more fuss when Ron said that of course Kit and Mark should take their purchases with them, because I could replace them with two more tomorrow, and it would be less trouble all round. So the pictures had to be wrapped . . . But at last we could go.

I can't remember much of the dinner. We all drank too much, except Mark, who reminded us that he was driving. He and Kit kept up their elaborate pretence of being just colleagues, although it was obvious to the whole table that they were in love. There is a flame between lovers that their body language reflects like a sconce, no matter how much they may try to snuff it out with public words. So the gaze is held just a second longer than it need be, and the heads incline together more than they should, and the fingers brush as a menu is passed. Their flesh flickers. Meanwhile, outside in the dark, the rest of us watch them within their circle.

Despite myself, I was fascinated by this man my friend adored, knowing exactly why she did. I was almost jealous, certainly unreasonably irritated when my daughter began to flirt with him. Why should she not? He was good-looking and young, after all, while the rest of us were middle-aged. Kathy's giggles, and the way she curved her body, and let her hair fall over one eye only to toss it back, and the little self-deprecating remarks which begged to be refuted, were the familiar opening rhythms so ancient they transcended cultural boundaries. Mark in his turn responded with the gentle politeness of a man only ten years older who is flattered by her attention but loves someone else.

That someone else was watching too. I was shocked to see Kit – the confident and sophisticated one, the one men turned to look at when she entered a room – frown. As Alan talked to her about the press, and Christine berated them both about media intrusion into private life, Kit kept looking across to where Kathy was teasing Mark about a feature he had written about rave culture, leaning so close to him that her head was almost on his shoulder.

'You're too old to know anything about it,' said Kathy.

'Yeah, well, I've asked the editor to send me to cover bowls clubs next,' he grinned.

'Turn all the old ladies on?' giggled Kathy. 'Mmmm, I expect you'd like that!'

'Darling, he'd love it,' interrupted Kit, too loudly, breaking into poor Christine's habitual earnestness.

Kathy screamed, 'What – he'd love *old ladies*?' with all the arrogance of her unlined skin and smooth body. At the same time Kit added, 'Wouldn't you, Mark?'

Her voice was harsh but the eyes that normally laughed at or challenged the world were pleading. *Love me*, they said, *and never look at anyone else. Because I know this is finite, this is passing even as we sit here, I beg you to tell everyone that you will love me even when I am old, no matter what young girl may perch next to you to blow her sweet breath in your ear.*

'It would depend who was playing,' he murmured, 'and if I was in love with her.'

Clever, clever boy, I thought, as Kit visibly relaxed and smiled, and Kathy subsided. Mark smiled across at Kit. They shared a secret. Once more I was playing witness to an exclusive love, watching these two just as I had read Simon's letters, and pressing my nose against the glass.

I remember nothing else of the conversation, except that everyone broke off from time to time to talk about my work, and Ron said he was very satisfied with the sales. Then it was over. Outside the restaurant, Kathy retrieved her backpack from Mark's car and put it into mine, and we all said our farewells.

'We'd better move,' said Mark. 'At this rate we won't be in town before twelve-thirty and I have to be up at seven.'

Kit crushed me in a hug that left me breathless and laughing. 'Goodbye, old thing,' she said. 'I'll call you tomorrow. But I just have to tell you that I'm really, *really* proud of you, you know that?'

'It's a great show,' said Mark, after a moment's hesitation pecking me on the cheek.

'I'm so glad Mark could make it – aren't you, Rosa?' Kit said.

'It was good to meet you,' I said to him.

All of us, except Kathy, knew she was asking for my

approval, not of the boyfriend but of the affair itself, and that she had received it. When at last they drove off, honking the horn and shouting goodbye, Kathy asked me, as we got into my car, 'Are those two having an affair?'

'No, of course not,' I said.

'She seems pretty keen on him – though can't say I blame her. He's wickedly good-looking.'

'It's just Kit's way,' I said. 'She's always like that with men. They've worked together; they're friends; that's all there is to it. Now – you haven't told me about France.'

When we arrived home we sat in the kitchen with a mug of coffee and Kathy told me about her holiday, and how she was bored by the boyfriend. 'You know, Mum, travelling with people, you see all their most horrible ways. He's got no sense of humour, that's the worst thing. And he's so possessive! It's like being on parole, with your jailer watching every move – yuk! I told him we're not married, for God's sake!'

'So you think being married is like being in jail?' I murmured.

'No . . . Well, it depends,' she replied, suddenly uncomfortable.

'Oh, don't worry – I do!' I said airily.

There was a pause. Then, given courage by the wine, my daughter asked me something that was clearly torn from her, making her draw in her breath slightly before she spoke.

'Mum – do you think . . . ? I mean, would you have started painting again if Dad hadn't – you know?'

'You mean, was I set free by his death?'

'I don't like that way of putting it . . . but yes.'

'Oh, without a doubt,' I said harshly, knowing she would flinch and look away.

'I like your paintings,' she said in a small voice, the child again.

'I'm glad,' I replied, as soft once more as any mother. There was a pause then I added, 'Darling, I don't see any point in that sort of speculation. None of us knows what might or might not happen, ever. Who's to say that if Dad had lived I mightn't have done just the same? Or even much better!'

Liar.

Kathy looked at me and smiled, a tell-tale moistness at the corners of her eyes. Yes, I lied to our daughter to make her feel better, but where is the harm in that? Most lies are for a greater good, after all – aren't they, Simon?

At last we went to bed. By this time I was quite drunk, and fell at once into a deep, drugged sleep. When the telephone rang I heard it as from a great distance, and for a second thought it was next door. Then I heaved myself up, and saw that in fact I had pushed one of my pillows on to the bedside table, knocking over my water and covering the phone. I looked at my watch. It was ten minutes past two. The muffled ring insisted its way into my fuddled brain, on and on. When at last I picked it up it was with a sudden spurt of fear.

'Rosa?' said a man's voice.

'Yes?'

'Look, I'm sorry to wake you up. It's Paul. Is Kit staying with you?'

I made a non-committal sound, as one does when dragged from sleep, struggling to sober myself enough to address the problem. My first quick thought was that Kit had lied to her husband because she intended to spend the night at Mark's flat, thereby dropping me into trouble. What was I supposed to say? Or maybe they had gone to a hotel on the way. But surely she would have told me? Kit was too practised in deception not to think of an eventuality like this.

'Rosa – are you there? Look, I hate disturbing you, but I'm a bit concerned.'

'No, it's OK . . . I . . . I . . . I'm just a bit bleary,' I stuttered, playing for time.

'She *said* she was coming back tonight,' he said, solving my problem, 'so I just thought you might have an idea where she is.'

'I'm sorry, Paul, I don't,' I said, trying now to think of an excuse for my friend, who had probably gone back to Mark's flat to make love, and fallen asleep. 'She did leave quite late . . .'

'What time?'

'Er . . . I can't remember,' I lied. 'We all went out for a meal, and I left before her.'

'Oh.'

I heard him sigh heavily. There was a short silence, then he said, 'Well, I suppose I'll just have to wait. Maybe she broke down . . . but she'd have phoned, wouldn't she? Oh, maybe she dropped in on someone when she got back to town . . .'

'Probably – you know what she's like!' I said.

'Well, I'll let you go back to sleep,' he said, sounding depressed.

After I had replaced the phone, and gone for a towel to mop up the spilt water, I lay back, unable to go to sleep. The details of the evening whirled round in my brain, residual pleasure at the success of my show mixed with fragments of the restaurant conversation, mixed with curiosity about what on earth Kit was up to.

And all the time Simon was there too, not speaking, just watching me. I focused my eyes on a point in the darkness, sensing his essence, like breath.

'Well, I did it,' I said. 'Aren't you pleased with me? Aren't you proud of me?'

There was silence, but I knew that he was. How could he

be anything else? Whatever his faults, Simon was a generous man . . .

I imagined him suddenly as an angel. Where do the dead go? It had pleased me to think of his soul unquiet, haunting my house, wandering perpetually in limbo waiting for me to make him suffer. Or make him better, by forgiveness. Ha! Ghosts and spirits I knew were real, but an angel . . . ?

What if he had already been forgiven? What if the struggle for his soul in the tomb had been won by the angel of goodness, leaving him redeemed? I remember reading somewhere that angels are messengers, intelligences from God. Ah yes, my mind added, doing somersaults of rage at the thought, but they are also spirits of darkness, Lucifer and the fallen ones, brought down by lust and pride. That was more like it.

You can be a fallen angel, Simon.

Stop thinking.

My need to stop thinking about him was acute. He exhausted me in death as he had never done in life, and had already spoiled my post-show triumph. The struggle in my mind between Simon and myself seemed, in the darkness, to be as vast and eternal as that between angels of good and evil.

I hauled my mind away, fixing on something else far more seductive. When at last I dropped off to sleep, my fantasies were about Mark Parsons making love to me, slowly and exquisitely, so that I squirmed with desire. There was no room for Kit or Simon in these waking dreams. In my mind I composed a note (no, a letter, beautifully written, of course) to Mark, inviting him to come and see my new work, and allowing the old dance ritual to begin all over again. It would, I knew. You can always tell; there is no such thing as innocence. Proving myself to myself again, it would *show* HIM – it would.

Then I realised the truth, with a bitterness that made my saliva curdle, running off my tongue like gall. Mark Parsons, be damned. What attracted me to my friend's lover was something about his look and his voice which reminded me of Simon, years ago when we first met.

Chapter Nineteen

Paul Jordan telephoned me at eight the next morning to tell me. He was at the hospital. It had taken the fire service two hours and twenty minutes to cut Kit Jordan and Mark Parsons from the wreckage of Mark's car, where it had ploughed into the back of a motorway repair vehicle, parked on the hard shoulder with its huge hazard arrow and flashing lights.

Perhaps he fell asleep for a few seconds. Perhaps he was distracted by a tipsy Kit's caress, and was simply driving too fast to control the car. Whatever the truth, the driver had no chance of survival, and the passenger's life was strung out like a web in a hedgerow.

With Simon it had been a policeman on the doorstep. Then, as now, disbelief was the first response, the urgent desire for there to be a mistake or for this to be a particularly sick joke. Yet Paul's voice was in my ear, as echoey as a room with all the furniture gone. There was no mistake.

'She was with somebody called Mark – a friend . . . er . . . they've worked together . . .' he stammered. 'Giving her a lift, I suppose. But I thought she was going in her own car. That's what she said. So where is her car?'

Outside Mark's flat, I thought, but said nothing. What did it matter now? Kit the beautiful one, the one who threw back her head and laughed, the one I had sat up with all night when we were twenty, arguing about the existence of God and whether Art was the nearest we could ever get to him; Kit the bad one who smoked and drank too much and who attracted men like jam attracts wasps, yet whose fearless, accusatory photographs of the black ghettos in the late seventies had won her acclaim; Kit the life-enhancer was struggling with death.

Paul's voice trembled as he told me it looked very much as if she would lose. 'All I can do is wait here,' he said. 'I have to hope. They're going to operate . . .'

I wondered if she knew, in the second before the impact, when maybe they both screamed, that all the miserable hours she had lain awake, with Paul asleep beside her, longing for Mark with the intensity of blood and bone, had now reached their apotheosis, and the man she was not allowed to live with would die beside her.

Paul and I were both silent. Then I heard his breath shudder, as if he were being choked. There were no tears in my eyes, and from a distance I heard my own voice, flat and weary, tell him, 'I'll come up – today. I'll come - and sit with you. I want to see her.'

'Not today, Rosa. I . . . I need . . . Ah . . . Later would be kind. Later in the week. She might not make it, you see. And I want to be alone with her. We've been apart so much just lately . . . So much . . . If you can come and see me in a couple of days? And her . . . if . . . it would be kind. I'd appreciate it.'

His tone made me want to scream. That was Paul – always so understanding, so reasonable. Why should he thank me? No wonder Kit loved somebody else. No wonder she was bored by her husband. As soon as the thought crossed my mind I felt guilty. Paul Jordan was not 'up to his wife', as everybody agreed, but he did not deserve this. And nor did I, when the policeman was at the door.

I lay in bed until nine-thirty, not crying, simply thinking about Kit and Mark. I fancied (because I had not bothered to wash the night before, but had hastily removed my eye make-up with pads) that I could still feel the imprint of their goodbye kisses on my cheeks.

When I went into Kathy's room and told her what had happened, she became almost hysterical. Her repeated sobs of 'I don't believe it' gave me a headache. I held her, stroked her head, murmured comforting sounds – and wondered why human beings always take refuge in disbelief, when there is evidence of random cruelty each minute. Or, if you prefer, of the malignancy of God.

That night Paul telephoned again. He sounded frail; his voice had lost all resonance, and he articulated his words slowly, like someone who had spent too long abroad and had forgotten the inflections of his native speech. He was at home; they had sent him. Kit was still critical; they told him it was better for him to go home and rest to conserve his strength. I told him firmly I would come to London the next day – although in truth I did not want to. I quailed, not just from his grief, but from any questions he might ask about Kit's companion in the car. I did not want to be responsible for her love or her lies.

I got the 8.27, after arguing furiously that Kathy should not come with me. There was something bothering me, something I knew I might have to do – and I did not want my daughter around. I told Alan Grierson the same thing, brushing aside his desire to 'look after me'. I told him it did not suit him, and hung up quickly when he protested. He seemed irrelevant to me; I could hardly recall the touch of his flesh. I clutched those last fantasies about Mark Parsons to me like a shameful, pathetic secret. Maybe Death puts a mark on your door, like a gypsy, to announce that it's all right here, they will buy your lucky heather, poor *giorgio* fools.

All through the journey, I found myself staring at the faces of fellow travellers and wondering if they knew what I knew. It was as if I existed in some science fiction fantasy, and my eyes were cursed with a vision that could penetrate to the bones of human pain. And in the brutal rhythm of the tube there was no escape; it rattled out a monotonous lamentation. When I reached the hospital, I saw in the taut face of the woman selling flowers outside, and in the expressions of the people going in and out, and the staff on the corridors, only an exaggerated version of what I had seen on the journey, invisible to most observers, but worn like a badge of membership.

Unbidden, a vision came to me of Simon's face, when I went to identify him. Smooth, at peace, he showed no outward sign of the breaking within. 'His heart gave way,' they said, and Simon was indeed not waving but drowning that morning when he drove away and looked up at the window to see me watching him. I had pretended not to see that feeble flap of his hand, withdrawing into the room to punish him a little more.

Looking at his face on the slab, I had seen the world around me melt and swirl, losing form, so that I had to grip with both hands to steady myself. Then two words had broken from me, the only two words in the language at that moment.

'Come back,' I had said. 'Come back.'

Come back.

I paused by the lift and closed my eyes. In the red darkness I tried to recapture my husband's face, but whereas before it had bobbed before me with the grave perfection of a Piero, now it broke up into jagged daubs like a bad Bratby. It was so ugly; everything was ugly. I realised that I was terrified of seeing Kit mutilated too, and wanted to flee.

'Are you all right?' said a voice.

I opened my eyes to see a young nurse looking at me with concern. I nodded. 'Yes, I'm fine,' I said. She smiled, did not believe me, yet still moved on. I could see it in her eyes. She recognised in me the knowledge that's as certain as a London cab-driver's mental map.

Of course they would not let me enter the Intensive Care Unit. I sat in the corridor, smelling antiseptic handwash, for about twenty minutes until Paul came out to see me. He looked haggard, as if some alien force were sucking at his blood and pulling his flesh downwards. We studied each other gravely, but did not kiss, such social niceties irrelevant.

'How is she?' I whispered.

He shook his head and spread his hands helplessly for a second, before letting them drop to his sides.

'I wish I could see her. Won't they let me in?'

'They'll only let me . . . Oh, Rosa, I think she's dying!'

This burst out of him, but still his eyes were dry. I shook my head furiously and gripped his arms so hard it must have hurt. 'I don't believe that, Paul!' I hissed, knowing at the same time that I did believe it. I believed anything now.

He told me that Kit had multiple injuries, that both legs were crushed and a rib had punctured her lung. A head injury was causing concern. The next few days would be critical.

'Her face?' I asked fearfully.

'Just surface scratches from broken glass,' he said.

'Has she recognised you?' I asked.

He smiled briefly, and for the first time his eyes grew

moist as he nodded vigorously, not trusting himself to speak for a few seconds. Then he told me of the moment when, thinking she was unconscious, he had felt her fingers curl around his own, and hold on. 'She wouldn't let go,' he said, 'and when I saw her eyes open – and she was just staring at me as if pleading with me, do you understand? – I felt sure it was going to be all right. She said my name . . .'

'It will be all right,' I said quietly, not feeling any conviction in the words.

'I could say you're her half-sister,' he said suddenly, after a few seconds silence. 'I mean, they're not to know, are they?'

He left, and I sat down once more, leaning back against the shiny cream wall. There was that in me which wished to be delivered; I wanted the staff to forbid my visit so I could run away.

Within fifteen minutes I was inside the Unit, scrubbed and gowned, walking on tiptoe from instinct, following Paul towards my friend's bed. Green dots and dancing lines beeped out the mysterious rhythms by which the woman clung to life, anchored to earth only by the tubes into her hands and nose. Awe was the only response to this sight – awe, and pity, and terror.

'Hallo, Kit – it's me, Rosa,' I whispered, close to the bandaged head.

'It's Rosa come to visit you, darling,' said Paul, in a foolish, high, almost-hearty voice, as if he were speaking to an old person needing reassurance.

The eyes did not open, nor did her fingers curl around mine when I laid my hand on hers. Paul and I sat each side of the high bed, our heads level with Kit's shattered body, drawing back in silence when the nurses came to do the observations, jumping in fright when the saline drip clacked out a brief alarm. It went on – until I could bear it no longer.

He saw. 'Why don't you go, Rosa?' he murmured, not shifting his eyes from her face.

'I want to talk to you, Paul,' I said. 'I can't just leave you. Leave you both.'

'Go and spend the day. Go to a gallery, or something. I won't stay here around the clock because they've convinced me it's pointless. So I'll be home tonight . . . You could come round?'

'I'll bring pizzas,' I said.

'I've told them – I'm on the end of the phone,' he said, but not to me. Kit made no response. Her skin was turning yellow, like a leaf without the light.

The afternoon crawled by. I bought a salad and a glass of white wine at a café in Soho, then walked down St Martin's Lane to the National Portrait Gallery. When Simon, Kit and I were students we had haunted the Tate, believing in the new, rejoicing in the spareness of Klee and richer rhythms of Kandinsky. We knew the collection inside out, from Blake to Lichtenstein, and always stopped to smile, with an affection bordering on patronage, at Rodin's 'The Kiss'. What we had were feelings of freedom, of being at the start of things. We were not to know that everything becomes old hat in the end, time catching up, Lucien Freud shading skin tones so bravely to colours of decay.

Now I wanted only faces. I paced the galleries, looking at the faces of the dead and remembering the memorials on the walls of Bath Abbey. Were they lied about too, these faces? Would nobody ever convey the truth about another living soul, and damn the conventions? I saw the sadness on Charles I's face, and the arrogance on Cooper's Cromwell; the sidelong slyness of Hawker's Charles II, and the appraising sensual knowledge of his pudgy Nell – an early version of my Kit. All of them seemed to me – wonderfully, miraculously – to be true.

True.

'Oh, what would you know?' I said aloud.

I looked for more versions of Kit, and found her in Emma Hamilton's sweet flirtatiousness, as well as in Gwen John's haughty determination. The latter was almost unbearable.

Chapter Twenty

The strange thing was that in all the years of our friendship I had rarely visited Kit's home. The house was furnished with a predictably eccentric mixture of good second-hand furniture, amusing oddities (like the fox's head over their sitting-room door), modern pieces like a glass coffee table, and bold prints. There were ethnic hangings, and African tribal masks, too – and in the sitting room, a wall of Kit's own black-and-white prints, so that as Paul and I talked we were observed by the sad, silent eyes of people famous as well as anonymous, caught within her lens as if to say, 'Yes, look at me, for heaven's sake!'

'You know how this feels, Rosa,' said Paul, twisting his hands together. 'You of all people. It's so . . . *such* a lonely thing.'

'I know,' I said, reaching forward awkwardly to take his hand.

Paul Jordan was two years older than Simon, which made him about fifty. He was very tall with the slightly stooped shoulders of someone who had been teased and called Lanky in school. His hair was grey at the temples; he had the look of the successful solicitor that he was – which is to say, he looked dependable and pleasant, but not the sort of man you would cross a room to meet. Holding his hand, I saw how thin and mottled it was, and how the veins stood out like blue-grey worms. It was impossible to avoid the flash in my memory of Mark Parson's hand – tanned and chunky, as it lifted the menu. It made me shiver.

All afternoon, as I had wandered about the gallery, and sat killing time with tea, something had been at the back of my mind, and now it pressed forward with urgency. Not far from where we were sitting, in Kit's tiny 'den' at the end of the corridor, Mark's love letters to Kit were hidden in the cupboard by the window, in an envelope marked with my name, and the word 'gardens'. It must have been true; she would not have joked about something like that. What if Kit did die? I had promised, jokily, to go and retrieve those letters, and destroy them; would there be an opportunity better than this one? Yet it might tempt fate to do so, in advance of actual need . . . I wondered for a second if perhaps she had had a premonition, that all this was preordained, then dismissed such superstition. I believed in the random, as she did: the perpetual possibility of joy – and pain. My friend had simply made proper provision – as much as all those sensible souls who went to her husband to make their wills.

My mission in carrying out what might well turn out to be her last wishes would not be to protect her, but to protect this man who sat next to me, his head bowed with anxiety and disbelief. She had said that, in justification. He must be spared. He must not be slapped with the cold fact that he had torn her in two, as surely as Simon was torn. He must be protected from the awareness that he became her jailer. And later, if the miracle occurred (and if she wished to be so foolish), Kit could retrieve the precious letters from me.

So it was decided. My heart beat so loudly I thought he must hear.

'Would you like some coffee?' he asked.

I nodded, offered to make it, then realised that while he was occupied in the basement kitchen, it would give me the chance to go to Kit's room. But I dreaded it. Among her idiosyncratic collection of things bought from foreign trips and in antique shops I knew I would meet my friend, and I was afraid of crying. I would not cry any more. To cry would help no one, let alone Paul.

When he had gone downstairs, walking very slowly like someone on the seabed, I slipped along the short hall, and opened the door of Kit's study.

The room was such a mess I actually gave a half-smile. There were boxes of prints on shelves, and a filing cabinet with one door open, and a file laid out on top, and a desk so piled with correspondence, briefing notes, cuttings and opened envelopes that the computer was like a rock washed by a sea of paper. Behind the desk was an enormous pin-board, every inch of its surface crammed with postcards, cartoons, and photographs. On the floor by the desk was a carrier bag from Harvey Nichols. Unable to resist, I took out the tissue, to find a short wrap skirt made from soft red suede.

Suddenly, unbearably, my eyes stung, and I had to shove the skirt back in the bag quickly. The extravagance of the garment, and the statement of its colour, reminded me so acutely of Kit, and all that was glorious about her existence. 'Please don't die,' I whispered.

Quickly, hardly seeing where I was going, I went to the cupboard by the window, knelt, and easily found the envelope marked with my name, just as she had said. I was in the act of shoving it into my handbag, when Paul's voice said quietly, 'What are you doing, Rosa?'

I rose quickly, blushing as if caught in the act of committing a crime. 'Oh, I meant to tell you – Kit and I had been talking about doing a book together. *Gardens in the West Country*. I'd written down a sort of synopsis, and, well, I want to have it, you see,' I knew I was babbling.

Paul looked at me for what felt like a very long time, standing in the doorway, tray in hand. His face wore an expression so bleak and weary it was shocking, even in the context of that day. Then he nodded, as if some agreement had been reached between us, and said, 'Rosa, you went to look for Mark's letters, didn't you? But it doesn't matter, don't you see? Come through and have your coffee.'

Scrambling to my feet, I felt guilty, and for a second resented the confidences that turned me into an accomplice. Confused and embarrassed, I followed Paul back into the sitting room, and sat down opposite him this time, the envelope on my knee.

Calmly he handed me a coffee, then sat down and smiled slightly. I told him I was sorry – aware as soon as the words were out of how inept they were.

'What are you sorry for?' he asked.

'Or who?' I said.

'Or who,' he repeated, nodding as if I had said something wise.

'Maybe I'm just sorry to be sneaking about, when all the time . . .' I began.

'It's not your fault, Rosa,' he said.

There was silence. I had nothing to say, and waited. When it came, Paul's voice was matter-of-fact. 'I heard an interview on the radio once. It was a man talking about his sister who'd gone travelling in the Far East and been murdered. Afterwards her family found a letter in which she'd given careful instructions about what she wanted to happen if she died – how she wanted her ashes scattered, and things like that. Why would a young woman in her twenties do that? Do you think people *know*?'

'I think they just dread accidents, especially if they've got something to hide.'

'Tell me about that evening. Every detail,' said Paul.

I did as he asked, interrupted every now and then because I was going 'too fast'. He wanted to know how his wife looked as she entered the gallery, when I'd arranged for her to pick up Kathy from the airport, whether I had met Mark Parsons before, what they both wore, how they seemed, what they said. It was, obviously, important to him that Mark had not been drinking – except for the first glass of champagne. He asked what we talked about at dinner; I struggled to recall every word Kit had said. The whole exercise was miserable for me, and yet I could see why it mattered.

All this time the packet of letters burnt on my knee. I wanted him to be the first to mention them, and a part of me did not want them mentioned at all. Cowardly, I wished I could simply rise, stuff the envelope in the bag, and walk out of that house, turning my back forever on Kit's husband and his pain.

'Poor Rosa,' he said suddenly.

'Why?' I asked – guilty, as if he had read my thoughts.

'It must be hard for you, sitting there, not liking to ask me how I know about Mark.'

I just nodded, knowing he would need no more prompting. When Simon died I wanted to talk about him to anyone who would listen, but found no one. People advise you to 'try to get over it', then change the subject. They demand release. They think that if grief goes unmentioned it will dissolve into the spreading saccharin of a benevolent universe. They fail to understand that it will throb just beneath the surface of your skin forever, or reflect in a certain stoniness at the heart of your gaze, immediately recognisable to others similarly scarred. You have gazed down into the darkest fires, and their image is imprinted on the retina forever.

I know. I know. I know.

The place was furnished, you knew it, it was home, but suddenly that day, you turned the doorhandle and walked into an empty room – and you are still there, voice echoing, trying to find the exit. Or perhaps the most frightening thing is when you want to remain there, in the cool twilight, finding solace with your ghosts forever. How can they know that – the well-wishers and passers-by? Should they be bold enough to try? Is it stupidity, or desperation that causes their ignorance? Paul was preparing himself for all this. He was shoring himself up.

'I met him once, you know,' said Paul. 'It was at a party about a year ago, or not so much. She handed him a drink, and I knew right away. A sort of light between them. Do you know what I mean?'

'There was always a light around Kit,' I said, not answering him. Because although I knew what he meant, I did not want to remember my friend and her lover at the private view, and my own envy at their glitter.

He nodded. 'That's why people have always loved her. Oh God, Rosa – we're both using the past tense! We've got to stop it! Anyway . . . I used to think, years ago, when I knew she'd had her first affair, that it was impossible to imagine a man who wouldn't fall in love with her. She was so . . . so . . . *rich* in things. She gave so much, didn't she? I remember when I first met her, she was freelancing and would take any work then, and she came to my firm to do portraits of us all, because the senior partner had the bright idea that it would give the clients confidence to see all these black-and-white prints in gilt frames in the waiting room! I thought it was a stupid idea, until I saw the photographer was the most stunning girl I'd ever seen in my life. I hadn't got a chance. Do you remember all that?'

'Simon and I were already married,' I said.

'I know. And she wouldn't marry me. I asked her I don't know how many times. She'd go out with me for months then just go off with someone else.' He paused, frowning with remembered pain. Then he grimaced: an apology for a smile. 'But I got her in the end . . . persistence pays off, you see . . . Anyway, I don't know why I'm telling you all this, when you know what Kit was like. People couldn't help loving her, could they?'

'They couldn't help it,' I said.

Paul Jordan was sitting perfectly still, with his hands resting on the arms of the chair, his coffee forgotten on the little table at his elbow. He was no longer looking at me, but at some point beyond my head. 'I never thought I deserved her, Rosa. Sometimes I thought her friends – like you – thought that too.' I shook my head but he was not interested in my response. He knew what he knew. 'Although I could see that there'd be others who'd say she was lucky – because I gave her a good home and put up with God knows what. But the point is – I *didn't* deserve her. I could adore her and look after her and do everything for her, but I couldn't make her adore me. And she needed that. She needed to *love* – not just be loved. But I wasn't the sort of man who she could love – like that. Really love. That kind of passion was in her, but how could someone like me have the key?'

He spread out his hands, as if to take in his own unprepossessing form, and the comfortable room that he had created for her – Paul the domestic one, who would always be there (she said) when she came home. Then the hands flopped down again, tired.

'She always loved you, Paul,' I said, unnecessarily, to fill the silence.

'Oh, I know. So many different ways of loving. That's one way, but it's not Grand Passion, is it? People want that; they want to be on fire, don't they? Anyway, back to Mark. When she met him I sensed something was different. She was so brittle with me I thought she'd break. And there were just too many jobs away – suddenly, when she'd been saying she didn't want them. She was different. *It* was different. One night, she was in France – probably with him – and I was here by myself, and I thought I'd go mad. I walked from room to room, just crying and wanting her so much I knew I would always go on taking her at any price. Her terms. I went into her study and did something I'd never done before – started looking around for evidence. That's when I found his first few letters.'

I found myself trembling, and wrapped both hands round the warm mug as if it could save me. As I listened to Paul, the cold, bad side of me wanted to walk away, feeling no sympathy, saying instead that I had been there, and done it, and wanted no more of this cruel synchronicity. Yet at the same time I longed for the courage to rise, to rush across the room and embrace this man, telling him we were both deceived.

I did neither.

'There's one thing you can say for Mark Parsons – he can write!' said Paul. 'I read them and put them back, and knew I just had to put up with it. That was it. There was no choice. I don't think she ever knew that I knew . . .'

'She didn't, Paul,' I said.

'But in a way I wished she had. Then she would have known how much I loved her, you see. That I could be strong enough not just to carry her on my shoulders, but her lover as well. I lived with both of them. I thought about them when I woke up and last thing at night. I gave her the ground they could grow on. It's funny, isn't it, that I wished she knew that? At least she'd have proof then of how much she meant to me.'

'She didn't need proof. She knew,' I said.

'Did she feel guilty – about Mark?' he asked suddenly, looking at me directly.

I didn't know how to answer, because I did not *know* the answer. Did someone like Kit feel guilt? No – she was too caught up in the immediacy of experience to reflect on its implications. Besides, she took Paul for granted. She knew he would always be there – and he was. Was that how Simon felt about me? Guilt is irrelevant, he wrote in one of those letters. Maybe it would have been truer to say that guilt is the ultimate cement – binding the wall when the ground is shifting beneath it. Without it chaos would rule.

'Yes, I think she did,' I said at last. 'She did love you, you realise that, Paul? When she told me about Mark she used a phrase I still remember. She called it a "terminal doting passion". Is that the same as love? I don't know. She made it sound more like a fatal sickness.'

A wry smile hovered at the corner of his mouth. 'But people don't die of love, do they, Rosa? They die from stupid accidents. Or maybe that's not right. Maybe we don't know why they die, or if it's meant. Maybe they intended to die.'

He spread his hands again, looking suddenly confused. I shook my head vigorously. 'That's not true. It's impossible to imagine. Not Kit.'

'You're right. But what about *him*? What if he wanted to die with her? When they first told me there was someone with her I prayed it wouldn't be him – you know, she might have been giving one of your friends a lift – although I knew it would. Then I hated him. I wanted him to burn in hell for killing her.'

'I don't think he did it deliberately, Paul,' I said quietly.

'Why the hell did she have to take him? Or if she had to, why didn't they go on the train?'

'Don't. It's a waste of time,' I said.

He shook his head vigorously. 'Nothing's a waste of my time. I've got all the time in the world. I keep thinking the door's going to fly open, and she'll come in with her gear and a shopping bag, demanding coffee because she needs her fix of caffeine. She'll be like the wind coming in here, driving out my cobwebs. Waking me up.' He paused. Then his voice was pitched higher with the strain as he added, 'She will come, won't she, Rosa?'

'Yes,' I said.

'And if . . . you know . . . if it's only because he is dead, and she's nowhere else to go, I won't mind. That's how it's always been. I don't mind the price.'

The face turned towards me was so desolate, and so much a mirror of my own soul, that the last selfish restraint disappeared. The packet of letters slipped from my lap as I rose, and crossed the room to kneel by Paul Jordan's side and embrace him. He leant into me as he wept with great juddering breaths, shaking my whole body. I breathed in the unfamiliar smell of this man whom, in truth, I hardly knew, throwing back my head and screwing up my eyes because I knew that to cry myself would not help him.

But what could help him? Perhaps my presence did; at any rate he became calmer after about five minutes, and raised his head. Our faces were very close. I could see the minute blue throb at his temple, the fine web of wrinkles starting, the veins of blood in the whites of his eyes, a recent nick where he had cut himself. He was getting older and so was I. As he looked at me, Paul simply shook his head – a gesture of such infinite bewilderment and helplessness it stung me.

'I know,' I said.

'Yes,' said Paul.

'I love Kit, but God, you're good to her. She's lucky.'

'Yes,' he repeated.

I hesitated, but telling him about Simon had become necessary. I needed him to know how much I understood. Or perhaps I became aware of how much I fell short of him, and needed help.

I took my place in the armchair again, picking up the brown envelope marked with my name, and holding it as I talked. Every so often I would run my fingertips tentatively over the bumpy brown surface, as if the paper might burn. He listened, occasionally nodding but making no comment. I told him everything, omitting only my relationship with Alan Grierson. He had no need to know that.

When I had finished he was silent for a while. Then he asked, 'So you hate Simon? You won't forgive him?'

'No,' I said. 'I'm not as good as you, Paul. If ever I feel in danger of letting it go, I call up the letters and imagine him with that bitch and remember how when he was in France with us he was thinking about *her*, wanting to be with *her* . . . and then it's like someone threw petrol on a bonfire inside me. I go up – whoosh – most of the time, anyway. Other times I feel quieter – almost smug. I jeer at him and say, Look, you did all that, you thought you were so good deceiving me, and now look at you! Then you know what? I'm glad he's dead.'

Paul shook his head. 'You don't mean that, Rosa.'

'Maybe what I mean is I'm glad I'm alive, instead of him.'

'I think what you're saying is you still love him,' said Paul.

'I don't know what I mean,' I said, tired suddenly, and wanting to creep away and sit in the chilly summerhouse of an English garden at twilight, listening to the harsh melancholy of rooks in distant trees, and knowing it would all go on forever, without me. We sat in silence for a long time.

'Listen to me, Rosa. There's nothing left to do but forgive him. And her,' said Paul at last. 'Everything else *is* a waste of time.'

'I'll never forgive *her*,' I said.

'Oh, I meant my Kit,' he said, 'and I was talking to myself.'

'What about Mark Parsons?' I asked harshly. 'Are you telling me you forgive him too? I don't believe you, Paul!'

'I don't think it's got anything to do with forgiveness,' he said. 'It's just . . . how everything is. And if you're asking me if I accept how everything is, then I'd say, My God, what choice have we? It would drive you mad if you didn't.'

Drive you mad.

'I suppose,' I said.

'You might think I'm stupid, but the truth is, I simply can't find it in me – not even now – to hate someone for falling in love with Kit,' he said. 'I did – so why shouldn't someone else?'

'But she needn't . . .' I started to protest, then stopped, ashamed.

'Don't,' he said quietly.

'Shall I take these away?' I said, patting the envelope on my knee.

'Oh, do what you want with them,' he said. 'Actually, you know, I've found myself thinking they should be kept. Isn't that incredible? But, they're such beautiful letters. Kit was convinced that one day he'd be a great writer. He was about to start a novel, I believe. He wrote about it in there. But now . . .' He shrugged and nodded at the envelope.

'Are you going to tell her that you knew about him all along?' I asked.

'Let's wait and see what happens,' he said bleakly. Then added, 'Oh, take the damn things away. Do what you like, keep them for her, whatever. Go for it, Rosa! Do you remember she'd always say, Go for it!'

'Her philosophy all over,' I smiled. 'She wanted everything, and right away. I remember once she was interviewed in *Cosmopolitan* – one of those articles about successful women in a man's world, or something. And she was asked what she attributed her success to, and she said—'

'An awesome greed,' Paul supplied, with a smile. 'Yes, I remember that.'

'Talking of which, I'm going to feed you,' I said.

After the pizza he took me upstairs into the hall. Two parcels leant against the wall by the front door, unnoticed by me when I entered. I knew immediately what they were; the police had delivered what they found in the boot of Mark's smashed car. To my horror there were spots of blood on the paper that wrapped my paintings. I grasped Paul's arm, not wanting to touch them.

'For God's sake, take them away and put them in the dustbin,' I gasped at last.

'No – I'll open them. I want to see.'

Shuddering, he made himself pull off the paper. Silently we each picked up a painting, and walked through to the light. I had forgotten the paintings Kit and Mark had chosen. Now the desert burnt in Paul's sitting room, and I remembered Mark's voice saying, 'The one that looks like the ocean's boiled up to burnt sienna, and each rock has a black shadow.' He had gone on to quote T S Eliot, 'I will show you fear in a handful of dust.' He had promised me he would write and send me the passages . . . Would he have done so? Would he have ever thought of me, as the painting became part of his furniture, dumb witness to his writing, his passion, his life?

'I prefer this one,' said Paul.

Kit had chosen one of the mazes – the one with the white wraith at its centre. The hedges were dark; there was no way out for that creature; it would flutter there in its blind panic for eternity.

'That one was Kit's choice,' I said.

'Good,' he said. 'I'm pleased it's the one I like best.'

'Shall I take them away?' I asked.

He shook his head vigorously. 'No – I want to keep them. Did they pay for them?' I nodded, thinking the question oddly mundane. 'All the more reason then!' He went on, 'Look, Rosa, quite apart from the fact that they're by you, these paintings are a sort of legacy, aren't they? Look, let's be realistic for God's sake. This might turn out to be the last choice Kit ever made, so I'll hang them together. They'll always be together.'

'Not the last choice Kit made, Paul,' I said softly.

'What do you mean?' he asked.

'Don't forget, whatever else was true, she was choosing to come home to you.'

Chapter Twenty-one

Just over a week later, Kit was out of the critical stage, though still very ill. When I visited her she was able to grasp my hand. She started to say something but I shushed her. It was enough to sit for thirty or forty minutes, then go.

I had tried to imagine the moment when Kit was told by Paul about her lover's death, but quailed from it. Nor did I ask him for details. Since that day we had only exchanged practical information; it was as if neither of us really wanted the closeness to extend beyond our brief exchange of weakness. In any case, Paul was jealous of his time with Kit; the constant stream of her colleagues and friends was kept moving by him with possessive and protective firmness. It was as if he had come into his own at last.

I found out from Kit's office when Mark Parsons was to be cremated, and travelled to Golders Green for the sparse ritual. Alan Grierson came with me; they had worked together once and he insisted. There was talk of a memorial service later, but for the moment these inadequate obsequies were all the living could offer the dead. I sat among strangers in that bare, modern chamber in North London and wondered if there was a God and if he was watching with a smile at our determined omission of his name. Thinking of the beautiful (for yes he was, as Simon was beautiful) young man who was dead I remembered with shame my lust for him and remained dry-eyed. When Alan attempted to tuck his hand in my arm I leant away, knowing that his mouth would tighten at the rejection. I did not want him any more, and he knew it. You grow as much from those you leave behind as from those you cling to – and I had done with him now.

Again I found myself brooding, Where have they *gone*? I longed for there to be a room, a definable space within my imagination, where I could lodge the beloved dead, close the door on them until the time when I would turn the key myself and walk in and greet them. In my unhappiness I even caught myself wondering if he and Simon might meet and recognise each other by instinct, and what they would say if they did. It was absurd, I knew that. The dead do not converse. If anything I can see them as isolated spirits, whirled in the storm like skeins of birds. Or hung about the necks of the living forever as symbols of guilt.

I felt that weight on the back of my neck as I travelled back with Alan, afraid the road might leap up and destroy us both. My head ached with the effort of keeping upright. My goodbye to him was brief. I put out a hand to indicate he should not get out of the car.

'What is it, Rosa?' he asked.

'I think you know,' I said.

'Jesus, I don't believe this,' he said, clicking his teeth.

'Things can be true without you believing in them,' I replied, 'like God, for example.'

He stared at me bleakly, then smacked the wheel with both hands.

'I'll call you in a while,' I said, opening the door. 'We can still be friends, Alan.' The door slammed on his obscenity.

As I walked to my front door, part of me wanted him to

follow and persuade me to change my mind. How? By the physical, of course. Hardly by appealing to my better nature or my love, for Alan must have known by now that both were all used up. But he drove away at speed as I was on the point of turning round, and so it was too late. I was saved from my own weakness. He was saved too. It occurred to me that dumping my lover so unceremoniously was an act of nobility. Why should he – who had seen and done so many things – be allowed to humiliate himself further by trying to insert vulnerable flesh between me and my ghost? And why should I bow to the conventional notion that a woman alone needs a man?

Go now, said the bird . . .

I thought: I have never been very good at closure, until now. Closure brought to mind enclosure; then – borders, boundaries, banks. Deep lanes between fields. The safety of separation. Simon knew about that.

Putting the key in the lock evokes secrets. Suddenly I wondered why he had burnt her letters and yet kept his own. What did that say about him? Was it massive ego that made him cling to his own words, avoiding the delete key each time, filing his outpourings – or simply delusion? Perhaps he was lulled into viewing the computer itself as a barrier which could not be breached. Do not secrete your illicit letters in a locked drawer or the hidden compartment of an old desk, or at the back of a cupboard in a misleading envelope, for some-day, some time, you will be discovered. You will be dust, yet the screams of fury, the sobs of betrayal will follow you into your grave. And so . . . the match spurts, the paper crisps at the edges, flames, then folds inwards to grey. Yet people fail to destroy, and Simon filed. Maybe it was because knowing his intimacies were 'safely' on microchip made him feel less lonely when he was separated from her.

He was a fool. But then, so was Alan. And Mark Parsons. All gone.

At home I moved from room to room, dazed by the multiplicity of grief. If I had not felt I had to live for Kathy's sake, I swear I would have chosen to die – somehow. But how do you die? They were lucky: *his* heart gave out and *he* was killed instantly in a car. But me – I don't even know how to take my own life. Where do you buy poison? How do you tie a proper knot? Gas is useless now. 'You might as well live,' Dorothy Parker wrote, and God knows she was right. Yet it is hardly a way of accepting life. I felt like a child in an orphanage, opening my one parcel on Christmas morning, knowing I should be grateful for the charity, yet not wanting what I had unwrapped.

Several times I sat for a long time at Simon's desk, thought about switching on the computer, then stopped. I listened for him in the silence, but heard nothing. Staring at the mysterious Charlie Fitzgerald's number, I allowed my finger to hover over the telephone, knowing somehow by instinct that I could solve my small mystery, but lacking the courage to begin. Or perhaps I did not really want to, now. Maybe I was used to living with both these ghosts and dreaded the corporeal. 'What shall I do?' I asked aloud, with (for once) no clear idea of who it was I addressed.

Go, go, go, sang a bird in the garden.

Two days passed before I could act. By then I had no choice. Without some sort of action towards closure I would become unbalanced again. I knew it. And I was committed to travelling up to town again to visit Kit. Kathy phoned me every other day from Edinburgh, and told me she would meet me in London. Knowing Kit since childhood, she was obsessed with her recovery. The impending visit acted as a spur.

It was a day of light, high cloud when I made the second journey. I knew I should not telephone first, feeling that if the woman was absent that was meant to be, and if she was there something would tell me what to do. In preparation, I had driven to the churchyard to look at Simon's grave. It was immaculate, as I expected. She had even added a buried vase for cut flowers, which was stuffed with an extravagance of purple sweet peas, their scent intolerable in the stillness. I stood breathing it in, knowing that before long I too would be bearing gifts to this shrine, whether I liked it or not.

I parked my car by Winterstoke Church, and walked back towards the house, standing for a while at the gate looking in, as I had done before, and wondering if someone returned my gaze from behind those seemingly blank windows. The village was quiet, apart from the whine of a far distant strimmer. It seemed the street must vibrate to the drum beat of my heart.

The gate made a dull clang. I stalked up the wide path to the dark green front door, flanked by old lions covered in lichen, lips drawn back in a silent snarl. I was wishing at that moment that I had telephoned and heard the answering machine – anything to have prevented this visit. It was as if my footsteps, going up that drive, were marked out in the pattern of the universe, indelible.

I reached the front door, hesitated, then rang the bell. After a few minutes I heard brisk footsteps echoing inside the house, and at last the door was opened. There was a silence a thousand years long as the woman stood looking at me with an unfathomable expression. I stared back. A bee buzzed under the porch. The sound of the strimmer had ceased.

The person who stood before me, one hand on the door handle, was older than me, about five or six years older than

Simon, I guessed. She was tall and thin, with grey hair swept up into a precise chignon and the hawkish elegance that speaks of old beauty. But the lines on her face were deep. She wore denim jeans with brown loafers and a blue and white checked shirt. Her hands were weather-beaten and ringless.

This could not be the *She* of my imaginings. It was all wrong.

'I'm sorry . . . are you . . . Charlotte Fitzgerald?' I asked, my voice sounding faint and tinny, in anticipation of feeling foolish.

'Friends call me Charlie,' she said. Then, calmly, 'Come in, Rosa – I'm quite surprised you haven't been to see me before now.'

I tasted decay. This was indeed the woman - That Woman, the Bitch, the Slut, the Whore – and her coolness astounded me.

'Oh, really?' I said harshly, hearing my voice rise.

She nodded, and stood aside to let me walk past into her house, with such ease you would have thought she had rehearsed this moment. Perhaps she had, just as I had myself. But she had the advantage of knowing exactly who would confront her, whereas I had been deceived by a chorus-line of mistresses, a cliché of seductresses, a universal image of shameless sexuality.

I could not believe it. She was *old*.

Old and middle-aged.

Which is to say, she was not young.

The hall was wide and flagged, with a polished staircase curving upwards. In a flash of my inner eye I saw Simon there, walking up those stairs hand in hand with this woman, like teenagers snatching the time when the parents are out. It was obscene. I closed my eyes for a second, feeling faint, and stopped on the pretext of allowing her to catch up and lead the way. She did so, not speaking. The silence between us threatened to shatter the china bowls, the glass chandeliers, the Staffordshire ornaments.

Charlie Fitzgerald led me into a spacious drawing room that contained none of the eccentric details of Kit's or my own – the bits and pieces which proclaim self-conscious individuality. This room was formal with grave, grown-up beauty like its owner, who indicated, with an imperious sweep of her hand, that I should sit down. It was as if I had come for an interview. The rage I had felt when I first saw what she had done to my husband's grave rushed through me once more, so I did not sit down, but I turned to face her instead. This time I thought I saw a glimmer of dread in her eyes, which spurred me on.

'What I've got to say won't take long,' I said loudly. 'I just wanted to see you for myself, and let you know how miserable you've made me. Just tell me this – why didn't you leave us alone, for Christ's sake? Why didn't you leave *him* alone?'

She sat down in the nearest chair as if a silent shot had ended her life, right then, as I watched. The change was so sudden it jolted me out of that rage. I suppose I had expected her to shout back at me, to play the mistress, to say she had equal claim to my husband. But she said nothing. She just sat slackly in front of me, face hidden in her hand. Not knowing what else to do, I sat down opposite. These are the moments when you expect drama, but there is nothing. There is the great ache of disappointment that even this is not right – not like literature, still less like movies. Inaction and inertia. Both of us slumping there with nothing to say.

At last she lifted her head. Her eyes were dry; the skin seemed stretched more tightly over her cheekbones; a salt-and-pepper wisp had escaped and hung down over her forehead.

'I thought you'd find out,' she said.

'How?'

'People do. Don't they say, the truth will out?' Her tone was dry – inappropriately so, I thought.

'You said you expected me to come?'

'Yes, I did. In the end. Or rather, I hoped you wouldn't. He was careful.'

We stared at each other, with a sort of . . . wonderment, I suppose. How many times had each of us fantasised about this confrontation? Now it was like walking through the grille into the arena, filled with the suicidal terror of the martyr, only to find the slavering beast transformed into the most vulnerable of rodents. The roar of the crowd dwindled to nothing. We tolerated this silence together.

At last I said, 'I found all his letters to you, on the computer. I read them all.'

I saw her wince. Then she looked down, as if ashamed, and said quietly, 'I'm sorry for you if you did that. Just so sorry. It must have been . . . You must have felt so unhappy.'

'Don't give me your pity,' I said.

'But I do,' she replied.

'I'm not sad, I'm bloody angry!' I said, like someone waking from a dream. 'Not unhappy – just furious! I know you probably feel sorry now, but don't feel sorry for me! I hated him for what he did, for all those lies, for the whole bloody thing. And I still do. Sorry's got nothing to do with it.'

'Ah, Rosa,' she said softly, shaking her head, 'you did feel unhappy. I know you did. You must have done. There's nothing else to feel.'

'Thanks for telling me. So – what about you?'

'I wake up each day and imagine that I'll hear his voice on the telephone, or find a letter on the mat. *Still.* I'm locked in, Rosa, and I can't find the key. Sometimes I don't think there is a key, not even a door any more. I feel as if I've been walled in, like an anchorite. But do you know something? In a way I don't mind. I've grown used to it. And it means that, even if I am walled in, Simon is in there with me. Perhaps we're both buried, only he's dead and I'm alive.'

This was not said in a voice that asked for sympathy, or even understanding. Charlotte Fitzgerald was matter-of-fact, describing her condition of grief as if she were discussing her choice of colours in this beautiful muted room, or what might be a possibility for lunch. Yet she was talking of my husband, and I felt the old surge of jealousy at her words: anger at the presumption that she could so easily annexe his ghost.

'Oh, I know he's dead all right,' I said bitterly.

'Don't hate me,' she said, and I thought how easily people slip into their lines.

I leant forward sharply. 'I suppose you'll tell me it couldn't be helped, you just fell in love and that was that. But put yourself in my place – finding out that for six years your husband was wanting to be with another woman. Thinking about her. Phoning her. Writing her such letters! How do you think that would make you feel? You were married once, weren't you?'

'He died,' she said in a flat voice. Then, 'Do you know that poem by Emily Dickinson – "My life closed twice"?' I shook my head. 'It says it all for me. I've read it so often I know it by heart. Listen . . .' (She took a deep breath and concentrated, but it was not the effort of memory, I could tell, rather the control of feelings.)

> 'My life closed twice before its close –
> It yet remains to see
> If Immortality unveil
> A third event to me

'So huge, so hopeless to conceive
As these that twice befell.
Parting is all we know of heaven,
And all we need of hell.'

I said nothing. Yet she was looking at me expectantly. Her
face was full of light and sadness and . . . *knowledge*. It dazzled
me. Suddenly I found myself thinking, Perhaps we fall short
of this woman, Simon and I.

'I was married to Sam for twenty years, and I was a widow
for six years – then I met Simon, and I didn't feel like a
widow any more,' she said simply, 'but I feel like a widow
now.'

'Sam Fitzgerald?' I said, remembering the name. She
nodded. Sam Fitzgerald had been a legendary magazine
editor in the seventies and eighties, famous for bringing on
young talent. I had read about him – and recalled that Kit
had worked for him from time to time.

'How did you meet Simon?' I asked abruptly.

'I moved here and wanted the garden done. So he came
here and . . .' She spread out her hands in that small gesture
of helplessness.

'Yes, but how did you find out about him? Did you read
about him, or what?'

'No,' she said, slowly, 'he was recommended to me.'

Something about her tone and expression set a flicker
going in my mind, a magic lantern in a darkened room, just
out of my vision.

'Who by?' I asked.

'Does it matter?'

'Yes – to me. I need to know the whole story. The beginning is important. The most important.'

'Beginning? . . . Sometimes I really don't know if the

present exists – or if being in this house, remembering how it was when he was here, is the only thing that's real. The beginning . . . that was so long ago.'

'I'm wondering who – who recommended Simon to you?' I insisted.

'Oh . . . well, it was Kit Jordan,' she said, with a weary shrug.

'KIT? But . . . how?'

'. . . and I suppose I don't need to say any more. You know the rest.'

'But – did she know – about . . . ?'

'Yes, she did. She phoned up three weeks later to see if I'd made contact, and already it was too late. I was in such a state I blurted it out to her on the phone. She was the only person in the world who knew. She promised that she wouldn't tell you, because she said you wouldn't be able to bear it.'

'*Kit?*' I said again.

'But I never spoke to her about it again, and nor did Simon. She knew, but after that she didn't want to know, do you see?'

'All the time, she knew,' I said aloud, talking to myself. 'And when I found the letters, with her – she knew. She knew it must have been *you*. And she didn't tell me! I can't believe this . . . Both of them betrayed me then. Both of them.'

The edges of the room curled in on me, as if smouldering. I could almost smell it; nausea made me hold my breath. The next thing I was aware of was a glass being put into my hand, very gently.

'Drink it,' said Charlotte Fitzgerald, in a voice so low and sweet it would have been loving had there been room for love, after so much misery.

I sipped pale sherry, spilling a little down my chin. She

took out a handkerchief and mopped me, as a mother might, sticking out her tongue a fraction as she did so, and whispering, '*There.*'

Yet her mouth did not move. I heard it in my head.

There.

'There's nothing true at all except lies and sex, sex and lies,' I said.

'And death,' she said.

I nodded. If I had been asked to get up then, and walk across the room, I couldn't have done so. I felt like a rag doll, discarded by its owner and flopping useless in the corner of a forgotten cupboard. I saw that Charlotte Fitzgerald, back in her armchair again, was surveying me with open pity. And I wanted her pity now. It was better than my loneliness.

'Don't be angry with her, Rosa – not now. What did you expect her to do? Tell you? It wasn't her fault Simon and I fell in love. She didn't bring it about.'

'She should have told me when we found the letters,' I said.

'What for? What would have been gained?'

'The truth. She could have helped me. Instead she tried to make excuses for him – to excuse herself. She made that clear enough. But all these months, when I was wondering who you were, she knew perfectly well and she didn't tell me. I'll never forgive her for that. I just can't believe it.'

She was shaking her head as if to stop me, but I would not be stopped. I could see quite clearly, in my mind's eye, Kit's expression when we found the letters, and could remember most of what she said. It was just possible that she really did believe, in the first second, that the letters were to me, but I doubted it. I doubted everything. She and Simon were united now, beyond redemption. I willed them to whirl in icy winds forever, if not burn. On second thoughts, yes, let them burn. Let them be consumed. Put them both to the torture, the flame . . .

And Mark, what of Mark?

No, let Mark be spared. But . . . what if Kit told him? What if he was feeling pity for me that night, because he knew I had been deceived not once but twice, just as this woman opposite me was moaning that she had been bereaved not once but twice? What if they all mocked me, behind their pity?

I rocked, and must have groaned aloud, because she started to say something. But I held up my hand.

'Don't speak to me. Don't. No more explanations or excuses. I've had them – up to here. Nobody's going to tell me any more things can't be helped. You know something? I've been having an affair at the moment with a man who's married; I know his wife and I know it's wrong. Do you hear that word? WRONG. I don't make any excuses. I don't say I couldn't help it. I admit that I did it deliberately, for my own ends. At least I'm bloody honest – not like the rest of you.'

'But . . . do you love this man?'

'No.'

She nodded, then said quietly, 'That makes it different. I don't expect you to understand. I'm just telling you it does.'

'Ahah, I see. It's OK if you love, but not if you want to fuck. Oh, so that's all right then! You two are excused. How convenient!'

She shook her head, and whispered, 'Oh, Rosa, I can see . . . Oh look, I want to tell you something – about Simon.'

'What?' I asked, hostile. 'Why should I want you to tell me anything about my husband? Why should I listen to you?'

'Come outside in the garden,' she said, getting up and making a sweeping movement with her hand.

I followed her through double doors into a dining room, moving through a continuum of perfect taste. Then she was bending to unlock french windows, and I found myself staring at her buttocks and imagining his hands cupped there. But *this* woman? No. It was all wrong.

She threw open the doors, as if glad to let in the air, and led me out on to a paved terrace. For a moment she stood quietly, looking around, as if she were the stranger and not I. Then the hand made its sweeping movement again, in front of my eyes. 'Look!' she said.

All around me was Simon's garden, or rather, the garden he had created with her, for her. It was perfect – an Italian garden in Somerset. There was such order there, such imaginative discipline of planting, such a balance of architecture, that I let out my breath. Despite myself I understood.

'Come on,' she said.

Silently we walked through this half-acre, where garden room gave way to garden room, all balanced, all harmonious. Shaped box and mowed lawn. A mini avenue of clipped trees leading down to an armillary sphere. Juniper in contrast with yew. Immaculate gravel and then a thyme walk, its tufts releasing their scent as we trod. Laxness of dahlias counterpointing the stiffness of sculptured privet. Circularity played off against crisp angles. Drifts of white roses, already in their death throes, set against rich evergreen planting that would defy the cycles, to swagger, even in winter.

'Separate spaces,' she said.

At the end of a path we came across a pond, its straight stone edges softened by growth. In the centre was an old statue, richly patinated. It was of a young woman, her hair caught up in a Grecian filet, one hand holding a palette, the other a brush. She gazed down into the water with blank indifference, and, as I bent to dip my hand, its surface broke her up, mixing her with the sky. My own reflection was distorted too, and the shape of the woman who stood behind me, also looking down, so that for a second we were united in a pattern of dancing light.

'Sit down with me, Rosa.'

I did as she asked, on a handsome stone bench by the pond, supported by carved lion ends. It was as if we had walked in a dream, she and I, and all the time, beside us in the box hedges and the waving mallow, and even within the settling water of the pool, Simon McKee flitted too, drifting across leaf and stem, but never settling, like a gnat at twilight. And now we had come to rest, but could he? I looked over my shoulder for a second, as though I might catch a glimpse of him hovering. But there was only the dark stillness of leaves.

'The thing is, Rosa, you can go on hating me forever if you like, but even if I never see you again I want you to know something very important. You must listen to me! Simon loved you. He would never have left you . . .'

'But that's why I killed him,' I said.

'What do you mean? Don't be silly.'

I swivelled so that I was facing her squarely. I wanted her to know the truth. 'I mean it! He loved you with such a – a *heat* he couldn't bear it. His heart gave out. But it was only because of ME! If I hadn't been such a bloody victim, if he had thought me strong enough, he could have gone to you, and been happy. He would have lived here and been happy. He would have been an old man walking in this garden, and loving it, because he made it. Don't you see? But I made it impossible for him. And so he died.'

I took a deep breath, trying to discipline my breathing, my eyes, my hands, my words, but none of it would be stopped.

I heard my own voice crack and wail, 'And I don't want him to be dead! I'd rather he was alive and with you! I would!'

'You said you hated him,' she said softly.

'I *do*!'

'It doesn't sound like hate,' she said. 'And anyway, if you blame yourself, there's something unjust in your hating him. Oh God – Rosa, can't you see that there're no rules here? Or rather, there's an order of things – but no rules?'

I didn't understand and told her so. What is an order and no rules? Can you have an order of columns or religion with no rules to set a context? Of course not! I rebelled against this impossible indiscipline. All self-indulgence, all of it. Intelligence can get away with so much.

Looking at her face close up I could see the deeply etched lines that he must have examined, in love, and where the mouth loses its precision – and yet I knew that she was beautiful. The mistress. It mocked me.

'Simon's life had a structure,' she said softly, 'and we were both a part of it. I tried to break away but it was impossible. I knew I had found my place, and if you were the other side of the wall that held him up, both of us buttresses, then so be it. That's how it was. I consciously accepted the shortfall in my happiness, knowing that you were ignorant of yours. But what does it mean? Dear God, Rosa, the world is full of suffering people who never even know what each of us has known! In the face of *that* – all the little strictures about fidelity fade to nothing.'

'Do they?' I said.

'YES!' she cried, and her face was actually alight. She believes it, I thought, and it is all right for her because she was not on the receiving end of the lie. At that moment I thought of Kit, and felt angry and betrayed again. There was nowhere to turn.

'I don't know,' I said, shaking my head.

'We'll all be dead a long, long time,' she sighed. It irritated me.

'Why you?' I asked. 'I'm not being rude, but why *you*?'

'Ahhh – so I'm not what you imagined, is that it? Greying hair instead of sexy blonde? Rosa, you should know better!'

This woman was patronising me now; it was intolerable. 'Well, maybe you were a good fuck!' I shouted, emphasising the obscenity, which echoed in the avenues of Simon's perfect garden. 'After years and years and years of practise! Well run in!'

She shook her head from side to side, as a cow does plagued by flies, and murmured, 'Don't . . . please don't.' Then, more loudly, 'This is no good for either of us, is it?'

'Nothing's good for either of us!' I shouted. 'He saw to that! Simon saw to that! He left us here – like this. He's probably watching us now! Laughing at us!'

'Don't say that,' she whispered, looking around, I swear, as if she were afraid.

I couldn't resist saying what I said next. (I know you will be disappointed in me. You want me to forgive, or at least to be understanding. But I say there is too much understanding. We run with compassion, weak and melting, all things losing definition. I despise your understanding, your forgiveness. I want some justice. And condemnation. I want suffering to take its place at the centre of the stage: suffering and passion two sides of the same coin, and let us not forget it. So why shouldn't I tell this woman the truth?)

'Does he speak to you?' I asked. 'I mean – now?'

'What do you mean?'

'I thought that was clear. Does he speak to you?' She shook her head. I smiled.

'Ah, well, he speaks to *me*.'

'Do you mean—'

'I talk to Simon all the time. He's still in our house. Does he come here too?'

Her eyes were huge, as large as my triumph. She shook her head, then got up abruptly, to stand by the pool. I was frustrated; I wanted her to speak but she just looked at the water lilies, standing quite still, as blue and silent as the shadows beneath the box hedges.

At last she glanced sideways at me and said, 'I think . . . people always think they can hear the people they loved.'

'But talk to? Actually converse?' I asked.

'Rosa, do you believe that?' She sounded panicky and averted her eyes.

'Truth is – he's sort of chosen me,' I said brightly.

She whispered, 'Oh God, Simon, what did we do?'

The last question was said almost under her breath yet she wanted me to hear, I know she did. Nobody ever does anything by accident. That is part of the sadness. There is no spontaneity. Only control . . .

Now I sound like him. I am the apologia for these hedges and paths. Borders, boundaries, banks. I saw it when I walked into the garden, and it made sense. But in the last few moments with Her I had lost that meaning. He kept me in one compartment and her in another, and that, I am afraid – simple and mundane and obvious to you though it may be – is the truth. Don't expect human beings, in extremis, to be original. They are not. They suffer in a totally ordinary way. They are not literary, still less experimental. The language of their pain is everyday, and the narrative hangs its head, as dirty as realism. Their experience is the stuff of chain stores, cheap and universal and necessary.

And yet . . . Oh yes, I am arrogant too. I felt triumphant that I would go on talking to my husband and her lover – and she would not. It was clear she had not. He had not visited this garden, he had visited our house – that she could not take from me. Perhaps it was because he was still on the rack, or at least pegged out for the winds of purgatory: the unquiet soul. And that soul belonged to me. For better, for worse.

She started to walk back to the house and I fell into step beside her. Charlotte Fitzgerald (I could not think of her as 'Charlie', no more than Simon as 'Macky'. To him she was my dear, my darling, my love, and so she would remain forever) paced, head down, quite fast, not talking. But our silence was oddly companionable. At last I said, 'I know you think I'm stupid, or hysterical, but I meant what I said. It's true. I do talk to Simon, and I think I will as long as I live.'

She said, 'I just read and reread the poems we read together . . .'

'We didn't read poems,' I interrupted.

'. . . and I walk here several times a day. I got rid of the gardener because I want to do it myself. And when I'm reading out here, I think I'm with him. Know I'm with him . . .'

She stopped and turned to me a face of such dignity, yet such pleading too, that I felt that I had seen a beacon in the darkness, thirty or forty miles away, marking the end of a war, and could not forbid the answering fire to kindle within me.

'I expect you are,' I said.

She put out a hand then, letting it rest on my arm for a long time, while I did not shrug it away. It did not matter any more, this rivalry. Not because Simon was dead – but because I was alive. That was the most important thing, and it would propel me. This woman existed – she had said so – within a cell. Perhaps that proved she had loved Simon more than I did. Perhaps that love was only a product of impossibility. So what? She said she accepted the shortfall in happiness, and there was no alternative for either of us, now – and maybe not six years ago either. The enclosing garden each side of us was dark and uncompromising in its geometry.

We walked back to the house without speaking. She led me into a pine and cream kitchen to make coffee. I watched in silence, but it was I who carried the tray back into the sitting room. We sat in the same places as if they had always been fixed.

'Well, Rosa,' she said, looking at me over her cup. We might have been village ladies with little to do but take coffee together.

'Well?' I said.

'I don't want you to leave here without telling me you understand, just a little.'

'Understand what?' I said.

'That Simon did love you – very much indeed. And that I accepted that.'

'And that his loving you was a separate thing?' I supplied.

'Yes.'

'Whether I understand it or not isn't the point,' I said. 'People always want bloody understanding nowadays. It's almost required. You have to be in touch with your own feelings and excuse other people's. On and on. And we're deceived into thinking it's easy . . . But the point is, whether or not I understand – and probably I don't - I will live with it. There's nothing else to do, is there?'

'But . . . do you forgive him? And me?' she asked after a pause.

This was as I had foreseen in one of my fantasies, yet more embarrassing, not because I did not know what to say, but because I did not expect my husband's mistress, the siren of the letters, the one who inspired such flights in the down-to-earth man, to be so predictable. All those words of

love, all the pain of that experience, their union, their endless celebration, the frustrated longing of their separate
nights, her loneliness in the garden, his battered, exhausted
heart . . . and all to ask for my little forgiveness? But how
can sin be forgiven unless it be redeemed? Why, I decided
a long time ago that if you deny God there can be no
Christ – and if there is no Christ, how then can sin be
redeemed?

Paradise is a garden, split formally into four. Yet within
that garden, making chaos of geometry, is the serpent. I
wanted my gardens to be wild. Such wildness provides cover
for a whole writhing coil of serpents, and the danger of them
is exciting. Ah, but not any longer. In those days, when I was
young, I did not realise how powerful the reptile is. Now I
do not want him in my home. Let stone walls and hedges be
thick, to banish him – please. Yet even that is impossible. No
borders, or boundaries or banks so well made, but he will
break through.

So I answered her. 'Charlotte, what is the point?'

She drank from her china cup, then put it down, and I
thought she looked ashamed – but perhaps that was wishful
thinking. (Shame? Mistresses don't feel shame. They have
spontaneity and sex on their side.)

'I went to see your show,' she said. 'It was good. Very
good.'

I had asked the point of forgiveness and she had started
to talk about my painting. Cunning! Again, she was in
charge.

'Why did you go?' I asked, resenting her insolence. To
look at my pictures. To look at me.

'I was curious. I didn't know if I would ever meet you, and
I wanted to see if the paintings were anything like the person
I had formed an image of, from what Simon said . . .'

'And?'

'They weren't. Not at all.'

'The thing is,' I said drily, 'I broke out of my box.'

'They're wonderful paintings,' she said. 'I think he would have loved them. Those garden ones . . . Well, looking at them, it was as if I could hear him talking, in my head. All his ideas. Except that the paintings have a . . . a claustrophobia about them . . .'

'And you're saying he didn't? Come on.'

'So you think you're painting Simon's soul?'

Her voice was in the distance, but I was not listening any more.

I'm sorry, Rosa, I'm sorry, my love.

I heard it all right. It was as clear as the ticking of the clock in her hall. He was there, but he had no right to be.

'He keeps telling me he's sorry,' I broke in.

'Then I expect he is, Rosa,' she said, in a tired voice.

'Are you?' I asked.

She seemed to grow a few inches as she replied. 'If you're asking me if I'm sorry you found out, then yes. I don't want you to hate me, or him. I'm sorry you were so hurt and disillusioned. It's all terrible. But if you're asking me if I'm sorry I loved him, and he loved me, and we had a small portion of six wonderful years – then the answer is no. I won't lie to you. I'm not sorry. I can't *deny* all that happiness. It was wonderful . . . and he was wonderful. He loved me for what was inside me, and in a way I think he knew me better than Sam did. So – I'll never be sorry. There'll be nobody else for me now, I know that. Only Simon.'

'What about me?' I asked.

'There'll be somebody else for you,' she said. I felt patronised once more.

I rose to go, and she made no move to stop me. As we

turned towards the hall, I caught a glimpse of our reflections in a beautiful gilt mirror that hung over a cherrywood table by the door. With a quickening, I thought, 'I am much more beautiful than she is!' And I wondered if Simon could see, and if he noticed it too.

When we were standing by the front door, I realised I didn't want to leave. Part of me wanted to find out more from this woman about the passionate man who had written the letters. I was still confused; there was still much to say. But the silence of eternity had to be accepted too. Would Simon accept it now? I wondered. It was all over.

'You can go on looking after his grave,' I said. 'You do it better than me.'

'Thank you,' she said simply.

Then she put a hand on my arm, gently, just as she had in the garden, as if to detain me. Her gaze was penetrating.

'Will you do me one favour? I know I haven't the right . . . but . . . Oh, please will you not read his letters any more? They were written to me, and they're private – not for anybody else's eyes. Letters are *private*. What went on between us is nobody's business – not even yours. Whether he was right or wrong . . . he's dead now, and those letters are mine – all I have. So . . . please?'

I wished she had not spoken, because the anger came back then, and I realised it would never go away. She had spoilt everything. She had no right to ask me that. She had no rights at all.

'And the rest of my life is all mine. So I'll do what I like,' I said.

I left Charlotte Fitzgerald standing at the open door of her elegant, empty house, a gaunt figure in blue who had received no reply to her request. At the gate I relented and turned to wave, but she had already closed the door. She would walk in her garden, then return to her books. That was all she had. It was foolish of her to have thought, even for a second, that she could have my compliance as well.

I drove back to the city through riotous hedgerows, and for the first time for months my mind felt empty, all sky.

Chapter Twenty-two

I cancelled my planned visit to Kit, to Kathy's obvious surprise. When she asked me why, I replied simply that I was too busy.

'But I've arranged to come down, and everything,' she protested.

'Well, you could go. I'm not stopping you,' I said.

The silence at the other end of the line was painful.

'Mum – what's wrong?' she asked.

'What's right?' I replied.

'You OK?'

'Clinging on.'

'But Kit's getting better, Mum!' she said reassuringly.

'Kit's a survivor. Hmmm – always has been,' I said, with a tiny laugh.

Survive.

Oh, I will. Don't you worry, I said, contemplating the telephone and thinking that when this next bit was done I would go up and spend a week in Edinburgh. Kathy needed me, and I had been absent. Soon I would return.

It took me a week before I could contemplate a conversation with Kit. I did something strange: I bought some freesias and spent days making meticulous drawings and watercolours of them, as if to prove to myself that I still could. The work brought me full circle. For some reason I was choosing to please my parents and Simon once again and yet the retrospective did not betray my metamorphosis.

Each time I thought of Kit being the means by which Simon met Charlotte Fitzgerald, I would stop whatever I was doing and stare into space, incapacitated by the irony – and my pain at the silent betrayal.

At last it was time. I telephoned Paul to say I would visit Kit on Tuesday afternoon. He was relieved, since the other partners had been putting pressure on him to pick up work again. He was torn, he told me, 'but I won't be in a position to support Kit if I get chucked out.' Kit was still very ill, but the doctors said she had been lucky. She would walk again; she would not be incontinent; her lung would survive; her battered body would one day wear the red suede wrap skirt.

As I walked through the hospital corridors I experienced the terror of the actor about to go on stage. My mouth was dry; my mind a blank. I had rehearsed my lines many times, but now I doubted my memory. Or nerve.

Kit was in a private room now; I was touched to see how carefully Paul had stuck up the many cards, as well as some of Kit's own photographs, and even a reproduction of a Georgia O'Keefe she had always loved. All this gave that bland hotel-like space the feeling of a teenage room. There was a scent of *Diorissimo*: a suggestion of honeysuckle on a summer night. Scentless white roses filled a vase.

As soon as Kit saw me open the door, she raised both bandaged hands six inches off the bed in greeting, before letting them fall back. The gesture carried within it a shadow of resignation. I bent to kiss her, suddenly aware of a faint trace of bodily odour beneath the perfume. Her face was parchment-

pale, the lank red hair harsh in contrast. Each movement
made her wince.

I sat in the chair, and for a few seconds we gazed at each
other, like passing acquaintances unsure of what to say. Then
we started at once.

'Well . . .' (My sentence had no syntax; I was glad to stop.)

'I . . .' (Her eyes grew moist immediately; she shook her
head.)

'I don't know where to begin,' I said at last.

'Look at that first,' she said, turning her head towards the
cabinet by her bed, where a solitary card stood among the
hospital paraphernalia.

I picked it up and studied the image. Contemplating that
picture was like hearing a note of music held high and clear,
and knowing that it would quiver always in infinity, beyond
human hearing. It was standing on a mountain top and gulp-
ing cold, clean air, so that the lungs can hardly bear the
purity. Like falling into sweet oblivion. It showed a wicket
gate painted the blue of Cretan doors, standing open
between its brown posts (green grass each side, the path
trodden to yellow), and leading to nowhere but the immedi-
ate cliff edge and the sea beyond, grey-blue under a sky
swirling with white and mauve cloud. I turned the card over
and read 'Winifred Nicholson (1893–1981) GATE TO
THE ISLES (THE BLUE GATE)'.

'It's lovely,' I said feebly. Its beauty transcended comment.

'Inside,' she said.

I opened the card, and read the small, elegant handwriting.

My dear Kit,

I cannot express my sorrow for you, and all you have

suffered. I have thought about you so often, and remember you in my prayers – prayer being something I have only recently discovered. Without wishing to add to your burdens, I thought you should know that Rosa came to visit me. If that shocks you I am sorry, but I did not want you to see her again without knowing what she knows. She can't blame you; you must not let her blame you. For nothing is your fault; indeed I see no point in the concept of fault at all, in these matters. God bless you – and I hope that within the next couple of months you will allow me to visit, even though there are others with a more pressing claim on your reserves of energy. All speed to your recovery.

    With warmest wishes,
       Charlie F

I replaced the card, and looked at Kit. She gave an imperceptible nod, as if to say 'You see?' then closed her eyes. Her face, once so sharp and full of life, so beautiful in its wide-mouthed, ravaged way, was gaunt. She looked frail, battered and old. For a second, like transparencies accidentally doubled-up, my memory superimposed the image of her entering Equinox with Mark and Kathy, laughing and dominating everyone around with her enormous energy. Then I saw her leaning forward to pour him wine in the restaurant, hair and eyes flaming.

Her eyes opened. She was waiting for me to speak. All the sentences I had rehearsed, and (more important) the accusatory questions, had melted away, and I was dumb. There was only one thing I had any right to ask her about.

'Kit, I . . . Oh God, Kit, I'm so sorry about Mark. So sorry,' I blurted at last.

'Yes, I know,' she whispered, then (oddly), 'Thank you.'

'Are you all right? I mean – can you bear it?' I asked.

'You have to. It's non-negotiable,' she replied, with a glimmer of her old toughness.

'Oh, I know,' I said.

'When Paul told me, I knew right away that he knew everything. All that time, and I thought I was being so clever – and he guessed. Yet he went on, I mean, he *let* me. I suppose he'd say he didn't have a choice,' she said, 'but . . . he's an amazing man – and I never really guessed it.'

I told her about my visit to their house. She reached forward and just touched the back of my hand with her finger, trailing the drip. 'You did that for me? But that day – when I told you about Mark's love letters – I thought you disapproved.'

'I did in a way. I didn't want to be your accomplice. But when . . . after the accident . . . I didn't want Paul to be hurt. You know?'

Kit nodded, and we were both silent for a few moments. I glanced towards the Nicholson card, and saw her follow my gaze.

'Like I was *her* accomplice – is that what you think, Rosa?'

I nodded. I had to be honest. Enough of lies.

Kit seemed to struggle to raise herself a little. Instinctively I reached forward to help her, settling the pillows. She looked paler than ever, and sighed before she spoke. 'Listen, Rosa, if I could have undone the moment when I gave Charlie your phone number, and said how brilliant Simon was, I would have. But when she told me . . . Well, I didn't think it would last.'

'She said she never mentioned it to you again,' I said.

Kit shook her head. 'That's not true either. She was trying

to make it better for both of us. Look, let's stick to the truth, for once. A couple of years ago I met her at a drinks in London and she told me it was still going on. She told me it was this very great love. Her face was . . . oh, never mind. I'd just begun with Mark at the time and thought the whole world was defined by my own passion. You know – anything goes.'

'But you were my friend,' I said.

'Yes, and that's why I wasn't going to say anything. What was I to do? Make three people unhappy – or just hope Simon kept up his balancing act?'

For the first time I felt a spurt of anger. 'Oh, that's all very well, Kit – but what about later? You must have known those letters were to her. You should have told me then.'

'Maybe I should,' she said slowly, 'but I bet you wouldn't have, Rosa. I bet you'd have chosen silence, and what you thought was safety. Anybody would – except the most arrant busybodies. There you were, still revering Simon's memory . . . I didn't want to take that away from you.'

'But it *was* taken away – by the bloody letters,' I protested. 'All you'd have done was help me. Saved me some of that torment. Maybe I'd still have gone to see her – I don't know. But you could have talked it through with me.'

She nodded, her eyes filling with tears. 'Oh, I know you're right. I suppose I was so obsessed with Mark, and the . . . the impossibility of everything, I couldn't face it. I was chicken, Rosa. All these years I never thought of myself as a coward. Now . . . I know how feeble I am. I lie here sometimes, trying to get my head around the fact that Mark isn't walking about somewhere, that I'll never see him again, that there's *nothing* . . . and I just don't know how to go on. I wouldn't – if it wasn't for Paul.' She gave a little wail, and flicked her head from side to side.

'So – not nothing,' I said softly.

'That's true,' she said. She looked like a little girl who has to accept second prize in the fancy dress competition: brave and grateful at least for her place. 'You've got my letters – Mark's letters?' she asked, after a silence. I nodded and asked what she wanted me to do with them. 'What do you think? I'm so torn . . .'

My voice was louder than I intended. 'Kit, I don't think you'll be doing yourself or Paul any favours by taking them back,' I said, 'because it's over.'

'It would have ended sooner or later anyway . . .' she said.

'Well, that's neither here nor there. The fact is, Mark is dead, and the letters are just a reminder. I think I should get rid of them. You should tell me to.'

'But they're so beautiful,' she protested.

'They had their moment,' I continued grimly. 'They can't bring him back to life. You can't publish them or anything. Let go, Kit – it's all over.'

She nodded, and murmured, 'You're right, you *are* right,' almost to herself.

I went on, 'Look – I came here ready to accuse you of betraying me, but it doesn't matter any more, either. You can see that, can't you? It's *all* been and gone. Finished. I don't care any more. You've got to get better, and I've got to get on. That's how it *is*.'

'You're right,' she said again.

'I know.'

'Non-negotiable,' she said.

'Exactly.'

'We'll both get better,' she said, with an attempt at a smile.

'Go to a health farm!' I said. The absurdity of that suggestion, given the reality of Kit's physical condition, struck us both at the same time and we actually laughed.

Then pain made her wince, and she gasped, 'Don't.'

'At least if it hurts when you laugh you know you're alive,' I said, 'and that's the miracle, Kit. We're both alive. And it's like walking through the blue gate, isn't it?'

'Falling off the cliff?' she asked.

'No – learning how to fly,' I said.

Chapter Twenty-three

This was the last letter in the file. It was undated. People in love do not need dates: their refuge is what Robert Graves calls 'uncalendared love'.

My darling,
I'm so sorry I couldn't come and see you yesterday afternoon. Jack let me down in the morning, and then I couldn't get the people delivering the slabs to change it, and then the summerhouse firm kept me on the phone at the site because there was a problem with the right gilding for the finial . . . and so the dominoes started to collapse, and took down with them my planned time with you. When at last I managed to ring you I got your answerphone. Yet I knew you were there – hurt and angry because you had been waiting and I had not come. Please forgive me. I couldn't help it.
Now this will have to be quick because R and I are going to see the Musgroves for the day (Oh tedium, but they used to know her parents, and there is a splendid garden there which we shall discuss), and I

know she's waiting for me. On the way I'll post some invoices with this among them. The thing is, I have managed to rearrange the day after tomorrow, but I remember now too late that you said you might have a lunch in Bristol. So this is to say please, please, *please try to get out of it*. If I don't see you then it won't be until next Tuesday, because, because, because. You know.

Oh what shall I do? I long to see you so much – so please try to get out of that lunch. I know I should not expect you to cancel things for me, but what choice is there? We both have to do it sometimes. Please don't be angry with me because of yesterday. I did try to call again when I got home but I kept getting the bloody machine and then R was with me, so what could I do? You aren't angry with me, are you, my love? I DO try, and you know I do. It's just that I carry all these things in my head all the time, and sometimes it is all too much. Rather than let you down, I'd cut off my arm. But then I couldn't hold you, could I? (Go on – smile!)

If you manage to cancel, and will let me come, then leave a message on our answerphone saying that you are a Mrs Masterson and you would like to make an appointment for me to come and look at your new garden. Leave any old number. All right?

I love you and I long to see you and take you in my arms, my beautiful sleek pussycat. Be understanding, my love. If you are not, then nothing is bearable for me.

With hundreds and thousands of kisses,

S

I realised the folly of romanticism. For all love is subject to the calendar, and illicit passion more than any other sort. What was this love letter but a tedious concatenation of arrangements? All the poetic rhetoric of the first letters had dwindled to a time and a place, and neither of them convenient. I had no way of knowing if she cancelled her lunch, or if his heart had given out before. Perhaps she bridled and refused him. Maybe that pushed him over the edge – poor, poor Simon with his trowel in his pocket, his roots split in two.

Why poor?

Because I pity you, Simon! That's where I've come to at last, not hating you but pitying you. I'm too tired now to hate you, or hate Her – or rail against God, or fate, or any other damned thing. She said you loved me, all the way through, and so I feel even more sorry for you. Because it's easy to leave your wife if you don't love her, isn't it? Some men behave intolerably, so that in the end their wives drive them out, absolving them from the responsibility of choosing. Were you ever tempted to do that?

Never. I could never have left you. I'd lie awake with you sleeping beside me, thinking about Charlie, and wanting to be with her so much it was as if my mind waved out on a stalk, driving me mad. Then I would hear you breathing, and every so often you'd give a little sigh, as if your soul were escaping into the gloom. And I knew my role was to watch over it against the darkness. I had to protect it . . .

It?

You, Rosa, you. But in the end the most damage to you came from me. I stayed because I wanted to look after you . . .

That's not the same as loving! She said you loved me!

Oh, but it is. And I did. What greater love than to cherish?

But her . . . you loved her.

Differently. Understand, Rosa. If you don't prune your capacity for love, it grows and sprouts until it overwhelms everything. But it's wonderful. Untamed and unkempt. I'm not ashamed of that, Rosa. Even though in the end it choked me.

God, you're still lying to yourself and to me. Do you want me to say it? The truth? It's small and plain and ugly. And *common*. You were unfaithful.

Does the Holy Spirit care more about faith – or love?

Such an atheist and going on about the Holy Spirit? Don't look for excuses, Simon, you lied and you deceived me. No matter what she says, or you, I keep returning to that simple truth – again and again. It's as if the words are burnt black up in front of my eyes. You know – a naff pokerwork motto: 'Trust in me!' And I feel bitter about that. I know you expect me to forgive you, but you have to know I'll *never* forgive you. Even though I'm too tired to hate you. Sinning is quick, isn't it? A loving impulse, or a flash of lust – and then you're burning in hellfire forever. That's what they used to believe, and it's what I believe. A version of hell. That's what you're in. You can't visit Her, and talk to Her – because the damned aren't allowed to approach heaven. So you're here with me. And as long as I don't forgive you, your sin won't be redeemed. Can't be. So, you'll be with me forever, Simon. You see?

I'm sorry, Rosa, I'm sorry, my love . . .

You could devise a modern set of punishments for the seven deadly sins, couldn't you? Instead of all those demons inflicting actual punishment on the body, the punishment would all be in the mind. So you'll be here, I know it, and you'll be watching me with Alan – if I bother any more, I haven't decided – and whoever comes after him, and after that, and it will really hurt you. Whereas she – she says there'll be nobody else for her, and she means it. What punishment there for you, in Her house and garden? None. Stay

with me, Simon! Watch me grow! I think I'll paint a Seven
Deadly Sins series next . . .

Clever, beautiful Rosa. I wanted to look after you . . .

And now you're doomed to haunt me forever, because I
won't let you go, Simon. Do you hear that? I won't allow you
to rest in peace. Will you tell me why I should?

But he was silent then.

In front of me on the desk, in front of the computer, lay
the brown envelope marked VAT (crossed out), and
ROSA/GARDEN PLANS. I had not looked at it before,
but now I pulled out the few cuttings about grand houses and
their gardens, and then about twenty letters.

Each was still in its envelope – large, thick, smooth white
envelopes, with Kit's name written in a strong black calligraphy. Obviously, most had been posted inside other
envelopes, probably businesslike brown ones, because of the
lack of stamps or postmarks. Some were badly torn, where
Kit had ripped them open in her eagerness to read what her
lover had written. Two had been opened very neatly with a
paperknife. I glanced at the dates, but they were not in order.
It seemed that each time she received a letter she simply
shoved it into the big envelope to take its place higgledy-
piggledy among the others. At least the computer imposed
order, I thought.

Perhaps I should not have read Mark's letters, but I had
already read Simon's, so what did it matter? People read love
letters when the writers are dead: Janáček, Carlyle and his
Jane, Keats, Oscar Wilde . . . all the illustrious ghosts who
were as sublime and trivial as us, all of them opened their
souls on paper, to be pored over by strange eyes. Kit would
not know I had invaded her privacy; in any case I felt I had a
right to curiosity. It would weigh in the balance with her
silence, and therefore, let me forgive it. All these letters, the

ones on the screen and the ones in my hand, were mine now. My legacy.

The letters written in Mark Parsons' bold, italic handwriting were, as I expected, sublime. He wrote of poetry, the weather, his sore knee, his work, his love, Kit's body, a painting he had seen, a meal they had enjoyed . . . and all became equal, lifted by language into a universe that rocked with hidden, silvery laughter, infinitely optimistic. He wasted no time on superfluous endearments, or on arrangements, still less on arraigning fate. His prose glittered off the page, his passion for Kit turned into a magnificent game, a celebration of *style* which was definitely hers, and obviously his – but abstract also. These letters were a testimony, not just to the love he felt for Kit Jordan or vice versa (although there was that in plenty) but to the idea of love itself. The power of his words rendered irrelevant mere personality, and transient emotion. They tapped out their dance upon the teeth of death.

I read each letter slowly, imagining how Kit had felt as the only begetter, siren *and* muse, and my envy of her was profound. All her lies by omission were irrelevant now. What else could she do? She wanted everything and understood that desire in others, consuming and destructive as it was. Of course she understood Simon. They were bound on the same wheel.

Paul Jordan's eyes had travelled this path too. It must have humiliated him, to know the quality of his wife's lover . . . Oh, but Paul Jordan was beyond humiliation. Most men would consider him a fool, a poor used drip; most men are crass; they straitjacket their spirits with certainty or ignorance. I knew the truth. The grey solicitor carried within him a greatness of spirit that made me humble.

When I had finished reading, each letter put carefully

back in its envelope, I sat looking at the little pile, and staring beyond it at Simon's last letter on the screen. At last I flicked back to the beginning of the document:

> My dearest,
> I have to steady myself. The unforeseen has happened. In years to come I shall look back, like someone staring at the sun, into the golden light of our meeting . . .

I tried to re-experience the shock of discovery, and my fury, but both eluded me now. Poor Simon's letters seemed frantic and overstated beside Mark's, and yet the thought was disloyal: there was no competition, no more than between me and Charlotte Fitzgerald, who measured solitary steps in her paradise garden. Both represented, in the end, just so many tiny flames in a vast, impervious darkness. Sitting there I suddenly imagined Simon and Mark as tiny handfuls of dust, bleating pitifully, 'I was real! I was flesh! I was loved!' and pleading for redemption, while all around, the empty sky vibrated to the opening bars, violent, percussive and threatening, 'O FORTUNA . . .'

But the point is, I was there to hear them. To join in the *Carmina*.

Transfixed, I felt my heart beat faster, and leant back in the chair, feeling its back cup my spine. I stared at the screen, which seemed radiant to me now, far beyond its function. Minutes passed, then at last I could act. I had learnt how to months before, once neither the machine nor its manual had the power to terrify me any more. I knew how to 'Select All' in a document – and how to delete. A flash of light. And it was done.

'All gone!' I used to say as a child, flapping my hand in

desperate, wishful farewell, at anything or anybody who frightened or annoyed me. 'All gone!' It made adults laugh, my mother said, even if they were on the receiving end of the insult. But they did leave me alone, I think. It's easy to look back on the nervous child, wilfully dreamy, and see how she stumbled along the path that led into this room, to this desk, and a screen now devoid of personality, or love. Or guilt.

Poor Rosa McKee.

'All gone.'

So she grew up then, at one remove from herself and able to embrace irony at last – alone.

Oh Fortuna.

That is what he had heard when he had knocked on the bedroom door to say sorry – ignored, the wooden panels vibrating to an increased volume of perversity. You had to stand outside it all! You had to flap your hand and say 'All gone' to the ghosts.

So Rosa McKee smiled at the machine, switched it off, gathered up the fat white envelopes, and went downstairs, pausing only to pick up a box of matches in the kitchen before walking out into the overgrown garden. The incinerator was full of dry leaves, but she did not burn the letters all in one go. It had to be savoured, this destruction of beauty: each envelope fed slowly into the fire, calligraphy collapsing, words dissolving, ashes falling – and the flame springing larger and larger, as the greeny-grey smoke scarfed up, making her eyes water.

'Goodbye, Mark Parsons,' she said aloud, making the words a sort of blessing on the ashes.

Then when it was done she turned her back on the whispering white pile, and re-entered the house. It was utterly still. She walked briskly up the stairs and opened her studio door, pausing on the threshold. The smell of paint was resinous and welcoming.

'OK, Simon,' she said.